Praise for

The Beauty of Humanity Movement

NATIONAL BESTSELLER

"A debunker of stereotypes and a seeker of the big picture, [Gibb] isn't satisfied with merely creating convincing characters and a bold plot. She educates and enlightens the reader. . . . Suffice it to say that the plot ignites around a scam in the contemporary art world, that a bittersweet story of old lost love is brought up to date, and that the beauty of humanity—sans irony—triumphs." —*The Gazette* (Montreal)

"There is a lot packed into this carefully balanced, delicately spiced novel. . . . Inspired by the real-life Nhân Văn affair, it achieves one of fiction's greatest aims: making the personal universal, and vice versa." —*The Independent*

"[Gibb] demonstrates an amazing ability to inhabit the headspace of people of other cultures living in different times. . . . [Gibb's] latest work slips like silk into the psyche of contemporary Hanoi. . . . Gibb's largely unadorned writing is rather like Hưng's phở, delicious for its austerity and complexities." —*Telegraph-Journal* (New Brunswick)

"Gibb carefully sets up the many strands of the story, shuttling back and forth from present to past. . . . Gibb brings *The Beauty of Humanity Movement* to a poignant close." —*Quill & Quire*

"Well written and engaging, with characters that represent the participants and consequences of a country in the middle of great change." —*Library Journal*

"Gibb fluidly takes the reader from the bitter years of war to the Hanoi that has emerged in the reform era, which, despite all its modernization, is still a mystery to many of us." —*Booklist*

"Great characters, expertly written...another winner from Gibb." —*Now Magazine*

CAMILLA GIBB

THE

BEAUTY

OF

HUMANITY

MOVEMENT

ANCHOR CANADA

Library and Archives of Canada Cataloguing in Publication
is available upon request.

ISBN: 978-0-385-66323-6

Printed and bound in the United States of America

Published in Canada by Anchor Canada,
a division of Random House of Canada Limited

Visit Random House of Canada Limited's website: www.randomhouse.ca

10 9 8 7 6 5 4 3

For Phương, Lan and Bao

THE

BEAUTY

OF

HUMANITY
MOVEMENT

A Note of Grace

Old Man Hưng makes the best phở in the city and has done so for decades. Where he once had a shop, though, he no longer does, because the rents are exorbitant, both the hard rents and the soft—the bribes a proprietor must pay to the police in this new era of freedom.

Still, Hưng has a mission, if not a licence. He pushes the firewood, braziers and giant pots balanced on his wooden cart through the streets of Hanoi's Old Quarter in the middle of the night and sets up his stall in a sliver of alleyway, on an oily patch of factory ground, at the frayed edge of a park or in the hollow carcass of a building under construction. He's a resourceful, roving man who, until very recently, could challenge those less than half his age to keep up.

When he is forced to move on, word will travel from the herb seller, or the noodle maker, or the man delivering newspapers, to the shopkeepers along Hàng Bông Road who make sure to pass the information on to his customers, particularly to Bình, the one who is like a son to him, out buying a newspaper or a couple of cigarettes in the earliest of morning hours, returning home to rouse his own son, Tư, slapping their bowls, spoons and chopsticks into his satchel, jerking the motorbike out of his kitchen and into the alleyway, and joining the riders of three million other motorbikes en route to breakfast, at least forty of them destined for Hưng.

His customers, largely men known to him for a number of years, are loyal, some might say dependent. He is loyal and most certainly dependent. This is his livelihood, his being, his way in the world, and has been ever since he first came to apprentice in his Uncle Chiến's phở shop at eleven years of age.

It was 1933 when his father sent him from the rice fields to the city, getting Hưng well out of the way of a mother who cherished him least of all her ten children. She'd kept him at a distance ever since a fortune teller had confirmed her suspicions that the large black mole stretching from the outer corner of Hưng's left eye to the middle of his cheek-bone was an inauspicious sign. Tattooed with the promise of future darkness, the fortune teller had decreed.

Hưng had come to his Uncle Chiến with no name other than "nine," denoting his place in the birth order, becoming Hưng only in Hanoi, under the guardianship of his uncle, a man who neither subscribed to village superstitions nor could afford to turn help away.

This morning, Hưng has set up shop in the empty kidney of a future swimming pool attached to a hotel under construction near the Ngũ Xá Temple. It has taken several attempts to get his fire started in the damp air, but as the dark grey of night yields to the lighter grey of clouded morning, the flames burn an orange as pure and vibrant as a monk's robe.

Some of his customers have already begun to slip over the lip of the pool, running down its incline with their bowls, spoons and chopsticks, racing to be head of the queue.

Hưng works like the expert he is, using his right hand to lay noodles into each bowl presented to him, covering these with slices of rare beef, their edges curling immediately with the heat of the broth he is simultaneously ladling into each bowl with his left.

"There you go, Nguyễn. There you go, Phúc, little Min," and off his first customers shuffle with their bowls to squat on the concrete incline, using their spoons and chopsticks to greet the dawn of a new day.

Ah, and here is Bình, greeting him quietly as always, bowl in hands, never particularly animated until he's had a few sips of broth. Although he is well into his fifties, Bình is a man still so like the boy who used to accompany his father, Đạo, to Hưng's phở shop back in the revolutionary days of the early 1950s. The world has changed much since then, but Bình remains the same mindful, meditative soul who used to pad about after Hưng, helping him carry the empty bowls out to the dishwasher in the alleyway behind the shop.

"There you go, Bình," Hưng says, as he does every morning, dropping a handful of chopped green herbs into his bowl from shoulder height with exacting flourish.

"Hưng, what happened to your glasses?" Bình asks of the crack that bisects the left lens.

Hưng, loath to admit he inadvertently sat upon them last night, shrugs as if it is a mystery to him too.

"Come"—Bình gestures—"let me fix them for you."

Hưng dutifully unhooks his glasses from his ears and hands them to Bình's son, Tư, who is waiting beside his father with his empty bowl. Tư tucks them into his father's shirt pocket, and Bình shuffles left, making way for his son.

Tư, just twenty-two years old but so full of confidence, greets Hưng with more words than Bình ever does and waves his chopsticks left and right as he tries to calculate the size of the pool. This is very much like him—Tư loves numbers in a way that seems to pain him. He used to teach math at a high school, but he has abandoned that recently in favour of entertaining tourists. Hưng is not sure all that foreign interaction is good for the boy, but he trusts Bình is monitoring the situation.

Hưng indulges Tư with a challenge this morning: "I'd like to see you calculate the pool's volume in terms of the number of bowls of phở that would be required to fill it."

Tư grins as he manoeuvres his way carefully across the pool, holding his bowl right under his nose, the steam rising like incense smouldering in a temple to bathe his face.

Hưng has taught Tư, Bình and Bình's father, Đạo, before

him that you can tell a good broth by its aroma, the way it begs the body through the nose. And *phở bắc*—the phở of Hanoi—is the greatest seducer, because of the subtle dance of seasonings that animates the broth. It is not just the seasonings that make *phở bắc* distinct, it is provenance, a lesson Hưng would happily deliver to anyone interested in listening.

The history of Vietnam lies in this bowl, for it is in Hanoi, the Vietnamese heart, that phở was born, a combination of the rice noodles that predominated after a thousand years of Chinese occupation and the taste for beef the Vietnamese acquired under the French, who turned their cows away from ploughs and into *bifteck* and pot-au-feu. The name of their national soup is pronounced like this French word for fire, as Hưng's Uncle Chiến explained to him long ago.

"We're a clever people," his uncle had said. "We took the best the occupiers had to offer and made it our own. Fish sauce is the key—in matters of soup and well beyond. Even romance, some people say."

It was only with the painful partitioning of the country in 1954 that phở went south; the million who fled communism held the taste of home in their mouths, the recipe in their hearts, but their eyes grew big in the markets of Saigon and they began to adulterate the recipe with imported herbs and vegetables. The phởs of Saigon had flourished brash with freedom and abundance while the North ate a poor man's broth, plain and watered down, with chicken in place of beef as the Party ordered the closure of independent businesses like Hưng's and a string of government-owned cafeterias opened in their place.

6

Terrible stuff it was, grey as stagnant rainwater in a gutter. Those who are old enough to remember it thank Hưng for getting rid of the mouldy taste in their mouths. Kids of Tư's generation probably can't even imagine it. Tư was born just before the government's desperately needed economic reforms of 1986, when the market was liberalized in order to alleviate starvation and independent ownership once again became a possibility. Only then could the true potential of phở be realized.

The challenge for Hưng now has less to do with the availability of ingredients than with the need for restraint. Hưng sees himself as a guardian of purity, eschewing bean sprouts and excessive green garnish in accordance with northern tradition. They may well have opened their doors to the world, but that does not mean they must pollute their bowls. *Ăn bắc; mặc nam*, they say—eating as in the North; clothing as in the South—something so fundamental must be respected through deference to tradition.

Hưng is a man governed by such principles rather than any laws, particularly those ones keenly enforced by the police that are of greatest inconvenience to him and those he serves. When the officers come to ticket him for trespassing or operating without a licence after he has had the peace of setting up shop in the same location for a few consecutive days, his customers will be forced to run off clutching their bowls, sloshing broth against their freshly pressed shirts, losing noodles to the pavement, jumping aboard their motorbikes and lurching into the day.

Hưng's crime is the same every day, but sometimes the

police are in more of a mood to arrest a man than fine him. "Where did you relieve yourself this morning?" an officer in such a mood had asked him a few months ago.

Hưng had shaken his head. The question made no sense. "Where did you pee, old man?" The officer raised his voice, threatening to arrest Hưng for resisting a police officer if he didn't answer the question.

Hưng reluctantly pointed toward a patch of grass and asked, "Has peeing now been declared a crime?"

No, but that very patch of grass, as he was no doubt well aware, was the consecrated site upon which the Ministry of Labour, Invalids and Social Affairs would soon be erecting a new monument to honour the revolution's martyrs and devotees. And so Hưng was promptly arrested for insulting the Communist Party, which is to say, the only party there is.

Hưng considered that night behind bars, lying on concrete and pissing into a communal bucket, mild punishment compared to the previous time he'd been charged with insulting the Party. Then, they had disciplined his mouth by punching out most of his front teeth with the butt of a rifle.

"Why this waste of money on statues?" he shouted after Bình had paid the bribe to release him from prison the second time. "Why yet another monument for the revolution? It's been fifty years of this. Oh, if they could read the insults in my mind . . ."

"They used to claim they *could* read minds," Bình said, and off they wandered, mumbling together like two old men despite the almost thirty years between them, two old men who had indeed once believed in the Party's telepathy.

Hưng serves the last man among today's early shift of customers and looks over at Bình and Tư, the younger still making calculations in the air with his chopsticks, the elder concentrating on his bowl. He wonders whether it isn't time for Tư to marry. He hopes Tư's mother, Anh, is giving this matter some attention; if not, Tư may well be the last in this family line Hưng will serve.

The comforting clatter of metal spoons against ceramic is suddenly interrupted by a booming voice that floods the bloodless kidney, bouncing from side to side. Noodles slap against chins and silence falls. "What the hell are you all doing here?" a man yells, stepping down in heavy work-boots. "I've got a project to supervise. I'll have you all arrested if you don't pack up and leave immediately!" He smacks a crowbar repeatedly against his thick-skinned palm.

Bình rises to his feet and all eyes turn toward him. "Sir, you have to smell this," he says, nodding at the bowl in his hands.

Hưng feels a hot rush of pride fill his cheeks. Bình really is a son to him, if not by blood, then certainly through his devotion. What is blood without relationship, without life shared, in any case? Hưng has come to believe it is little more than something red.

A hush vibrates around the pool as the foreman steps toward Bình and demands to know their business. This is private property; what are they all doing squatting here like it's mealtime on some communal farm?

"This is Hanoi's greatest secret," Bình says, his eyes lowered in deference. "Seriously. You have to know. It will change you."

Despite the threat of the rusty crowbar, despite his familiarity with the pain such an instrument can cause, Hưng knows this is his moment. He shuffles forth across the concrete in his slippers. He holds his own bowl under the foreman's nose, steam rising to envelop them both. His customers inhale as if sharing one set of lungs. No one makes a sound as the foreman licks his lips and takes the chopsticks Hưng offers. The foreman thrusts those chopsticks to the bottom of the bowl and lifts the noodles into the air, creating a wave that plunges the herbs to the bottom before they float back to the surface, infusing the noodles in the broth, just as every mother teaches her child.

The foreman proves he is just like every mother's son. He leans over the bowl and inhales as he lays the noodles back down to rest in the broth, then clutches a few strands between his chopsticks and raises them to his mouth. The construction workers stand around the rim of the pool, watching their boss in silence. The foreman slurps broth from the spoon, lifts up a few more noodles with his chopsticks, curls them into his spoon, picks up a thin slice of beef, lays it on the bed of noodles, tweezes a piece of basil from the broth and places it on top of the beef, then puts this perfectly balanced combination, this yin and yang, into his mouth.

And then he grunts.

"I see what you mean," he finally says to Bình, handing the bowl back to Hưng.

"Bring your bowl tomorrow. Tell your men, too," Hưng says quietly, squinting at the workers on the rim. His left eye is clouded over; his right discerns the outline of a row of men. "Half price for them," he says, "free, of course, for you."

"I'll pay you full price," says the foreman. "Just as long as you and your customers are out by seven."

"Yes, sir," says Hưng, shuffling back to the fatter end of the kidney to extinguish his fire. He feels a tremor of nervous laughter rattle beneath his ribs. He dares not look over at Bình. He smiles into the fire, sharing the victory with its embers instead.

It is not yet half past six—still plenty of time left to serve the latecomers who have just arrived, which Hưng does now with good humour and renewed concentration, laying noodles and beef into each bowl with his right hand, pouring ladlefuls of broth over top with his left, his rhythm as even and essential as a beating heart.

Hưng recognizes each man by the state of his hands: the grease moons under the nails that mark a mechanic, the calluses of one who works a lathe, the chewed nails of a student writing exams.

But then whose lovely hands are these amidst this parade of manly paws? The delicate hands of a woman who has, improbably, never engaged in manual labour. And the bowl. Shining. Translucent. Porcelain.

He looks up. The young woman before him is a classic beauty with delicate, balanced features, and although she is not one of his regular customers there is something familiar about her face.

Perhaps Bình sees it too, for he coughs in that moment and pulls his son away by the shirtsleeve—no time for gawking, time to get to work.

"You've come to me for breakfast before?" Hưng asks, turning his attention back to the young woman before him.

"No," she says, revealing herself a foreigner with just one word. Her black suit and crisp white shirt also set her apart; she is dressed like a serious businesswoman, and those teeth—white as the snow that used to fall on Quyết Mountain when he was a boy, straight as the pines that crowned it.

"Maybe I knew you when you were a child?"

"I don't think it's possible, sir. I grew up in the U.S. But perhaps you knew my father—Lý Văn Hai."

"Lý Văn Hai," Hưng repeats. The name is not entirely unfamiliar to him, but it is a sound far away, a temple gong ringing in a distant valley.

"He was an artist here in the fifties."

Hưng stops the movement of his ladle. Wait. Who is this woman? And what does she want? Does the government now employ beautiful young women with foreign accents as spies? Has she been hired to trap him, all these years later, to have him admit some collusion with the men of the Beauty of Humanity Movement?

Hưng straightens his back, ready to defend himself, when he suddenly sees all the colour drain away from her face.

This girl is no spy.

"I'm sorry," she says quietly. "I know this must seem like it's coming out of nowhere, but I heard you knew many of the artists back then, and I've spent a year searching and nobody knows anything and I just . . ." Her voice evaporates and her shoulders slump. "I just hoped that maybe you knew him."

Hưng clears his throat. He does not know what to say. The professional businesswoman has transformed into a girl defeated. A girl in search of her father. "A Hanoi man, was he?"

She glances up, turning Hưng into a frozen portrait of a man holding a ladle in mid-air. She looks so vulnerable— her eyes shining like rare black pearls, a slight tremor to her chin—her face far too revealing.

"He grew up in Hải Phòng, but he moved here to train at the École des Beaux Arts in the late 1940s," she says.

It has been decades since a beautiful young woman has looked at him in such a way. Not since Lan, the girl who used to raise her eyes to him for answers. It is almost unbearable. If only he could offer this young woman—and himself—some relief. But he cannot honestly say he remembers anything about Lý Văn Hai, except perhaps that combination of short syllables.

"His name is vaguely familiar," says Hưng, leaning in closer. "What else can you tell me about him, dear?"

"He was sent to a re-education camp in 1956."

"So many of them were," Hưng says quietly.

"He was in good company then."

"Oh, he would have been, yes," Hưng says. "Some of the very best." He feels the urge to tell her just how good, to boast about the poetry and the essays and the artwork the Beauty of Humanity Movement produced, the fearlessness the men he knew had displayed in the face of opposition, the reach and inspiration of their work.

"Come again," he says to the young woman instead. "Perhaps I will remember him."

She pulls a business card from her pocket and hands it to him.

Hưng squints at the English letters and bows his head respectfully, not recognizing a single word.

Tư sits behind his father on the seat of the Honda Dream II as they head back toward the Old Quarter after breakfast, wending their way through the congestion of motorbikes, bicycles, cyclos, pedestrians, cars, wooden carts and back-bent widows peddling food in baskets hanging from bamboo poles, blazing a trail through air thick with diesel fumes and morning fog.

"You've never seen her before?" Tư shouts, as his father slows down to turn a corner.

"I told you—no," Bình yells over his shoulder.

"But what do you think she was doing there?"

"No idea," his father yells. "Strange morning."

Strange indeed. Auspicious even. Tư's father seems possessed with the strength of the new moon—look at his victory over the foreman this morning, after all. Although his father is a naturally reserved man, Tư has seen him overcome his inhibition when it counts. It is their job to protect Hưng, particularly now that he is getting older. Hưng's eyesight has deteriorated recently, his movements have become stiff and slow; it pains Tư to realize that Hưng is no longer the invincible street warrior, but a man showing the vulnerabilities of his age.

Tư squeezes his father's shoulder affectionately before hopping off the back of the bike in front of the Metropole,

Hanoi's finest hotel, once the finest in all of Indochina. He skips up the steps and enters the lobby. The giant potted palms, chandeliers and ceiling fans keep the grand colonial air of the place alive. Phương, Tư's best friend and partner in capitalist adventure, stumbles in just after him, looking foul-tempered with the stink of late-night karaoke. He has neglected to shave and his lips appear glued together. Phương has clearly not been fortified with the bowl of phở that is vital for one's daily performance.

"You missed some real drama this morning," says Tư.

"I've had quite enough drama of my own already this morning," says Phương.

Phương is the driver, and Tư, because of his better English, is the guide, but together they are the A-team employed by the New Dawn Tour Agency in their matching company T-shirts and knock-off Chinese Nike Shox Jungas with soles the colour of ripe mango. On the job, Phương goes by the name Hanoi Poison, Hanoi P for short. He says it's for the benefit of the tourists who can only seem to spit his real name, but the truth is it's his rap name and he's planning on becoming a famous rap artist. Phương has solid musical training behind him, a growing reputation and many, many fans, but most of all, he's got talent. He tries to mess with Tư's name as well—Tư-Dangerous, TaTư—but Tư is not interested. "I'm old-fashioned that way," he says, "leave it be."

Tư met Phương a couple of years ago when they were both teaching at the high school in Đống Đa district. Tư was twenty years old and had just made the depressing dis-covery that loving math was a very different thing from loving teaching it. He was dreading the thought of the next forty-five years until retirement, but when he thought of the drudgery his parents had endured in their early working lives he was overcome with guilt.

Bình and Anh had been employed at the Russian KAO factory for years, dutiful proletariat manufacturing Ping-Pong balls for a pittance. Tư's father had worked with celluloid, his mother had tested for bounce and Tư had had a cardboard box full of misshapen white balls to play with as a child. But in the 1980s, the bones of the Soviet Union began to rattle. Soviet aid ran out and the factories began to close, leaving Vietnam friendless and hungry and in trouble. And so began Đổi mới—Vietnam's very own perestroika—the economic reforms that allowed a free market to develop and have since changed all of their lives.

Tư's father now has endless carpentry work. He employs two assistants, four skilled woodworkers and an apprentice, but still, with so much construction going on he must say no to jobs on occasion. Despite his enthusiasm for private enterprise, Bình is still more craftsman than businessman.

Tư's mother, meanwhile, had knocked on the doors of every one of the new butcher shops that opened in the 1990s until she found one proprietor who was obliged to listen because he came from the same village as her mother. The story is now legendary in their family. "Tell me nine ways to prepare pork for Tet and I'll consider hiring you," the butcher said. And so Tư's mother recalled the pork dishes they used to eat during the holidays at her grandmother's house. She described the sensation of her teeth

collapsing through fried rice paper into the soft ground
pork middle of a spring roll, the crisp saltiness of pig skin
fried with onions, the silk of the finest pork and cinnamon
pâté coating her tongue, the soft chew of pork sausages, the
buttery collapse of pig's trotters stewed with bamboo
shoots, the ticklish texture of pig intestines resting on vermicelli and the fill of sticky rice, pork and green beans
boiled in banana leaves. Just when she was about to falter,
she remembered how her father used to reminisce about the
dishes his mother made for Tet during his boyhood in Huế:
pork bologna, fermented pork hash, pig's brain pie . . .

The butcher raised his finger. "You're hired. Stop there
before I fire you."

Tư did not have to do time in a factory: he grew up in a
world where he was free to choose a career for himself. What
right did he have to complain about his teaching job? But
then he'd met Phương, a part-time music teacher a few years
older than he who taught classical đàn bầu two days a week.
Phương, moping in the teachers' lounge, had called theirs a
thankless profession. This had unleashed a sympathetic torrent
from Tư, marking the beginning of an illustrious friendship.

Phương had the spirit and imagination of an artist and
entrepreneur, enough to inflate the dreams for two. By the
end of that school year, once Phương had lobbied Tư's father
for consent, they had both submitted their resignations and
registered for a diploma course at Hanoi Tourism College.

You are the Đổi mới generation, the instructors at the
college told them, the children of the renovation, the future
of Vietnam—a future that depends on opening even more

doors to international trade and relations. Tư feels the elation of being poised at the vanguard of the future as a proud, fully fledged, nationally accredited tour guide shaking the hands of the world.

Tư's English might be better than Phương's, but Tư knows that in many ways it was Phương who taught him what foreigners really want. Tư prides himself on being an excellent memorizer, and initially relied on the vast and readily accessible number of facts stored in his brain. He has memorized, in particular, *The Big Book of Inventions*, so if a tourist comes from, say, Norway, he can impress him by asking, Do you know the invention for which Norway is most famous? The aerosol spray can.

The tourist will then turn his blue eyes to his companion and say, *Really*. I had no idea.

In 1926 by Mr. Erik Rotheim, chemical engineer, Tư might add.

He also attempts to wow with statistics—a communist education encourages such things—the land area of each administrative division in the country, for instance, the number of university graduates from various faculties, the lengths of the Mekong and Red rivers and the Great Wall of China.

Really.

It was Phương who pulled him aside one day and said, "When they say *really*, it actually means *that is very boring*."

"Really?" Tư asked.

"Really."

Tư believes it is shared wisdom like this that has made them the A-team. But he is still learning, and perhaps that is what he likes best about his job. No pain, no gain, as the Americans say.

This morning, he and Phương are escorting a middle-aged Canadian couple to some nearby villages. Tư likes the Canadians, even if their most exciting invention was only the garbage bag. (*Really*. In 1950 by Mr. Harry Wasylyk of Winnipeg, Manitoba.) They are generally kind, though it always amuses him how they introduce themselves with variations of: Hello, nice to meet you, we are from Canada, see the maple leaves sewn onto our knapsacks? Our country might be right next door, but it's a world apart from its southern neighbour; in fact, we offered refuge to a great many draft dodgers who did not believe the Americans should be in Vietnam—horrible, horrible war, horrible, horrible U.S.A., horrible, horrible George Bush, and Iraq, now don't get me started on Iraq . . .

Yes, yes, Tư will nod and smile, because he does not want to speak a truth they will find complicated or disagreeable. This is what is meant by saving face. The war was a long time ago, well before Tư was born, and besides, in his opinion, an opinion shared with most of his friends, everything great was invented in the U.S. Blue jeans, for example. And Nikes and Tommy Hilfiger. And MTV and Nintendo and the Internet. And furthermore, the Vietnamese *beat* the Americans; they don't go around boasting about it, but it's true. It wasn't like the Chinese, crushing the Vietnamese for a thousand years, or the French who tortured and killed for decades, making the Vietnamese slaves in their own country and taking every decision out of their hands.

While such thoughts might fly around like a Ping-Pong

ball inside Tu's head, none of his clients would ever suspect it. Tu works hard to impress them with his good nature and exemplary customer service, and is ever-ready with his New Dawn smile.

Today's Canadians are from Quebec, the first French Canadians Tu has ever met. "We too were colonized by the French, as I am sure you are aware," he said when he met them in the lobby yesterday, attempting to establish some common bond.

Their reaction had caused Tu to spend most of last night in an Internet café. Today he hopes to redeem himself with sensitive insights into their unique history and culture. He will need to, because Phương, green with hangover, does not look like he will be of any particular help.

Tu is indebted to his friend for changing his life, and he considers Phương a brother. He envies him like a brother too. Phương is taller and leaner, but it's not Tu's fault he inherited his father's slightly bowed legs. The baggy jeans fortunately help disguise this. And at least both his eyes are real; there is no danger of inheriting his father's glass eye. Tu doesn't have nearly as white a smile as Phương's, his upper teeth having been stained from taking antibiotics when he was a kid, but again—not his fault. And his hands? A little small, but surely more than made up for by the size and enthusiasm of his penis, as his future wife will discover.

Currently there are no candidates for that job. An introduction through family is always best, and even if Phương prefers random girls for himself, as Tu's honorary older brother, he introduces him to girls from time to time.

Last Christmas there was this one girl Phương kept chatting about, and while Tư was interested at first, the more
stories about her charitable work that Phương recounted,
the less interested Tư became. By the time Phương finally
introduced them, Tư was expecting someone with a shaved
head in a flowing saffron robe who had no interest in romance
or other worldly (i.e., carnal) matters. Instead, he was
introduced to a cute girl dressed as one of Santa's helpers.
She was wearing a short, fuzzy red-and-white miniskirt
and her hair was tied into flirty Japanese-schoolgirl-style
ponytails underneath her floppy Santa hat. Tư suddenly felt
very shy. He felt other things too, but very shy was perhaps
second on the list.

It was Christmas Eve and the three of them were standing among two thousand other Buddhists facing St. Joseph's
Cathedral with its blazing neon-blue manger. There were
balloons and streamers and ribbons of fake snow floating
through the air above, a rainbow of coloured lights beaming
off the top of the church and music blaring over giant loud-
speakers on the church steps, but all Tư felt was the fuzzy
warmth of the girl's skirt as she stood wedged between
them, all he smelled was her perfume beyond the plastic
scent of her clothes, all he felt, suddenly, was her hand on
his hand, her head on his shoulder, all he heard was her
whispering in his ear, "You can kiss me, you can touch me,
if you'd like."

Tư was shocked: there they were wedged together in the
crowd when she turned toward him, barely an inch between
their noses, and took his hand and placed it on her breast,

which was like a perfect brioche from a French bakery, the nipple like a hard raisin. She then slipped her hand down between them and, although she had no room to manoeuvre, she managed to rub his penis through his jeans. In thirty seconds he erupted, making a sound like a small sneezing dog.

He never saw the girl again. He tried to call her the next day but her cellphone number didn't even exist. It was only then that he asked Phương, "That girl, she wasn't . . . ? Phương, you didn't . . . did you?"

"Merry Christmas, my friend."

Tư had been extremely embarrassed about the whole thing and wondered if this is what Phương had meant when he referred to her "charitable work." Still, he does savour the memory of it and dream of the meal that will come when he marries, because if he ever does get that close to a *real* girl, he will certainly be marrying her, although he doesn't want to marry *that* kind of girl, he wants a quiet and traditional girl, one he can introduce with pride to everyone in his family, one who will belong among them, for she will come to live with him and his parents as tradition dictates, because Tư is the first-born and only son.

Above all, his future wife must show great respect to Old Man Hưng. The old man is patriarch of their family in a unique and complicated way, beyond blood. Tư's father has known Old Man Hưng since boyhood, since before he was Old Man and was just Hưng. He is the one who kept Grandfather Đạo's flame burning, holding it close through decades of poverty and war, and waiting patiently for the day when he could share it and pass it on.

Old Man Hưng has been present at every important occasion of Tư's life. From his birth to every Tet holiday to his graduation. Given how much the old man seems to have aged over the past few months, Tư worries the remaining occasions are numbered. He means no disrespect to Grandfather Đạo, but on such occasions, and even in the day-to-day, Tư feels Hưng to be more of a real grandfather to him than the legendary poet whose image sits enshrined on an overturned crate inside Hưng's rickety old shack on the shore of a manky pond.

Introducing a girl to Old Man Hưng would be the ultimate test of her moral character. Hưng is poorer than poor, and the wrong girl would be put off by the association and might begin to worry about the security of her future. Even if Tư is ashamed by the old man's poverty himself at times, the truth is, Tư is looking for someone who is a better person than he.

Mr. and Mrs. Henri Lévesque have just entered the lobby, putting an end to this introspection. "You've slept well?" Tư asks. "Had a satisfactory breakfast? You have enjoyed some of the amenities of the hotel such as the free Wi-Fi? You have your camera in your bag there? This is our driver, Phương, and he will be taking us to the ethnic minority craft villages this morning. First in our journey, we will be crossing the Red River via one of the city's three bridges. The Red River comes to us from China through the Honghe Autonomous Prefecture in Yunnan Province and runs in a southeasterly direction for a total of 1,175 kilometres before emptying itself in the Gulf of Tonkin."

"*Really*," mumbles Phương, as he leads the couple down the steps toward the van.

Hưng pats his shirt pocket. The young woman's business card is nestled there alongside Tư's, which the boy insists Hưng keep on his person at all times. He indulges Tư with the solemn promise to do so, even if he does find the implication somewhat patronizing.

Hưng uses all his strength to push his cart through the streets toward the Hàng Da Market, where he will visit Bình's wife, Anh, at her butcher stall. She is very good company, always up for a bit of conversation over a calming cup of jasmine tea, but there is a particular urgency to his pace this morning: he hopes the business card might reveal a clue. His desire to remember something, anything about this girl's father feels so acute it could lead a man to fanciful thoughts, if not outright fabrication. He needs to work with the few pieces of information he's been given.

When Hưng tires of pushing his wooden cart, he turns it around and pulls it, his arms stretched out behind him like the yoke that harnesses an ox. He can feel the road rough against the sole of his left foot; time once again to replace a slipper. Fortunately, being far from fashionable, these black vinyl slippers are cheap. He remembers a time in the not-too-distant past when everyone wore them and had no choice. For a few years they were the only shoes you could buy in the government shops. One was rarely lucky enough to find the right size or a matching pair, but since everyone faced the same predicament, people were always prepared to engage in a frantic yet good-natured exchange in the street.

Such communality is rare these days. Now Hưng passes a new shoe shop every day, where shoes with prices marked in both đồng and U.S. dollars hang like ripe fruit. The streets of the Old Quarter shine with imported merchandise, where not long ago they only gave off the fumes of disintegration, the smell of rot. At times the glare seems far too bright.

Hưng grinds to a halt in front of the market. He has over-exerted himself and needs a moment of rest. He lifts the biggest of his pots from his cart and inverts it, plunking it down with a hollow boom on the sidewalk. He plants his bottom firmly upon it, his legs spread wide apart, and waves to the sugar-cane seller, gesturing for a cup of juice. He rests his knees on his elbows and rubs his eyes with the heels of his hands. What a dramatic and emotional morning it has been.

Seeing Bình rise and approach the foreman had cast him right back to those heady days in the early 1950s when Đạo and the circle of artists and intellectuals who gathered around him would congregate for breakfast in the shop Hưng had by then inherited from Uncle Chiến.

Bình, tiny then, would sit on a low wooden stool at his father's side, looking terrified of splashing his white shirt as he bent his head over his bowl and tried to manipulate a pair of long chopsticks between his small fingers.

Đạo and the other men completely failed to notice the boy's travails, consumed as they were with news of the liberation struggle and engaged in heated debates about the future of Vietnam. After abandoning his bowl, little Bình would sit patiently beside his father, who was alternately scribbling in a leather-bound notebook or arguing a point by jabbing the air with the burning end of his cigarette.

Hưng, alone, saw the boy. And Bình's invisibility gnawed at his heart.

"Come," Hưng said at last, drawing Bình away from the table. "There is a bird nesting above the frame of the door."

The boy padded through Hưng's backroom after him, where Hưng pointed to the nest wedged under the eaves.

"Are there babies?" he remembers Bình asking.

Hưng had crouched down and encouraged the boy to climb up and sit on his shoulders. Hưng tottered upright, pinning the boy's calves against his chest. "Can you see inside?"

"There's a blue egg," Bình said, his voice full of wonder. "When will it hatch?"

"I tell you what," Hưng said. "We'll have a look every day until it does."

One night, Hưng took a pair of ivory chopsticks, sawed off their tips and sanded them until they were nicely tapered and polished. He pulled Bình out of the inferno the next morning to present these to him. The boy held them in one hand and clutched them against his chest as he walked back to the table unnoticed and resumed his seat. The glow in Bình's eyes as he turned the chopsticks over in his hands and admired them from all angles had given Hưng the sense, for the briefest of moments, of what it might feel like to be a father. He had felt it again this morning watching Bình rise to address the foreman: that same proud flicker of paternal love. Age is doing its inevitable though, and reversing their roles; the son is now defending the father.

How gentle and selfless Bình has always been. How bold and idealistic was his father. But perhaps the politics of a time determine the disposition of a man; perhaps a revolutionary is only a revolutionary in revolutionary times. Hưng cannot say with any certainty what makes a man. But he certainly knows what breaks one.

Perhaps the poor girl who turned up unexpectedly this morning knows something of this too. If Lý Văn Hai was among the men who used to frequent Hưng's shop, he is unlikely to have met a happy end.

Right, he says to himself, slapping his thighs. Time to tell Anh about the girl and the ghost who is her father. Hưng presses his palms into his knees and pushes himself upright with a groan. He really is getting old. He has begun to wonder what Buddha has in store for him in the afterlife, whether it be reincarnation as a bull or a bug.

Hưng offers the bird seller a thousand đồng to watch his cart. The bird seller bargains for double. Hưng passes over a greasy wad of small bills, then makes his way unburdened toward a pink pyramid of stacked pigs in the far corner of the market.

Anh waves a large blade in greeting. She puts the knife down and wipes her bloodied hands on her white smock before delicately taking the business card Hưng holds out to her by the edges. She does not read English either. They need someone of Tư's generation to translate. Anh calls over the fishmonger's son, but he shakes his head: he was in a boat as a boy, not a classroom.

The district propaganda broadcast is reaching its peak as the business card is passed from bloodied hand to fish-scaled hand to muddied hand throughout the stalls of the market. A voice backfires like an exhaust pipe through the loud-speaker, spluttering the names and addresses of those who have neglected to pay their garbage collection fee or renew their motorbike licence or turned eighteen and failed to report for military duty.

Having heard his own name so many times, Hưng is immune to this public shaming. He's more attuned to the smaller sounds, the burps of nature. Frogs croaking their final days in pans of slimy water; birds twittering in their lacy cages. Despite all the years he has lived in Hanoi, Hưng can still hear a canary sing above the propaganda broadcast, over the thrum and burr of engines and the orchestra of competing horns. He can still discern a note of nature's grace.

The card is a stampede of fingerprints by the time it is returned to Hưng, but someone has written a translation of the words on its reverse.

MISS MAGGIE LY
Curator of Art
Hotel Sofitel Metropole
15 Ngô Quyền Street

➢ luxury at the heart of Hanoi since 1901 ➢

A Seam Between Worlds

Maggie's taxi is now wedged into a jam of idling engines. She wants to reach over the driver, punch the steering wheel and join the chorus of horns. On any other day she would simply lean her head back against the seat, resigned to the futility of fighting Hanoi's traffic, but she feels renewed this morning, more hopeful than she has in months. That faint glimmer of recognition in the old man's eyes as he repeated her father's name had been like finally seeing a sliver of light peek out from under an iron curtain. She'd wanted to slip her hand underneath, whatever the risk of being crushed, to grope around for a hand to take hold of on the other side.

She's spent a frustrating and painful year combing through archives that have yielded no evidence of her

father. She's found no reference to him in the archives of
the Fine Arts Museum, not even a single catalogue for an
exhibition where his work might have been shown. Even
his presence at the city's former École des Beaux Arts is in
question—there's no record of his attendance at the school.
The censors literally cut the names of dissident artists out
of registries and publications. They've been systematic and
thorough revisionists, leaving a history full of holes.

The records would suggest Lý Văn Hai never existed.
But if that is so, whose daughter is she? And who was the
man with the hands gnarled like a boxer's from an accident
he refused to talk about, the one who taught her to write the
English alphabet with a pen gripped between the knuckles
of his index and middle fingers, the one who sketched crude
animals for her with his claw, trying to guide her own hand
in imitation as they knelt side by side on the floor of their
room in Saigon?

He used to hold her hand every morning as they walked
down the street together even though he had no grip. People
referred to him as her grandfather because he was relatively
old when she was born, the fourth and only one of her
mother's pregnancies to result in a child. His hair had turned
completely white during the three years he'd been interned
in a re-education camp after returning from the U.S.

For a Vietnamese man, Maggie's father displayed what
she knew even then to be an unusual amount of public affection, kissing her on the forehead when he dropped her off at
school on the base every morning—a school for the children
of the friendliest of friendly Vietnamese, those who were

working directly for the Americans. Her mother worked as a nurse, and her father as a translator because, although he could no longer paint, he could speak English thanks to the four years he'd spent studying in Chicago in the early 1950s.

"I missed you today," he would often say when he picked her up.

"But, Daddy, I was here at school the whole time. Just where you left me."

There were days when there was no school and the three of them stayed in their shuttered room, her father kneeling on the cracked linoleum floor, bending over paper and sketching a story for her with his claw while her mother cooked over a kerosene burner, the smell of rice mixing with the incense they burned to mask the stench of sewage beyond the bamboo curtain.

Her parents would whisper at night, Maggie lying on one mattress, her parents on another, discussing the progress of the war, making plans. Maggie's stomach would flutter as if full of fish. "*If* we have a choice," her mother would whisper, and the fish would get rough with their tails.

Only when they were standing on the tarmac at Tân Sơn Nhất air base in 1975 about to board a U.S. military plane did Maggie realize a choice had been made. Her father had stepped out of line as they approached the plane, joining the other men gathered to one side. Maggie broke free from her mother, running toward her father, mashing her forehead into his stomach and digging her nails into the back of his thighs.

"Little one," he said, trying to loosen her grip with his claws. "Listen." He squatted so that he could face her. "We have no choice, Maggie. The men who did this to my hands? The men from the North? They are coming to Saigon."

The heat rising from the tarmac wavered like water and the fumes of the plane made Maggie feel woozy. She buried her face in her father's neck and inhaled the peppery smell of his sweat and the starch from the collar of his shirt.

"It is women and children first to safety," her father said, patting her back with his claw. "I will be coming on another plane."

Maggie looked over her shoulder at her mother in her nurse's uniform, holding a baby that was not her own. Lined up behind her were hundreds of nurses and nuns holding the hands of children and cradling a great many crying babies.

"You go back to your mother now. You keep her company. Be strong," he said, giving her a gentle push.

"But, Daddy——"

"She needs you, Mouse."

When Maggie stepped out of the arrivals building at Hanoi's airport a year ago, the combination of jet fuel and sweat and the starched shirts of men had caused her to drop her bags and bury her face in her hands. The smell of home was indistinguishable from the smell of leaving home: each inhalation a mix of familiarity and fear.

The recognition ended there. Maggie entered a city so much brighter and busier than the cold and dark portrait of Hanoi she had inherited from her mother. The optimism and energy of the place, with its doors thrown open to the West, its new wealth and possibilities—her mother wouldn't have believed the spirit, the surging adrenalin of three and a half million dreams being pursued simultaneously with little concern for what is stirred up in their wake.

Maggie found herself in a world of teenagers, a generation fuelled by hopes and hormones, people who had no interest in being dragged back to the past. They face forward, the future, the West. The past is abandoned: the pain of it, perhaps; the shame of it. It's old men Maggie must turn to now, old men with their ailing, fading memories and their fears.

A few months ago, an artist whose work Maggie has on display in the hotel gallery had directed her to just one such old man, telling her about a café that served as an informal gallery of artwork from the dark days before Đổi mới. Maggie had made her way to Nguyễn Hữu Huân Street later that same day. She paused in the doorway for a few minutes as her eyes adjusted to the light. Huge cracks ran across the tiled floor as if the building had survived an earthquake, and the thick metal bars on the windows gave it a penal air. A few men sat on low wooden stools drinking coffee and a fluorescent light buzzed overhead, casting a greenish pall over the room.

The walls were crammed with pieces of art hanging so closely together it was as if they formed a continuous mural. Maggie moved around the room, looking at each piece in turn, noticing how many of them were neither signed nor dated.

As she neared the kitchen, the café owner, Mr. Võ, shuffled forth in black slippers, broom in hand. She introduced

herself, but he did not smile. Older Hanoians have recoiled
at her American accent before, but his lack of warmth made
her particularly cautious. According to the artist, Mr. Võ
was notoriously wary of foreigners, especially those interested in art. He'd been hounded by dealers and collectors in
recent years.

"I was told this is where you could see the real old
Hanoi," she said, which did at least soften his expression.
"You knew all of these artists?" She gestured at the walls.

"Of course," he said.

"Did you ever know a Lý Văn Hai?"

Mr. Võ's bottom lip curled upward. "He must have been
one of Hưng's," he said, with a shrug.

Maggie shook her head, not understanding.

"He's a phở seller," said Mr. Võ. "Years ago he had a
shop where a lot of artists ate breakfast, but now he's on the
street, always moving."

"Do you know how I can find him?"

"They say you find him with your nose."

But it had taken more than her senses. After three
months of asking virtually everyone on staff, every artist
and dealer she knew, every driver or tour guide she found
waiting in the lobby of the Metropole, she finally got lucky.
Yesterday she met the new sous-chef who has been hired in
the kitchen—a French-trained Indian woman named Rikia
Saddy who speaks enviably flawless Vietnamese.

"I've heard he makes the best phở in the city," the
woman said, pouring Maggie a cup of coffee as thick as
melted chocolate.

"But if it's the best phở in the city, why don't more people know about it?" Maggie asked, leaning back against the stainless steel counter.

"I don't think it's a secret, just something shared with a small number of people. My husband's driver takes his breakfast from him."

Rikia phoned her husband later in the day. She came back to Maggie with the name of a new hotel under construction on the east shore of West Lake. "He says to bring your bowl before seven. And be prepared to run if the police turn up."

And so Maggie had brought her bowl this morning and introduced herself to Old Man Hưng. And seeing that faint look of recognition on his face as he said her father's name? A seismic moment that revealed a seam between worlds.

Hưng leans all his weight into his cart to push it the last hundred metres down the dirt track to the shantytown. He parks his cart behind his shack and hauls his pots down to the bank of the pond, resting them in the mud while he goes to fetch the papaya milk he uses to wash his apron.

As he puts his key into the padlock, he sees a package jutting out from under the corrugated tin eaves. Bình must have come by, that was good of him—here are his glasses, the wonky arm straightened, the cracked lens replaced.

There is little that can be done about the eye with a cataract, but with glasses, the sight of his right eye is measurably improved. Hưng can once again see the Cyrillic letters stamped on the canvas from which, years ago, he sewed himself a straw-filled mattress. If he leans into the scrap-metal wall of his shack, he can make out some of the headlines of the old newspapers he stuffed into the cracks to keep out the winter draft. But he has given up reading, gave that up some time ago; it just reminds him of all he has lost.

Hưng carries his bottle of papaya milk down to the pond and douses his apron with it, then rubs the material back and forth against the washing stone before rinsing it along with his cooking pots in the pond's brown water. From where he squats at the water's edge, he can spy a nest among the reeds, two ripe eggs waiting to be claimed. He thinks better of it, though, thinks of the long term, a luxury that has only come about in recent years.

A pond has its own ecosystem, largely unobserved by humans, except when their lives come to depend upon it. Hưng, who had drifted like some one hundred and fifty others to this muddy, buggy shore in the middle of an industrial wasteland at the edge of the city, has long been a keen and attuned observer. Hưng came from the country and the country is still in him. He knows the exact conditions that will promote the spread of algae, the precise details of the dragonfly's life cycle and where the various pond and shore creatures bury their eggs. He'd been a student of nature as a child, a study encouraged by his father, in lieu of companionship, that he could never have known would be of such use in an urban life.

Like Hưng, the people who collected on this shore in the late 1950s had lost everything. They were eating rats and the lice from their hair. Their shacks were built of scrap metal, woven pond reeds and bamboo posts. The trees had been felled by government edict. The land had been stripped of its small dwellings and kitchen gardens in keeping with Uncle Hồ's promise of industrial revolution. The combination of the tire factory across the pond and the construction of blocks of socialist housing co-operatives to the east produced great burning clouds of tar that floated overhead so that on a good day the sun appeared a weak orange through grey gauze.

But nature is a fighter and Hưng was a man blessed with a cook's imagination. He had immediately seen the promise lurking beneath the surface of this pool of lazy, brown, mosquito-breeding water. No one in the shantytown would go hungry as long as Hưng was there, a fact that became apparent just shortly after his arrival when he caught a duck, the first duck anyone had seen in over a year, among the reeds.

Hưng had wrung the bird's neck and plucked it before applying a burning stick to the leeches that had affixed themselves to his feet and ankles. He then drained the blood to make a custard, peeled off the skin and fried it into golden strips, and used the fat he'd scraped from the inside of the skin to flavour and fry the shredded breast meat. He boiled and mashed the liver with a few peppercorns he had in his possession; he stewed the duck's feet in the juice of a single orange; he roasted the duck's eyes and brains on the sharpened ends of chopsticks; he boiled the carcass, heart and kidneys to make a broth; he chopped the boiled heart and kidneys and dark meat of the legs and wrapped the mince in betel leaves and sautéed the remaining meat with sliced pondweed and wild leeks.

The smells enticed neighbours, and neighbours enticed those beyond, and soon a lineup of people had formed in front of his shack—shabbily dressed, grime-encrusted men, women and children with sharp cheekbones and skin variously scabbed, pockmarked and grey. Each clutched a pair of chopsticks and bowed a head in thanks before sampling the elements of the feast Hưng had prepared.

But Hưng himself had forgotten to eat that day. He had been left without hunger or breath by the sight of the girl who emerged with her grandmother from the shack next to his, a girl with the graceful posture of a crane and skin as pearlescent as eggshell.

You do not belong here, he wanted to say to this vision. *My God. You belong on a throne.*

He watched her eat from her bowl like the daintiest of birds, and found he was still staring in the direction of the shack where she lived with her grandmother several hours after she'd disappeared into it.

People thanked him for the feast with small gifts the next day—a piece of rusted tin, a single palm frond, a stalk of bamboo, an old newspaper, a broken pane of glass—one by one the pieces to build his shack came together. The girl next door emerged, offering him two dried rinds of star anise, dropping them into his open hand without raising her eyes. "From my grandmother," she said in a voice as sweet as birdsong.

Hưng could scarcely believe the girl was real.

While he felt moved to thank his new friends and neighbours for their gifts, at least part of his motivation to repeat the feast the following month had been desire. He wanted to feed the girl and feel her near.

For that second feast he speared and threaded water snakes onto a spit; he grilled small, ugly fish with ancient mouths over the fire; he boiled tiny birds' eggs in salted water; he marinated layers of those eggs in the juice of fermented berries; and he boiled snails and crayfish, offering crunchy, sliced bamboo shoots on the side.

The woman next door thanked him with a deep bow of gratitude. "It was dignified and so delicious," she said, then pushed her granddaughter forward by the small of her back.

"Thank you, sir," said the girl, her eyes lowered to the ground.

"This is Lan," said the older woman.

Lan. She was the orchid of her name, as elegant and rare. Hưng looked to the ground himself, not wanting to sully her virgin whiteness with the impurity of his gaze. "Hưng," he said with a cough. "Just Hưng, not sir."

The gift-giving continued, his neighbours bringing him pieces for the interior of his house: assorted single bricks, strips of soft bark from a eucalyptus tree, a woven grass mat, a pot someone had fashioned out of clay, tins once discarded by the French army, coconut shells from the beautiful Lan and her grandmother for ladling water, drinking broth, serving tea.

He made tea from artichokes—their hearts dried and cut

like leaves—luring the grandmother and the girl with this brew, drawing them over from their shack to his, where it became something of a nightly ritual for the three of them to sit together on a grass mat under a starless sky. They said little initially. Sharing stories of the past, tales of where they'd come from, seemed an unnecessary expenditure of energy when survival in the present demanded such effort.

All around them were thieves stealing ration coupons, hawkers selling whatever they could, parents pressed into selling their daughters into prostitution. Hưng tuned his senses for early detection of those overdressed men who came prowling through the shantytown. As soon as he caught a whiff of hair oil he would call out to the girl and her grandmother: "Come and keep me company on this dreary day, will you? I've got another story you might like. Something that will put a bit of sun in this grey sky."

It was the fear of losing Lan to traffickers or, if he is honest with himself, simply losing her to another man that led Hưng to instigate conversation, entertaining the girl and her grandmother with anecdotes about the men who used to gather in his shop.

"I once knew a man who could look at the most ordinary sky and see such beautiful things hidden there. A river, a pagoda, a mountain, a man and his buffalo, a pair of sisters dancing in the sun."

Hưng, Lan and her grandmother would look to the sky just at the very moment the men in suits were snaking by, and Hưng would say, "Hard to imagine it now when it is such a grey blanket, but that line there between the clouds, can you see it? It looks like the tail of a turtledove, don't you think?"

"I can see the dove," Lan would say, her mouth hanging open. "The whole dove, not just the tail."

"This man would describe what he'd seen in the sky and then someone like my friend Đạo might find himself inspired and spontaneously give birth to a poem."

Admittedly, Hưng elevated his own status in these stories by referring to Đạo as a friend. He knows he was never the man's equal. Hưng had spent years in awe of Đạo, who, despite being five years his junior, had been something of a mentor to him. Đạo took an interest in Hưng's aborted education, encouraging his desire to read and engaging him in the debates of the time. He had shown Hưng a respect to which he was unaccustomed.

"My friend Đạo believed everyone had a right to an opinion," he told Lan and her grandmother. "Wherever he came from. Or she. 'Let's hear what Hưng has to say on the matter,' he used to say.

"The men seated at the table with him laughed at first. Laughed and pointed at me. Why was this learned young man they all looked up to soliciting the opinion of a simple country boy turned cook? they wondered.

"'Stop it,' Đạo would say, batting his hand in the air as if he was swatting at flies. 'I think his perspective could be useful here.' I remember him turning to me and asking, 'What do you think, Hưng? Should all things cost the same? One pair of shoes, one watermelon, one bowl of phở?'

"They were all staring at me, waiting for an answer,"

Hưng told the girl and her grandmother. "I did not know what Đạo expected of me, so I simply said what I knew to be true. 'You come here for some reason. There is cheaper phở.'

"'You see?' Đạo raised his finger and smiled. 'We are hypocrites where it suits us. We will always be willing to pay the difference for a superior bowl.'"

Lan laughed like a bird might laugh, a giddy twitter she stifled with her hand.

Lan's enjoyment of Hưng's stories made Đạo real again, leading Hưng to feel both the pain of Đạo's absence and the simultaneous relief from that pain. The girl was a balm to him: both her desire for his stories and her improbable beauty. Even though much of the latter was concealed by the government-issue black pyjama bottoms and shirt she wore, when she was bent over washing pots in the pond, her spine, as delicate as that of a fish, pressed into the back of her shirt, he would think how much better she deserved—an *áo dài* of luxurious silk to grace her frame, gold for her elegant wrists and fingers, a pearl necklace, a garland of jasmine for her hair.

Hưng prayed she was old enough to understand her impact, though he guessed her an innocent of no more than eighteen. She called him Uncle, but Hưng's feelings toward the girl were not those of an uncle. He was almost forty then—a middle-aged man in love with a girl half his age—an ugly man, a poor man, a man in love for the first time in his life.

Although the girl's grandmother would often fall asleep while they sat on the grass mat together, her dreams whistling through her nostrils, Lan would remain bright, nodding, asking questions in a voice as soft as silken tofu, causing Hưng to forget the squalor that surrounded them and transporting the two of them to some alternative plane.

"Tell me about the Hundred Flowers, Uncle."

"Teach me why you prefer poems that do not rhyme."

She would lie on her side, her heart-shaped face resting in her upturned palm, her perfect feet moving back and forth against each other according to some internal rhythm.

Tell me. Teach me. Poetry and politics. In the absence of both, she had made him feel he still had something to give. These had been exquisite moments: a brief respite from life on earth, a journey to some faraway Buddhist heaven. But it is not a place he has visited ever since. He has neither the means nor the desire. He turned his back to her long ago, and his heart became a stone. They do not even acknowledge each other, have not done so now for over forty years.

She has lived alone in the hut next door since her grandmother died, refusing to move. Whether this is motivated by a deliberate wish to torture him or rooted in some more benign and practical reasoning, he really cannot say. The effect upon him is the same, regardless.

There is a particular bird that sings in the same register as her speaking voice, but he has managed to so thoroughly block out the song of this bird that it may as well belong to a species extinct. He even finds the cataract that began to cloud his vision a couple of years ago something of a blessing. It limits his peripheral vision so that he can't see her shack when he retrieves the apron he leaves to dry outside over the handle of his cart. Why then does he find himself glancing briefly to his left this afternoon as he reaches for his apron? Why has he been thinking of her at all? It is because of the girl who came for breakfast. A beautiful girl, imploring. Maggie Lý, the daughter of an artist, Lý Văn Hai. *Tell me*, she might just as well have said, *teach me*.

Lan is hunched over a wicker basket now, picking dirt and stones out of a bushel of rice, or perhaps shelling peanuts for sale, or maybe she has been lucky enough to find a cluster of tree ear mushrooms from which she is brushing dirt.

Hưng shakes his head to be rid of her and looks to his right instead, toward his neighbour Phúc Li, a man who, as a boy, lost his legs to a land mine and perhaps a bit of his mind as well, sitting as he does with his hand cupping his genitals, his old mother trimming his hair.

The legless Phúc Li waves to Hưng, grinning like a child watching fireworks. His mother snaps the rusty shears shut over his head. "Do you want me to do you next, Hưng?"

"I'll give it another week," Hưng says, running his hand over his few remaining strands of hair.

Hưng crouches to enter the door of his shack, lays his dry apron down on his straw mattress and roots for the needle and thread he keeps inside an old rubber boot. He stares at Đạo's framed image on the altar as he digs around in the toe. The picture is all he really has left of Đạo, having forgotten all his poems over the years. It was drawn for him by a woman who had come begging decades ago. "Look, we're all poor here," he had said to her as she stood on the threshold of his shack. "I'm sorry, but I have nothing to give you."

Much to his horror, she unbuttoned her shirt then and tossed it to the ground, revealing a bony, scabbed chest. "Stop that," he reprimanded, picking up her shirt and tossing it back at her. "Cover yourself. What do you think you are doing?"

"You can lie with me and do what you want," she said. "Pay me anything."

"Woman," he said with disgust, "what did you do before life came to this?"

The woman said she had been a tea lady at the art school.

"And did you learn anything of art while you were there? Did you learn to draw, for instance?"

She nodded once and cast her eyes to the ground.

But Hưng had no paper. The only thing he could think to do was tear out one of the endpapers from *Fine Works of Spring*, the journal Đạo and his colleagues had published a few years earlier. And so Hưng had squatted beside the woman as she laboured her way toward some likeness of Đạo, using a piece of charcoal from Hưng's kitchen fire.

He attempted to describe Đạo to the woman as best he could, but found a simple physical description of the man could not adequately capture his spirit. Once she had a basic outline of his face, Hưng interjected, "His eyes were set a bit farther apart, almost as if he had a wider view than an ordinary man, that of a visionary."

Đạo had made references in his poetry to tragedies that had not even befallen them yet, as if he could intuit the future. He had sought to warn people of what was imminent, hoping to inspire them to action. And Hưng had marvelled at his ability to do so in such few perfect words.

"He was fearless," Hưng told the woman. "He had a scar, just here, a mark of courage that ran two inches across the bone of his cheek."

Hưng had offered the woman his bed for a week as payment, while he himself slept outside. The frame for Đạo's portrait—that, he hadn't been in a position to make for years, not until he found a way to sell phở again and someone paid him with a piece of glass.

Hưng notices a spiderweb glistening at the edge of the frame now. He can picture Bình as a boy, his face contorted in concentration as he counted the silk rings of a web. The fate of those on earth depends upon honouring the ancestral spirits, and Hưng has kept Đạo's memory alive for Bình, whose father disappeared when he was only six years old.

Hưng peels the silken web away with his forefinger, lights a stick of incense and offers up his hands in prayer. He wishes Đạo well on whatever higher plane he now inhabits and he prays that they will know each other in the next life. But there are things Hưng must impart before he allows the spirits to take him on that journey. At a minimum he has a recipe to pass on. "The taste of home" is how an artist had once, long ago, described his phở.

My God, thinks Hưng. That someone. His hungry eyes hovering above a bowl. The man had been travelling; he had come by ship from America and his legs were still wobbly. He was carrying his belongings in a sack and he said he hadn't had a bowl of phở in years. Hưng had wondered how the man could still be standing.

The man's name was Lý Văn Hai, Hưng is sure of it. He must tell Miss Maggie Lý that he did once meet her father, if only briefly. He will make his way to her fancy hotel tomorrow and do just that, he thinks, patting the card in his shirt pocket.

"Đạo," he says to the portrait in front of him, "do you remember Lý Văn Hai? Eating phở in my shop one morning? You must have been there too."

He needs Đạo's help. There is simply too much for one old man alone to remember.

New Dawn

Maggie had deliberated about returning to the old man for breakfast this morning. She doesn't want to push, but she's impatient. You left him your card, she reminds herself. He knows how to get in touch if anything comes to mind.

She stops in the kitchen to thank Rikia for directing her to Hưng yesterday, then battles her way into her office holding a cup of coffee at shoulder height. The room is a bit of a disaster, crammed with pieces of art she has pulled out of storage leaning four deep against each wall. She has to tear through a forest of cardboard and brown paper just to reach her desk, spilling half her cup of coffee as she does.

She's eighty-five per cent of the way through cataloguing the hotel's collection—an incomparable body of work from the colonial era found stashed in the bomb shelter beneath the hotel. The art had survived both the war and the decades of the hotel's service as a Communist Party guesthouse, during which the building had deteriorated into a rat- and bat-infested dump.

The story of the collection's discovery had reached her through a colleague at the Walker Art Center in Minneapolis. "There's a real opportunity there," he had said, and Maggie had known this to be true in her gut. A hidden vault of art in her father's city. The opportunity to bring its contents to light. Her mother no longer alive to dissuade her. And Daniel's feelings no longer a consideration before her own.

Maggie came up with a proposal, which she pitched to the French management company undertaking the Metropole's refurbishment, to open a contemporary gallery in the hotel. Her timing couldn't have been better. Interest in contemporary Vietnamese art has surged over the last decade— having a gallery at the hotel made sound business sense. So did having a Vietnamese-speaking curator with a master's degree in curation from the Art Institute of Chicago who could do the work of preserving and cataloguing the original collection.

She spent her first month and a half in Hanoi below ground in a metal chamber with a flashlight. Her first weeks were all cool surfaces, taut canvases and a pounding heart. She pored through work that spanned the five and a half decades from the hotel's opening in 1901 to the expulsion of the French in 1954—her father's era, the world into which he was born, the one in which he drew, grew up, painted.

She was hopeful then. But that hope grew heavy, canvas by canvas, sheet by sheet, until it hung above her like a leaden cloud. And then finally a sliver of light. An old man. A phở seller. Mr. Hưng.

Maggie lifts a black-and-white painting and props it on the arms of a chair. A string of barbed wire made up of Chinese characters runs across the canvas. She was looking for this piece yesterday; it's by the Hoa artist she represents. Maggie is a collector of lost sheep: artists like this one who fall between cracks. In Vietnam, her Hoa artist is not recognized as Vietnamese, but in China, where he spent his adolescence after his people were expelled from Vietnam, he isn't recognized as Chinese either.

Maggie can relate. While she might look Vietnamese, this only gets her so far. She has had shopkeepers quadruple their prices as soon as she opens her mouth, people mock her accent, gossip behind her back and treat her with a great deal of suspicion. They call her Việt Kiều—some watered-down and inferior species of Vietnamese—a sojourner, an exile, a traitor, a refugee. However people might regard her, Maggie has to content herself with the knowledge that her roots are here, the family stories, as remote and inaccessible as they might be.

Maggie's mother was not a storyteller. She revealed very little over the years, and it was only after suffering a stroke two years ago that she offered anything unprompted. "Your father didn't feel entirely Vietnamese," she said one day from her hospital bed. "His experience in the U.S. changed him. He felt it had made him a better artist and a better person, and he wasn't going to let anyone take that away from him."

They had been speaking about apples just the moment before; she was craving the tart juice of a hard, green variety she had eaten as a child. It had taken Maggie a minute to follow: to move from the taste of fruit to this rare mention of her father. She seized the opportunity then, exhaling the question that had haunted her for the thirty years since that day she had said goodbye to him on the tarmac.

"What happened to him in the camp? His hands?"

Her mother turned away at the question.

Maggie sat down on the bed and leaned her chin upon her mother's silken head. She felt a tremor run through her mother's body as if she had just exorcised a small ghost.

The truth her mother revealed to her that afternoon is one Maggie has since kept caged in her chest. There was a time when she might have shared that painful story with someone—with Daniel—but that time had passed.

"They might have broken Hai's hands but they could not touch him inside," was the last thing Maggie's mother said before she drifted off to sleep that afternoon, the weak sun through the blinds casting prison bars across her bed.

Her mother died in that bed, suffering another stroke in the night. Maggie felt she had been struck down as well, made an orphan.

The phone rings once, twice, three times before Maggie makes a move to answer, bending at the waist and prostrating herself over the corner of her desk in order to reach it. There's some kind of problem, though the young man at the front desk is having difficulty articulating precisely what it is. From what Maggie can make out, it seems someone has been involved in an accident in front of the hotel. But why would they call her?

"Is it one of our guests?" she asks.

"No," says the young man.

"One of the staff? An artist of mine, a client?"

"No. I think he is some kind of homeless man."

It's one of the uncomfortable truths of working in a hotel like this that the doormen are under instruction to clear the street of beggars and the homeless. The official line is that it's done so that guests don't feel uncomfortable, but it's part of both the government's efforts to promote tourism and a wider Party policy that sweeps the streets of humanity periodically, particularly in advance of the arrival of foreign dignitaries.

"Did he injure himself on hotel property?" Maggie asks, still unsure why this is being brought to her attention.

"No, on the street," says the young man at the front desk.

"Is he okay? Does he need to go to hospital?"

"I don't know," he says. "He's asking for you."

Hưng feels like his leg has its own heartbeat. He's ashamed to be sitting here in this room with his trousers muddied and torn, particularly since his little accident seems to have knocked the reason he was coming to the Metropole in the first place right out of his head.

A taxi had swerved to the right as he neared the hotel, tearing a corner off the front of his cart and causing it to roll backward, trapping his trouser leg and sending him crashing to the ground. He rubs the back of his head now—sticky, a bit of blood. Perhaps the reason he is here at the Metropole is still lying out there on the street like a log parting a river of traffic, just as he was for a few minutes before the doormen hauled him to the pavement and onto his feet.

He came to tell the Việt Kiều girl something, but what? It must have had to do with her father, something compelling enough for him to wheel his cart around and push it in the opposite direction from the pond, barrelling his way toward the hotel after breakfast with a great sense of urgency—and recklessness, it would appear.

Now he is just a mess of pain and shame and frustration. How humiliating it is to be here in this condition. He has never stepped inside this building before; this is not a building for men like him with its grandeur and ghosts of Indochina.

He cannot now even recall her father's name. He could tell her what he remembers about 1956, he supposes, the year she said her father was sent to a camp, but as he used to feel with Lan, he would rather tell her about the decades that preceded it, the years of the liberation struggle, a time when people still believed they had the power to influence the course of history, that words could change the world.

What an unfamiliar and intoxicating new world Hưng had discovered upon being sent by his parents to work for his Uncle Chiến in the city in 1933. At eleven years old, Hưng found himself in the midst of a noisy, boisterous circus where men shouted at one another over breakfast, leaping to their feet in mid-sentence if the spirit moved them. The air was filled with competing voices, and great clouds of cigarette smoke spiralled with the dizzying rotation of the ceiling fans above.

Hưng had initially cowered in the corner, overwhelmed by the sheer volume of their voices. There was none of the polite bowing and deference toward elders that he was used to. Nothing he had been exposed to in village life had prepared him for the heat of such exchanges, their speed.

"Come," his uncle said, luring him out of the shadows. "They might roar like tigers, but they have the soft fur of kittens, I promise you."

Uncle Chiến seemed immune to the volume and violence of the men's voices. He darted around the room, ducking under gesticulating arms while balancing a full bowl of phở in each hand, sidestepping sudden movements, changing his direction mid-step. Uncle Chiến was a dancer, keen to teach his nephew the steps.

"Your height is an advantage," he said kindly. Hưng hardly had to bend to lift empty bowls, replenish water glasses and bottles of fish sauce, replace clean spoons and chopsticks in canisters and wipe sticky rings off the surfaces of the low tables.

Under Uncle Chiến's calm and steady direction, Hưng grew accustomed to the tone of the room. Soon it was no longer a wilderness of ferocious animals, but an orderly zoo. The same people congregated at the same tables each morning, certain men commanding more attention than others. They spoke of liberating the peasantry, the class struggle, the proletariat and bourgeoisie—ideas that might not have meant anything to Hưng, but certainly became familiar to him through their frequent repetition. As did the names of foreign men with big ideas: Stalin, Marx, Lenin. Zhū Dé, Zhōu Ēnlái, Máo Zédōng.

Hưng no longer flinched when someone stood up abruptly, throwing back his chair and bursting into spontaneous verse, or set the spoons on a table jumping as he pounded a fist for emphasis. He performed his tasks proudly and began to find the grace in his own feet. His height also gave him a further advantage his uncle had not foreseen. He could study the texts the men placed on their tables, make out the words they jotted down in their moleskin notebooks, marvel at the sketch of a tablemate's likeness—the magic of pencil on a page.

Hưng was captivated. These men were different from all the men he had ever known, and it was not just the absence of ploughs. Their foreign ways piqued his curiosity and he took it all in, eyes and ears aflame.

Hưng's limited education had given him the basic ability to read, though he'd had little opportunity to use this skill since arriving in the city. His uncle, illiterate himself, looked upon an abandoned newspaper as nothing more than good fortune for his fire. As he got older, Hưng found himself attempting to read over the men's shoulders. He found himself repeating, furthermore, some of their more well-worn phrases at night before his uncle came to bed: We must overthrow the forces of oppression and degradation. Communism is key to our liberation. By means of guerrilla warfare, if need be. Our allies are the Comintern and the

Communist Party of China, but the future must be fashioned by Vietnamese hands.

Through years of repetition, Hưng shed his provincial accent, acquiring some sense of the liberation about which these men always spoke. He never revealed this transformation to his Uncle Chiến, who still spoke with a peasant's accent, still betrayed his humble origins as a matter of principle perhaps, despite all his years in Hanoi. Not until his uncle passed away did Hưng dare to speak in the clipped tones of the Hanoi dialect to which he did not feel entirely entitled.

Hưng was twenty-two years old when he inherited his uncle's shop, and while he missed his uncle more than he knew it was possible to miss someone, he was ready to do his memory proud after apprenticing under him for eleven years. It was 1944, a world war going on. Hồ Chí Minh's Việt Minh, the People's Army, were fighting the Japanese who had occupied the country three years earlier, displacing the embattled French, but people still needed to eat breakfast, perhaps more so than ever. A bowl of phở can offer critical sustenance and a reason to get up in the morning, even in the most troubling of times. Certainly, a wife or mother could provide breakfast if need be, though most did not and still do not bother with the effort of phở, and wives and mothers, furthermore, did not have the news.

Under his ownership, Hưng is proud to say, the phở shop continued to be as much a place for conversation as for food, much of it by then bubbling up in the dark, southwest corner of the room around an outspoken young man named Đạo. There was something special about this young man—Hưng had noticed it immediately—an aura of light seemed to spill from him and suspend anyone in the vicinity in a state of grace.

Đạo was the most articulate critic Hưng had ever heard. "Yes, of course we must rid the country of the French," he said to his colleagues when the colonialists returned after the Japanese withdrew in 1945, "but we must fight just as hard against the Confucian norms that have enslaved our people for centuries. The enemy lies within us as much as it lies out there."

Hưng found himself forgetting his tasks whenever Đạo commanded the room; he stopped and listened along with everyone else. Đạo made the complicated politics of the time seem perfectly intelligible. "Politics must not be the domain of the learned and the privileged," he insisted, "but that of every man and woman, especially the ones behind the ploughs." No longer did the conversations in the shop strike Hưng as somewhat removed from the experiences of people of humble origins; Đạo was speaking both about him and to him.

Hưng found whatever excuse he could to be near the man—replenishing the fish sauce on his table more often than necessary, making sure to clear his bowl the moment Đạo laid his chopsticks across the rim.

When he wasn't speaking, Đạo was writing in his notebook. Hưng would cast his eyes discreetly over the man's shoulder and take in some of his lines. One day Hưng read a poem he found particularly striking. It was Đạo's ability to capture something between bitter and sweet that caused Hưng to speak directly to him for the first time. "The balance of yin and yang," Hưng said.

Đạo turned in his chair and looked up at Hưng. "Just like your phở," he said.

Hưng felt the rare heat of flushed cheeks in that moment and averted his eyes. Đạo, meanwhile, copied the poem onto another page of his notebook, tore out the page and pressed it into Hưng's hands.

This single gesture made Hưng want to improve himself. He began to gather the newspapers the men left behind each morning and read them for company at night, the company he had longed for since his uncle's passing. He read them by lantern light, lying on the mattress he used to share with his uncle in the windowless room at the back of the shop.

One morning, Đạo handed Hưng a package. "I brought you these," he said. "I noticed you have quite an appetite for reading."

"You are too kind," said Hưng, all but silenced by the gesture. He had never been the recipient of a gift in his life.

The package contained a collection of mimeographs. Essays about the history of the Vietnamese alphabet and the birth of modern Vietnamese poetry. Articles about the Russian revolution, the theories of the German thinker Marx, notes on Leninism by the great revolutionary Hồ Chí Minh.

It took months of Hưng's labouring at night to finish reading them, longer still to really understand them. On certain points he needed clarification. He would underline the relevant sections and look to Đạo the following morning.

"Here," Hưng would point, "where Hồ Chí Minh speaks of revolutionary ethics, is he appealing to Confucian notions of duty?"

"It's his way of communicating new ideas without alienating those who are very attached to the old," said Đạo. "You'll find he does the same with certain elements of village culture."

Where Hưng could not follow the path from a concept to its realization, he would put it to Đạo. "But we are not a nation of factory workers," he said one morning. "Where will the Party find the proletarian masses?"

"Ah, this is just as Mao said of China," Đạo explained, taking time to sit with Hưng after breakfast and explore how the various theories of communism could be applied in Vietnam. "Mao shifted the emphasis away from industry to agrarian reform, tailoring it to the Chinese situation," Đạo said. "Our man will no doubt do the same."

Their man was the great Hồ Chí Minh, who had further escalated the intensity of the war against the French with the declaration of the Democratic Republic's independence in 1945.

"What is this Atlantic Charter Hồ Chí Minh keeps speaking of?" Hưng remembers asking Đạo.

"It's an agreement between the Allies that nations have a right to self-determination. It's the chairman's way of convincing the Americans that they have to recognize our independence."

"He's very smart to use their language," Hưng had said. "It's just like he did when he began our Proclamation of Independence with the words of the American Declaration: 'All men are created equal; they are endowed by their Creator with certain inalienable Rights; among these are Life, Liberty, and the pursuit of Happiness.' Uncle Hồ strengthens his case by appealing as much to their sentiments as to their political sensibilities."

"Nicely put," Đạo said, eyebrows raised. Hưng had surprised them both with this first expression of opinion. "And good memory," Đạo added, tapping his temple.

"I've memorized many things," Hưng said. "I know most of your poems by heart."

"You honour me," Đạo replied.

Silence fell between them. Hưng had meant to honour, but Đạo's attention made him glow with embarrassment. He did not mean to boast.

There was so much Hưng did not know, leading him to study in even greater detail the essays contained in the pamphlets Đạo shared with him. In part, he felt the need to compensate for the fact that he was not out there alongside the Việt Minh soldiers, risking his life in battle.

In 1954, the war was won. The French were finally defeated by the Việt Minh at the battle of Dien Bien Phu. Hưng was prepared to give his soup away for free, to keep the shop open all day so that the men could drink and play games in celebration, but they would not relax, would not linger, least of all Đạo, who immediately turned the conversation to the realities of a free Vietnam and the role learned men like them would play within it.

It appeared the Workers' Party had already given some thought to this question. In the days immediately after liberation, the Party issued a series of proclamations calling upon artists and intellectuals—people literate and educated in ideology—to lead the masses toward awareness of their enlightenment and teach and disseminate the principles of Lenin and Marx. Spokesmen sought to recruit them by shouting about revolutionary duty from rooftops; officials plastered posters onto the walls of Hưng's shop.

"But wait a minute," Đạo was the first among the men in the shop to say. "Is this really the job of the artist? To be a Party mouthpiece, a sloganeer?"

In the end he was punished for posing such questions.

Had Miss Maggie's father also risked his life in this way? Hưng wonders. In all likelihood yes, since he was sent to a camp the same year Party officers came for Đạo and his colleagues. But if he suffered the same fate as Đạo? Then Lý Văn Hai never returned.

Old Man Hưng is sitting in a chair in a linen closet. He is snoring, his mouth wide open and toothless, an untouched glass of green tea sitting on a shelf. Maggie closes the door quietly and the old man wakes up, looking froglike and confused.

"My teeth," he says, patting his lips.

"The doorman found them lying beside you on the road," says Maggie. "I don't think they'll be of any use now, I'm afraid."

"Never fit right anyway," Hưng mumbles.

"And these," Maggie says, offering him the battered remnants of his glasses.

The old man turns the glasses around in his hand as if they are unfamiliar to him, then tucks them into his shirt pocket with a self-conscious word of thanks. He cups his knees as if he's about to stand up. His pant leg is torn and grease-stained, and Maggie sees a nasty cut running down the length of his thin, hairless leg.

"Don't get up," Maggie says, her hand against his shoulder. "You're bleeding, Mr. Hưng. I'm going to get the doctor to see you."

The old man dismisses this with a wave, saying he's quite all right, nothing broken, just a little scraped and bruised. He apologizes for wasting her time.

But what was he doing pushing his cart up Ngô Quyền, one of Hanoi's busiest streets? Maggie wonders. Surely this isn't the route he takes home after breakfast. "Were you coming to see me?" she asks tentatively.

The old man hangs his head. The thin grey hairs barely cover a scalp battered by decades of sun and rain. Yes, he was coming to see her. Unfortunately he still has no recollection as to why.

"Did you have something you wanted to tell me?" she asks hopefully.

"Perhaps I did," he says, nodding at his knees.

"Listen. I'm going to get you a room so you can rest up a bit. Get off that leg."

"No, no." He waves his hand. "That really isn't necessary."

But she doesn't want to let the old man go. She made the mistake of assuming she would have more time with her mother; she's not about to repeat it.

———

Hưng has never seen a bed so big. Even after bathing in hot water, he fears dirtying these white sheets. He rubs the balls of his feet into the thick, green carpet and opens all the cupboards one by one. Empty but for two lonely white robes and matching pairs of slippers. So much room. Everything he has ever owned could fit into one of these cupboards, but nothing he has ever owned would be good enough to be kept here.

He pulls on the trousers of the bellhop's uniform Miss Maggie has left hanging behind the door. They're too long and a bit tight at the waist, but he admires the gold piping that runs down each leg. Very smart indeed.

He tests the corner of the bed, which yields unexpectedly to his weight, then lies back against a cloud of plush pillows. He stares at the wooden beams of the sloping ceiling and wonders how one's back fares with such a lack of support and how many ducks lost their feathers to the pillows on this bed. He reaches for the booklet on the pillow to his left. It is a menu for something called room service. Miss Maggie had said he could just dial nine and order anything he wanted to eat. Anything at all. But Hưng has never used a telephone. He has never operated a television either and is reluctant to press any of the buttons on the device she referred to as the remote control.

When Miss Maggie stops by in the early afternoon to check on him, she presses a button on the device and turns the television on for him. "These arrows," she says. "This is how you change the channel. Now, what can we get you to eat?"

On the last page of the room service booklet, he finds a list of items translated into Vietnamese, but unfortunately, little of the food is familiar to him. He has never tasted Club Sandwich or Caesar Salad or Cheese Plate. He opts for phở, curious to know what a phở might taste like when made from ingredients where money is no object.

Fatty and sweet, in his assessment. Really rather unappealing. Designed for something other than Hanoian tastes. Still, he is surprisingly hungry and spoons the broth into his mouth while staring at the television. A channel called CNN broadcasts news of the Americans in Iraq. They are always at war, it seems. He presses an arrow. Black men dance on a channel called MTV. Hưng has never seen a black man in his life. Look at all that gold jewellery. And their lady friends, *ôi zồi ôi*, they are nearly naked! Where is the Bureau of Social Vice Prevention now? Busy arresting people for making jokes about the Party when naked ladies are dancing in the rooms of the Metropole?

Someone knocks twice, then pushes open the door to the room. Hưng places his bowl aside and quickly presses the arrow that takes him back to the war on CNN.

Today is a day of many firsts. Hưng was forced to endure a dentist once, but this is the first doctor who has ever examined him. The doctor wears a white coat and tie and seems ridiculously young to have such an important job; he may be even younger than Tư. Not that Hưng believes western medicine to have any particular authority. He's rather suspicious of all its pills and gadgetry and its lack of regard for yin and yang.

The doctor asks Hưng to bend forward so that he can examine the back of his head, then has him take off his trousers so that he can look at his leg. But why is he interested in Hưng's eyes, his armpits, his tongue, his testicles, and why is he making him count backward from one hundred?

"How old are you, Mr. Hưng?" he asks.

Hưng honestly doesn't know. He's not even sure what year it is. What does it matter, after all? He marks time in months, following the phases of the moon; it is months that are meaningful, seasons and tides. Years are little more than an invention of a government fond of marking anniversaries by building monuments to revolutionary martyrs.

"Old enough," he says unhelpfully.

And here the doctor goes with gadgetry, pressing a metal disc against Hưng's chest, some amplifying device through which he listens to his breathing.

"Do you smoke, Mr. Hưng?" the doctor asks, pulling the pipes out of his ears.

"No, sir."

"Have you been having any chest pain, shortness of breath?"

"I have been feeling a bit weak recently," Hưng admits.

"I can hear some fluid around your lungs. I think it might be a good idea to have an X-ray," he says. "I'll write up a requisition for the hospital."

The hospital. The hospital was bombed to bits during the war, and the memory of that carnage is still uncomfortably vivid. Hưng has neither the money for such a visit nor the will.

"How is my leg?" he asks.

"Your leg is fine," says the doctor, "it's just a superficial injury. Keep that cut clean with soap and water and I'll give you some antibiotic ointment you can apply twice a day. But," he says, writing something down on a notepad and tearing the page out for Hưng, "I really would recommend an X-ray."

He doesn't need an X-ray. He needs the right food; food is the best medicine. Obviously his qi has been depleted. He needs to eat congee with tofu and perform some yoga or tai chi; he has neglected to do his exercises of late.

He is relieved when the doctor departs and Miss Maggie returns. She brings a cup of tea for each of them. English tea in a china cup. She pulls a chair up close to the bed and sits down. She asks him how he is feeling and what he thought of the phở.

"Just fine," he says, "just fine." He does not want to be impolite or seem ungrateful.

"You're being polite, aren't you," she says.

He is taken aback. Is this the American style? He can only imagine so, having never met an American before. "Well, ahem," he says, clearing his throat. "Of course there is always room for improvement."

"Do you remember why you were coming to see me this morning?" she asks.

"I regret, Miss Maggie, that my memory is not what it once was. It is no doubt a consequence of my advanced age."

"The doctor seems to think there might be something more serious going on, Mr. Hưng. Maybe it's not your memory, but something to do with the amount of oxygen getting to your brain."

Breathing exercises, he thinks. Tai chi. Flow.

"Perhaps you know this already," Hưng begins, "but back in the days when I had a phở shop I had a regular group of customers who came in for breakfast—artists and intellectuals all. You said your father was sent to a camp in 1956? Well, that is the same year that these men began to publish their work. They produced a literary journal and six issues of a controversial magazine. They saw these publications as platforms for artistic expression and political debate, but of course the Party was not interested in such things and they were condemned for squandering their energy on something other than the revolutionary message. They refused to produce the socialist realism the Party demanded of them. This was their crime."

"Are you suggesting that my father might have been part of their circle?" she asks, leaning forward in her chair, her delicate hands on her knees, a hopeful smile on that lovely face.

He is reminded again of Lan in the days when she was eager for his stories, the way she looked to him for more. *Tell me*, she would say. *Teach me. Why does Đạo say love is like a game of Chinese chess?*

Hưng has a horrible dawning realization that it may be this intoxicating similarity to Lan that has led him here to the hotel. He might have remembered something about her father, but the urgent need to make his way here could just as well be rooted in something more selfish.

He feels ashamed for thinking Miss Maggie beautiful. For the fact that her desire to know something about great men of a lost time reminds him of someone else. He still cannot actually say with any certainty that he knew her father.

"My shop was not the only place where such conversations took place," he says, "but it was known. It had a reputation. It attracted people interested in art and debate, but I'm afraid it's impossible for me to recall all of their names."

"Do you know if any of them are still alive?" she asks.

Such a painful question, made all the more so by its directness. Hưng searches, but can find no poetic device that will serve him here.

"Those who were not successfully re-educated were either killed or tortured to such an extent that they soon died from their wounds," he says plainly. "That is the tragic truth of it."

"Or they managed to escape," says Miss Maggie.

What a notion, Hưng thinks, as he leans back against the cloud of pillows and casts his eyes upward. This is the top floor of the hotel; beyond it, perhaps some colonial idea of heaven. Escape is not a possibility Hưng has ever considered before. He has never even heard it suggested, not even in a whisper, that anyone ever escaped from the camps. But then it would hardly have been in the Party's interest to advertise such a thing, to suggest re-education was not always successful, that there were those who would have preferred to flee south or even board a leaky boat heading out into the treacherous waters of the South China Sea than submit themselves to a course of ideological enlightenment.

"So your father—he managed to escape?"

"My mother was a nurse at the re-education camp," she says. "She got him out and they fled south. He lived for another fifteen years."

Isn't that interesting, thinks Hưng. All these decades later a Việt Kiều girl raised far away in America has offered the possibility of an alternative outcome. In fact, she has gone beyond possibility and offered proof. What if Đạo had managed to escape their clutches? What if Đạo had had fifteen more years?

"What happened to your father in the end?" Hưng asks.

"The Fall of Saigon," she says.

So the man escaped the North only to be killed later in the South.

"Was he much older than your mother?" Hưng asks.

"Eighteen years."

There had been twenty-one years between him and Lan. Was it a matter of just three less? Could they have had a daughter like the lovely young woman sitting in this room with him right now? Might something between them have lived?

Tư has just dropped off his new German clients at the Metropole two hours earlier than scheduled. He doesn't know whether it was the couple or the driver he was forced to work with since Phương called in sick to work this morning, but the day has lacked any particular joy. The couple seemed unimpressed with his list of famous German composers. "Ich glaub, mich laust der Affe," they said, which Tư thought must be the German equivalent of *really*, except with more words.

Tư finds himself at the bar where he and Phương have a beer at happy hour on days like this when tourists have had their fill and just want to leave the dirt of Hanoi behind in their hotel pool. Sometimes, if Phương has some thinking to do, you can find him here alone. But happy hour isn't particularly happy for Tư without Phương. In fact, everyone in the place looks rather bored and unhappy, and Tư feels like a very big loser until he is relieved by the ring of his cellphone.

He answers it loudly. But who is this speaking? It is some lady called Miss Maggie Lý who speaks Vietnamese with a strange accent. She says she's calling from the Sofitel Metropole. Have the Germans complained about him to the hotel management?

"It's about your Mr. Hưng," she says.

Oh no, thinks Tư, is the old man in some kind of trouble? Has he shamed himself on hotel grounds?

"I'm afraid he was in a bit of an accident."

Tư throws some đồng on the table, then jogs down the street. He has been dreading a day like this. The traffic has no mercy for an old man pushing a cart. A moment of hesitation or misstep can prove fatal for a spry sixteen-year-old.

Tư bursts through the front doors of the Metropole, beer riding up his throat. He quickly scans the lobby. Everything is giant: the pillars, the potted palms, the guests. The man behind the front desk directs him to take a seat. Tư feels tiny sitting in the gilt-edged chair, his feet barely touching the floor. He whistles nervously and swings his legs until he notices the concierge scowling at him.

The man from the front desk approaches and asks if he might like to have a cup of coffee in the courtyard while he waits; Miss Maggie will be just a few minutes longer. Tư is about to decline, but something about the situation tells him not to. This is a highly unorthodox invitation. He is a tour guide, not a guest. They don't even like to have tour guides sitting in their expensive chairs; they certainly don't invite them to have coffee. He worries the stage is being set for the delivery of some very bad news.

The bellhop escorts him through a bistro and onto the teak deck of a poolside bar. Tư plants himself in a giant wicker chair that looks like a prop out of a movie. He would much prefer a beer at this hour, but a waiter serves him coffee—coffee in a cup and saucer rather than a glass as he is accustomed to. Tư looks slyly to his right and left before stuffing the piece of chocolate resting on the side of the saucer into his jacket pocket. He eyes the sugar cubes next, both white and brown.

He suddenly floats to his feet at the sight of the light-skinned beauty in the trim black suit who is entering the bar—it's her, the mysterious woman who appeared at breakfast yesterday! Before he can think of what he might say if he were to approach her, she is standing before him.

"Tư?" she says.

Tư nods, stunned by the coincidence. "Miss Maggie Lý?" he asks tentatively.

"Thank you for coming," she says, hand outstretched, her manner crisp, professional, American, her accent strange. "I'm sorry you've been kept waiting."

"Is the old man all right?" asks Tư.

"He's okay. I sent the doctor to see him and nothing's broken. He's a bit shaken by the whole experience though, and his cart's quite bashed up. I don't think he can manage to get it home. I asked if I could call anyone for him and he gave me your card. He was carrying it in his pocket."

Tư is relieved the old man hasn't been seriously injured, but he's also a bit ashamed by the situation. The staff probably think Hưng is some kind of homeless person.

"Do you, uh, know Mr. Hưng very well?" Tư asks.

"Me? No. We met for the first time yesterday morning."

This only increases Tư curiosity, but before he has had a chance to pursue this any further she is standing up and smoothing her trousers over her thighs in a way Tư finds a bit too sexy. "If you don't mind waiting in the lobby," she says, "I'll just bring him down."

Tư watches Miss Maggie Lý leave. Tư does not have a lot of experience with Việt Kiều, at least not of the up-close-and-personal variety. Until very recently the Việt Kiều were not much welcome. This one has a nice slim body and a musical sway to her hips, though she's tall for a Vietnamese woman. It must be all that milk in the American diet. This would also explain her perfect teeth. Milk and hamburgers. He wonders what she looks like naked. Whether she strips off all her clothes before crawling into bed with her husband. But no, she is a Miss, not a Mrs. Her boyfriend then. An even dirtier thought.

Tư reaches for the sugar cubes and pops a few into his pocket. A waiter catches his guilty eye.

Old Man Hưng has never looked so smart: he is wearing black trousers with some gold piping down the side like he belongs in a military band. Rather than sticking to his head as it normally does, his grey hair is a bit frothy. He smells good, too, if a bit feminine, like flowers. He looks far better for having had this accident, in fact.

Tư leaves Miss Maggie with a New Dawn business card and a confident wave, saying, "If you ever need the services of a tour guide in future." Friends in high places, he thinks. Hưng waves a confident goodbye of his own, saying, "I hope to see you again at breakfast."

But why does he hope to see her again at breakfast? What the heck is going on?

"Hưng," says Tư as they walk down the hotel steps, "what happened?"

"Taxi cut me off," he says, limping and gripping Tư by the forearm. He wades straight into the traffic, pointing over at his cart lying on its side on a traffic island, its front panel completely torn off.

"But why were you here?" Tư shouts. "This isn't on your way home."

"Maybe I get bored of the same route," says Hưng, lurching up onto the island. "Now help me pull this upright."

"Hưng, I think we should get my father to fix your cart before we try and move it."

"Come on, Tư," he says, stubborn and determined. The old man tugs one of the handles while Tư crouches down and leans his back against the side of the cart, grunting as he tenses his thighs and strains upright.

Hưng pushes the cart forward on the traffic island and it careens to the right. The wheels are askew.

"Seriously. My dad can fix this," says Tư.

But the old man refuses to accompany Tư home, insisting he needs to get back to the shantytown. He always insists on this point. Even that time when Tư found him in agony after he had anaesthetized himself with rice wine and pulled out the broken stumps of three teeth after being punched by a police officer, Hưng had refused to come back to their house. He hadn't eaten for at least two days. Tư's father sent for a dentist instead, one who, at considerable expense, relieved Hưng of the rest of his upper teeth and gave him a set of rejected dentures designed for a much smaller mouth—dentures that seem to have gone missing in the mysterious course of today's events.

Several times over the years Tư and his father have insisted the old man come and live with them—it is the Vietnamese way—but Hưng always wins in the battle of insistence, offering no other reason than "a man knows where he belongs."

Tư feels no man belongs in such a dirty, shabby place, least of all Old Man Hưng. He has always wished the old man's goodness could be rewarded with a better standard of living, a decent place to live, but he knows it is useless to keep trying to convince him to abandon the shantytown. He lives a quiet life of routine, remaining loyal to the people and places he knows, serving breakfast each morning, then returning home to his shack on the shores of a dirty pond.

The Beauty of Humanity

Hưng agreed to take Tư's money for the taxi fare, simply to put an end to the boy's questions. He is mortified by every aspect of this situation, and with Tư involved now, Bình and Anh will also worry. Worst of all, he can offer none of them a coherent explanation of what happened.

The taxi crawls through streets crowded with people making their way home. They are carrying babies and groceries and news of the day, looking forward to a meal with their families, Hưng supposes, the type of life he might have lived if circumstances had been different. The view through the window unsettles him, detaching him from the streets he knows.

Today's incident has, furthermore, prevented him from fetching the supplies he needs for tomorrow's breakfast. To come from a poor place and make a better life means marrying yourself to the work that will improve things. Phở is Hưng's rightful wife and mistress, just as it had been for his Uncle Chiến.

"You should caress the beef as you slice it," he remembers his uncle instructing him as he got older. "If you treat it tenderly, it guides you toward the grain. Tend your broth as if she is a sleeping beauty; keep watch over her, only waking her in the final hour with a splash of fish sauce."

Although he has been loyal to Uncle Chiến's recipe, Hưng has had to adapt to the vagaries of circumstances over the years. There was a time when he'd made phở from almost nothing. He hadn't known it was possible, but inappropriate love for a girl had driven him to it, had drawn him back into the bosom of phở, his willing mistress and reliable wife.

He had been sitting outside his shack with Lan one evening long ago, a full moon straining through the clouds, when he first admitted to himself that he was in trouble. Lan's grandmother joined them less frequently by then, saying the poems and the stories just lulled her to sleep and what good was she to anyone with idle hands? She nevertheless encouraged her granddaughter to spend evenings with Hưng, saying the girl needed an education and where else was there any chance of that.

Hưng thought this quite an enlightened attitude on her grandmother's part, perhaps choosing to not consider the possibility that she might be looking to relieve herself of a burden by pushing her granddaughter into the arms of a man, even one as old, blemished and poor as Hưng.

Hưng focused on the matter of education, an issue he took very seriously, having learned as much as he had from Đạo. Hưng had held onto all the poems Đạo had copied down for him, even though the poet later came to throw away most of his early efforts, dismissing as adolescent and naive his laments for a stolen country with recurring images of weeping mothers and flowers blooming without scent.

As Vietnam struggled toward independence, Đạo's poems reached into an uncertain future, contrasting images of Vietnamese peasants in Parisian zoos with those of human pyramids shaped like pagodas; allied Vietnamese workers with hands raised toward yellow skies. Some of these poems were eventually published in *Fine Works of Spring*, the first publication Đạo and his colleagues produced.

Upon reading that journal by the bitter melon light of the oil lamp in the backroom of his shop, Hưng had felt the words do a perilous dance on the page. The illustrations vibrated with hidden meaning. His skin tingled and his ears burned as he read a poem about the hard times that had befallen the North since 1954. It was a risky topic to raise, one that might lead the Party to charge a person as an agent acting on behalf of the imperialists in the South.

When Hưng tried to return the journal to Đạo the following morning, Đạo insisted it was his to keep. "Because you are one of us," he said. "One of our movement to keep the beauty of humanity alive."

Hưng, filled with a mixture of pride and fear, held the inky pages to his chest. He bowed his head. He was humbled by the honour, but with honour comes responsibility. Being part of their movement meant the risk was his to share.

Five years later, in the interest of Lan's education, Hưng found himself sharing the journal with the girl, retrieving his well-worn copy of *Fine Works of Spring* from the stack of papers he kept wrapped in plastic inside his shack, safe from rats and rain. He handed her the mimeographed volume, wanting her to feel the paper, smell the ink on its pages, hoping she might experience it with all her senses just as he had when he'd held it for the first time.

"But, Uncle, I cannot read," she said, holding the pages in her delicate hands.

Hưng was surprised to hear it. He had left school at eleven, but he was a peasant boy from the country, this was to be expected. This girl was a Hanoian, born and bred, with the sophistication of the city about her despite the indignities of her current surroundings.

"Have you had no schooling?"

"My father was killed in the liberation struggle when I was very small," she said. "After that we had very little money, only enough for one of us to go to school. We sent my older brother."

And so Hưng began to read to her—the essays, the stories and the poetry—doing his best with the latter to infuse the lines with some approximation of Đạo's intonation and cadence.

Hưng read the contents of *Fine Works of Spring* to her, then those of *Fine Works of Autumn*. She took it all in and appeared to want more, and so he proceeded to read the *Nhân Văn* magazines to her, as well as the poems Đạo had copied down for him with his own hand.

Through poetry, Hưng conveyed to Lan a world of allegory and metaphor, and just as he had once not understood such concepts, the multiple layers of meaning at work, she did not at first understand.

"How can he claim his love for her is so great if he is only willing to feed her one cherry a month?" she asked. "It is very selfish of him to leave her hungry, is it not?"

"But he does not want to overwhelm her," said Hưng, speaking his own truth through Đạo's lines.

Where Đạo described the country as the smallest in a nest of red-lacquered Russian dolls, she recalled a promise her grandfather had once made to buy her a toy from Paris.

She understood things only in literal terms, but it did not matter. He loved her for her innocence, for her sensory appreciation, for the fact that when she heard a lemon described she could taste a lemon. And he loved her proximity. While he read Đạo's poetry to her, she would study the illustrations in the journals, leaning in close to him, smelling of the coriander flowers she used, when she could find them, to wash her hair.

"But you are not reading," she said one day, as she looked up from an illustrated page.

"I have it memorized," he said of the poem, a favourite.

"Teach me," she said, placing her hand on the page lying between them.

He stared at those graceful fingers, their beautifully tapered tips and natural polish, and thought, Oh, but, my dear girl, I cannot. Surely my heart would break.

Hưng had studied Đạo's poetry with his untrained eye

and found his heart moved. His heart had then begun to educate his eye. He had recited certain poems so often that they had become part of him, as familiar as the tongue in his mouth. To teach the girl one of these poems would be to give himself to her. To see himself in her mouth.

He quickly changed the subject, pointing at the moon. "Did you hear the Russians put a man in the sky this week?"

"But why would they do such a thing?"

"Perhaps so they could prove once and for all that God does not exist."

News of the wider world could not distract her for long, though; it was far less compelling than the world they were creating between themselves.

One evening, as she reclined on her elbow, hair loose about her shoulders and bare feet interlaced, she said, "Maybe one day you will have a shop again and all the artists will come back. And I will work for you. I will chop the herbs and wash the dishes."

The scenario was so impossibly perfect that Hưng knew this exchange could not continue. It was torture. It would cause him to dream the impossible, will the dead to life, act on impulses better left buried. He would lose his way and perhaps destroy her in the process. And look how thin the girl had become in recent months: what had he been thinking feeding her only poetry? He needed to find his way back to making phở.

But how did one make phở from nothing? Even the rice ration, when it was available, did not fill more than the palm of his hand—and that included the maggots. And so he was forced to experiment. One day he pulled weeds from the pond and laid them out to dry in the sun until they were as crispy as rice paper. Then he ground the dried weeds in a makeshift mortar until he had a fine powder, to which he added enough water to make a paste. He poured the paste onto a grid of dried, woven grass and left it to bake in the weak sun. When it had set, he cut the sheet into fine strips for his first batch of pondweed vermicelli. He improved upon the vermicelli the next time, making sure to use only the white hearts of the weeds. The slightly muddy taste was easily masked with a dash of *nước mắm*. He had to make do with fish and wild leeks for the broth.

The girl and her grandmother were the first to taste Hưng's communist-era phở. From the looks on their faces, Hưng knew he'd been successful. The broth tasted nothing like it should have, but it was pleasant enough, and the vermicelli was quite convincing.

"You could sell this," said the grandmother, and in fact, this was already in Hưng's thoughts.

He spent the next month building a stone grinder he could operate by pushing a pedal. Then he made himself a cart out of wood scraps and twine, and set out into the streets, launching himself as a roaming phở seller.

Up until that point, Hưng's sense of Hanoi had been fairly circumscribed, his routes dictated solely by the needs of the restaurant, but times had changed, and with them both the city and his way through it. His route meandered as he went in search of new clientele. How quiet the city was in those days, how devoid of people. Streets that had once bustled with commerce had become graveyards. Just a few entrepreneurial souls like himself had something to sell.

Without distraction he began to see the layers of the city. Craft villages had first arisen on this site a thousand years before, when the capital had been moved to Hanoi. The wall of the citadel, which these villages had served, still marked the western edge of the Old Quarter. The inhabitants had built walls around their villages as they evolved into guilds, and though those walls had since come down, Hưng could map their respective territories by discerning which temple, which pagoda, which communal house or *đình* belonged to which of the thirty-six guilds.

He had walked around the perimeter of the Old Quarter and come to rest his cart at the East Gate, the only original gate still standing. Hưng reasoned that a gate was an invitation to traffic, even in the absence of a wall, even in the absence of traffic, and so this is where he waited with his cart.

Several people passed by him on foot that first morning, none of them even glancing his way, but eventually two men on bicycles, curiosity or perhaps hunger getting the best of them, turned around and asked what he was selling.

"But there's no rice," the older of the two said, "no noodles. How on earth can you be selling phở?"

"Come," Hưng said with a nod and an inviting smile. "Taste."

He pulled the lid off one of his pots. Even he found the aroma tempting. He lowered a handful of his pondweed vermicelli into the broth with his bamboo ladle. He had one bowl and one bowl only—they would have to share. They held the bowl between them, accepted the proffered chopsticks and grasped at the noodles. They drank from the bowl in the absence of spoons.

"Ahh," the younger one sighed, wiping his mouth on the back of his hand. "That is excellent."

"That is the best thing I've tasted in years," said the other, burping loudly.

"I'll be here again tomorrow morning," said Hưng. "Bring your bowls and your friends."

"But how much are you charging?" asked the younger.

"How much can you pay?"

"Not much now, but next week I am old enough for the army."

"Me, I could pay in leather," said the older one. "I used to be a leather worker, that is, before all the cows disappeared. But I still have my scraps. Hey, a belt—do you need a belt?"

And so Hưng found himself the proud owner of a new belt, and soon thereafter, of quail feathers and palm fronds and lumps of northern coal.

He would share these things with the girl. Present them as small gifts. "You deserve so much more," he would say, handing her a speckled duck's egg or a smooth piece of cow horn.

She had tried to reciprocate where she could. One morning he found her sitting on the threshold of the shack she shared with her grandmother sewing a man's shirt out of a piece of tarpaulin. In the absence of news, of underground papers, of anything other than propaganda shouted through megaphones and plastered on walls, one had to rely on signs like these. There must be threat of another war, Hưng thought, if there are enough military vehicles for her to risk tearing a piece of tarpaulin off the back of a jeep. Who is it now? he wondered. The French or the Chinese? The Saigonese or Japanese or Khmer?

He had to resist the urge to reach out and wipe the smear of grease off her cheek with his thumb. "You deserve a better life," he said instead.

"We had a better life," said the girl, breaking a piece of thread with her teeth. "Of course we didn't realize it at the time. We had a very large apartment, and before my father was killed, plenty to eat. Even croissants and chocolate."

Hưng had felt all the communism in his body drain out of him as she spoke. All the colonial resentment too. The politics and history of Vietnam lay in a puddle at his feet. "You deserve the best pastries and the finest chocolate," he said. "You deserve a man who adores you and spoils you with such things."

"But I have a man who adores me and spoils me, don't I?"

Hưng had stood there feeling stripped naked. He was powerless in her presence; this was now clear to them both.

"Here," she said, holding out the shirt to him, "try this on. It only has one sleeve, but I'll find the material to make the other one eventually."

By the time she did finish making the shirt they were no longer speaking. The silence between them was as deafening as the raining bombs of the American War, but where the latter came to an end, the former waged on. He could not believe she was capable of such destruction, but in hindsight, the seeds had been there all along.

———

Hưng interrupts the driver as the taxi nears the shantytown, asking if he could just stop and let him off at the end of the dirt road leading down to the pond. Hưng would feel ashamed to arrive home in such an extravagant manner.

"I wasn't going to drive down there anyway, my friend," says the driver. "Bad roads. Bad people. You be careful."

What do you know of it? Hưng wants to say. The taxi driver has obviously mistaken him for a visitor. Hưng slams the car door and stomps down the unlit road in his bellhop's trousers, determined to look forceful and confident despite the pain in his leg. It has started to rain, and as soon as Hưng is out of sight of the taxi he reaches down, brushes his hand against the mud at his feet and runs a streak of it across his cheek and through his hair.

Father and son are taking turns pushing the cart toward the shantytown, but Tư is losing patience by the time they get to the track leading down to the pond. It has taken them an hour and a half to get this far, and it takes the strength of both of them—two hands on each handle of the cart. How the hell does Old Man Hưng do this on his own? Tư is grateful that it is at least dark; he really wouldn't want anyone mistaking him for a food seller with a rickety old cart.

They discover the track muddy and difficult from the early evening rain, and Tư is pissed off that his Nikes are getting dirty.

"It's a pair of shoes, Tư," says Bình.

"You don't understand," Tư mumbles.

"No, you're quite right. I don't," says his father.

They manoeuvre the cart to the edge of the track. As they near the pond, they see several small fires throwing sparks into the damp night. Black smoke spirals upward and the smell of kerosene stings Tư's nostrils. He hears the murmur of talk, the howl of an unhappy baby, the clang of metal pots and the drone of hungry mosquitoes and, as they approach the old man's shack, the distinct soft tenor of his voice as he talks to the man next door, a halfwit who honks like a goose.

Hưng is the heart of this small community on the banks of a polluted pond; he is good to these poor people, keeping them fed and entertained. He treats everyone with respect— from people in high places, like Miss Maggie Lý, to people without sense or legs, like his neighbour. It is humbling to have an Old Man Hưng in your life. It makes you want to be a better person.

The old man thanks Tư and his father for the return of his cart with his hands clasped together and a bow of his head, and insists they stay and eat something. He apologizes for having little to offer: rice, a bit of fried pork belly and fish sauce, that is all.

"Hưng, Hưng," says Bình. "Honestly, it's fine. What a day you've had, huh?"

"It's been quite an adventure. Come. Let's get out of the rain. You'll at least stay for a cup of tea."

They bend through the entrance to his shack and take a seat on his hard, straw-filled mattress. Hưng places the kettle over a small kerosene stove and rummages for his tea canister.

Tư and his father always visit the old man here on the first day of Tet. Even though his shack is normally dark and dank, at Tet it is always bright with fresh flowers, flowers he travels kilometres to collect. The room is swept of dust and evil and is fragrant with incense and plump fruits.

Few words beyond the customary pass between them on these occasions. They will wish Old Man Hưng prosperity, and he will return the good wishes and offer them square packets of *bánh chưng* which have been cooking overnight in a pot on the fire, his callused fingers unaware of the heat as he pulls each packet from the boiling water. They will eat the sticky rice and mung bean paste that hug the prized fatty pork middle, and Tư will share this treat with Grandfather Đạo by placing one of the square banana-leaf packets at the base of his altar alongside some white rice, rice wine and crisp new bills in a red envelope.

Đạo's altar still shines like a bright star today, a candle lit to keep him company. Tư and his father both bow to their ancestor before taking the cups of woody brown tea Hưng offers.

"So what took you over that way this morning, anyway?" Tư tries again.

"That Việt Kiều girl has lost something," the old man says, his eyes milky in the candlelight. "She thought maybe I could help her find it."

"And can you?" Tư prods.

"I don't know yet," says Hưng.

Bình asks Hưng about his leg and the visit with the doctor, changing the subject just as it's getting interesting.

"Leg will be fine," the old man says. "Just need to restore my qi."

"I'm glad it wasn't worse," says Tư's father. "For you or your cart."

They hear a sudden sharp cry outside the shack. "What was that?" Tư asks, getting to his feet.

"What was what?" says the old man.

"It sounded like someone in pain," says Bình.

Bình and Tư poke their heads out the door of the shack and see a woman lying on her back about a metre away. Tư rushes forward and helps her into a sitting position. She curses the mud on her backside. "It's the only decent skirt I have. So stupid to be wearing these things in the mud," she says, pointing at the flip-flops on her feet.

Tư's father follows him outside. "It's okay, Dad. I've got her." Tư lifts the old woman by the elbow, light as an egg. She leans the yolk of her weight into his forearm. "I'm all right, son," she says. "Thank you. You go on back to your grandfather now."

Tư and his father stoop to enter the door of Hưng's shack. It takes a minute for Tư's eyes to readjust to the dim.

"Did you know that at the Metropole you can pick up the phone and order anything you want to eat?" the old man says. "Imagine. Anything at all."

Tư wipes the rain off his face with his shirtsleeve and wonders if the old man has lost his hearing along with his qi. That lady couldn't have been more than a couple of metres away and that was a sharp and distinctive cry of pain. He wouldn't just ignore her. He is clearly not himself.

Whole Fruit

Maggie moves through the faded glory of the marble lobby of her apartment building. She steps into the rattling iron cage of an old French elevator and presses the top button. Gears click, wheels hum.

Her mother grew up in a building just like this on another tree-lined boulevard in the French Quarter. It was quite grand, though she used to lament how much it had deteriorated after her father was killed in the fight against the French. The cracks in the plaster, the leaks and broken windows, none of which they could afford to repair.

She never did see her beloved home again. Despite all the years in Saigon and Minneapolis after that, Nhi never stopped referring to Hanoi as home. It was the Hanoi of her childhood she missed, not the world it became after independence, a place where "everybody a snake, a spy." She had never con-templated returning. She had never forgiven her family for rejecting her because of her relationship with a dissident artist. She could not believe the country had really emerged from darkness; not even Bill Clinton lifting the trade embargo in 1994 could convince her.

"Don't you want to see it for yourself?" Maggie had asked when they were watching the news of Clinton's visit in 2000.

Nhi had turned her head away at the suggestion, cover-ing her mouth.

"I could go," Maggie said, "and if it's safe, which I'm sure it is, you could join me."

"Please don't do this," her mother had whispered through her hand.

Maggie had been reminded of her father's words from long ago in that moment: *You keep her company, be strong, she needs you.* Those words had been prophetic. From the moment they arrived in the U.S., Maggie had led the way.

They were resettled in Minneapolis in 1975 with clothes for winter courtesy of the U.S. Army, but with little evidence of home beyond the piece of paper upon which her father had written the phone number of Margaret McGillis, his former landlady in Chicago, after whom Maggie had been named. "You call her," he had said to Maggie's mother. "You call her and give her your address. That way I'll be able to find you."

But Nhi could speak no English, and Maggie was largely limited to letters and numbers. Their first task was survival, feeding themselves from tins of things they recognized by the pictures on the labels: sliced pineapple, sections of mandarin oranges in syrup, carrots, tuna, button mushrooms. Maggie's mother stockpiled these cans just in case—a mantra she never let go of in all her years in the U.S. Every night, for this same reason, she wedged a chair under the handle of the front door of the subsidized apartment they had been allocated.

About a month after she and her mother arrived, Maggie had been lured by the sound of a bouncing ball into the stair-well, where she discovered a Vietnamese girl very close to her in age playing a game by herself. She counted to ten in English before switching to Vietnamese. Maggie taught her new friend, Mei, the English words for eleven through thirty-two before they gave up the game and returned to the girl's apartment, where her mother, Mrs. Minh, was making spring rolls. It was the first thing Maggie had eaten in a long time that didn't come from a can.

Mrs. Minh took Maggie's mother to a Chinese grocery the very next day, and both their meals and her mood began to improve. Soon after that they had a visit from a social worker accompanied by a Vietnamese translator who gave them a lengthy set of instructions. Nhi would attend English classes in a church basement, and Maggie would start first grade at the school in their neighbourhood in the fall.

"Please," her mother had said to the translator that day, pulling the piece of paper with Margaret McGillis's phone number on it out of her pocket. "Please will you call this lady and tell her we are here?"

But the number was out of service. According to the

operator, the line had been disconnected for some time. They learned then that Americans do not stay in a house for generations, that there are few generations and little continuity, something her father must have failed to understand about America in his time there as a visitor. The future her mother had envisioned was rewritten in that instant. They no longer had the certainty of reunion with Lý Văn Hai.

Her mother had smiled and nodded politely at the translator that day and escorted her and the social worker to the door. She then wedged the chair under the door handle and lay face down on the floor of the hallway. Her back arched and contracted in undulating waves; she was soundless, her fists clenched against her temples.

Maggie rushed to the balcony, hoping to catch sight of the translator in the parking lot, but saw no trace of her. She ran back inside and picked up the phone, yelling for help over and over in Vietnamese to a dial tone.

There was a knock at the door. Maggie dropped the receiver and climbed over her mother, unhooking the chair from under the door handle. It was Mrs. Minh, Mei's mother, from down the hall. Mrs. Minh looked at Maggie's mother on the floor with some surprise before sitting down very calmly beside her and resting her palm on her back. "I was going to ask if you wanted to play mah-jong," she said, as if this were the most ordinary scene in the world.

Maggie unhinges the metal gates of the elevator and tiptoes to the end of the hall. She flicks the light switch and kicks off her heels in the foyer, padding across the parquet squares of the reception room into the kitchen in her stockinged feet. The sound of her heels on the wood floors makes the place feel too hollow and lonely. The flat came furnished with some heavy French antiques, but apart from a few kitchen utensils, Maggie has acquired nothing, uncertain of her place, or how long she will stay.

Her mother had accumulated very little over the course of thirty years in the U.S., as if her life there had only ever been temporary. Maggie realized just how true this was after her mother died. She stayed at her mother's apartment in the weeks that followed her death, sleeping in her mother's sheets and wearing her mother's bathrobe, still smelling of her Chanel No. 5. She sipped tea from a chipped year of the cat mug and spent hours staring up at the peeling border of poppies her mother had glued to the walls sometime in the 1980s, bracing herself for the task of disposing of her mother's things.

She drank a bottle of wine one night, destroying any resolve, and called Daniel. She hadn't spoken to him in months. "My mother died," she said blankly.

"Oh, Mouse," he said, piercing a heart already broken.

The regret she felt the next morning did at least give her the push she needed. She packed up her mother's mah-jong tiles to give to Mrs. Minh, and donated her clothes and scant pieces of furniture to charity. She kept her mother's watch and the rarely worn *áo dài* she'd had made for special occasions. It was then that she discovered her mother's secrets. Five years' worth of unsent letters from her mother to her father lay bundled in a shoebox at the back of the closet. Maggie had knelt down on the green carpet with the box in her lap and pulled one letter at random from the pile. The envelope was addressed to Lý Văn Hai at their old apartment in Saigon.

My dear husband,

Maggie has just lost her fifth tooth and will be starting third grade in the fall. In just two years, she is speaking English as if she was born in this country. She is an enormous help to me. Who could have imagined when you began to teach her the English alphabet, that soon she would be using it every day? I am taking a night class called Basic English for Newcomers, but it is not easy and sometimes I miss the class because of my shift at work. I think it will be some time before I know enough of the language to retrain as a nurse here, but I am thankful for the good job that I have. The head matron has been very patient with me and she has just hired two more Vietnamese cleaners because she says I have shown her how hard the Vietnamese work.

I am enclosing Maggie's second grade photograph. My dear husband, can you see how much she is starting to look like you? I worry about you so much, but when I look at our Maggie it makes me feel you are not so far away. I remain hopeful for our happy reunion.

Your loving wife
Nhi

Maggie, still kneeling on the carpet, had wept. Her mother's handwriting was so frail, so hesitant. She put the letter back in the shoebox with the others. They really weren't meant for her to read. She cleared out the rest of the closet, emptying a basket of greying, utilitarian bras and underwear into a green garbage bag, only to discover more secrets her mother had withheld. At the bottom of the basket were several pieces of paper: sketches Maggie's father had done for her as a child in Saigon. Gifts of lumbering animals he'd drawn with his clumsy claw. But her mother had taken nothing with them when they left; they had even been ordered to leave the small bag they had packed on the tarmac. Had she hidden these pictures in a pocket? They are creased and stained, perhaps with her sweat.

Why her mother had never shared them with her, Maggie will never know. But they are in Maggie's possession now. Much the same way her mother left Vietnam thirty years ago, Maggie has returned: carrying six of Lý Văn Hai's drawings.

Hưng lies in the dark listening to the gentle patter of rain on his corrugated tin roof, wishing he could pluck whatever it was he had hoped to tell Miss Maggie out of the weeds cluttering his mind. He falls asleep only to awake startled an hour later, the rain thundering down violently from above, catapulting him back to the time of war. The worst of it was in December of 1972, what the Americans called the Christmas bombing, when the B-52s rained bombs for eleven days, destroying railway yards and warehouses, factories and airfields and roads and bridges and hospitals and schools and blocks of communist housing, and wiping out entire neighbourhoods like Khâm Thiên. It had seemed then that all of Hanoi was burning.

The Old Quarter fortunately was spared, but the bombs had landed so close to the shantytown you could feel the heat rising from the northwest. The squatters were saved by their dirty pond. The tire factory on the far side of the muddy water exploded and lit up the sky for several days before engulfing them in an oily black cloud. For weeks the city was dark and smouldering, and people were coughing up blood and crawling on all fours because they could not see their way.

Finally, the sky faded from black to smoking grey. For several sunless days, Hưng and the other men and women of the shantytown waded through the oily pond, tossing debris onto the shore. He remembers pausing a moment at the sight of Lan there among the foragers, a brief look of recognition passing between them as if to say: all the pond weed is gone, all the fish, frogs and birds too, but somehow, whether by accident or design, we have survived.

It would take eleven years to rebuild the hospital, a generation to rebuild the neighbourhood of Khâm Thiên, but less than a year before the pond, without human intervention, began to show signs of new life. A film of algae appeared on the surface. The colour green returned to the palette of Hanoi.

Somehow it was only after the shock of the devastation of that winter bombing that the fear really set in. Hưng held his breath, listened for the drone of another wave of bombers. He prayed for an end to the war, prayed for the mercy of a God who was said to no longer exist.

Hunger forced him to breathe again, to venture beyond the shantytown to forage among ruins, to dredge muddy craters, to drag home dead dogs, to eat the roots of upturned trees. There were losses in the community: those who died of the blood in their lungs, of the rot in their intestines, of septic shock and suicide and starvation. Hưng did what he could to keep himself and his neighbours alive, turning over rubble in search of snails, digging for earthworms, boiling and reboiling rank water and making a weak green broth from the lichen he scraped off rocks.

Though Hưng no longer spoke to Lan, he would not let her go hungry. If she did not appear among those survivors who gathered for one of his neighbourhood suppers, he would simply wrap a portion of his share in a banana leaf and leave it on her doorstep in the middle of the night. He did this throughout the years of the war.

In April of 1975, black vans drove throughout the city, announcing the withdrawal of American troops. The Liberation of Saigon was imminent and victory would belong to the People's Army. The puppets of the South would be crushed.

"Rise up, comrades," Party spokesmen shouted through the windows of the vans, "for the homeland will soon be unified in the name of the revolutionary father. There will be new life in the new dawn. New light."

They had been waiting more than twenty years for this moment. *The skin of a fruit, discarded; a skinless fruit*, Đạo had once written of his divided country. Hưng has not since had the heart to abandon an orange peel, or even the useless dull-red rind of a lychee. Because of Đạo's words, Hưng's life has been governed as much by metaphor as economics.

How Hưng wished Đạo could have been there to see it. A future united. Whole fruit.

Of course, the deception of whole fruit is the rot that can be concealed beneath its skin. The victory of 1975 was tainted, as victory always is, by opportunists. Smugglers of uncertain origin came to the squatter settlement on the edge of the pond. A team of sharply dressed men and women walked past the shacks, luring people into the light with shouts of "Who wants a future for their children? Who wants relief from suffering?" The Americans are crazy for Vietnamese children, they said, they are scooping up all the orphans in Saigon and giving them medicines and making them strong. Sell yours to us and we will take them south and get them onto the planes and they will grow up rich.

Hưng was struck numb as he watched one young woman after another pass a swaddled newborn into the arms of an uncertain future. Where the young woman could not do it herself, her mother or mother-in-law stepped in. Whatever their feelings about the war, they must not have hated the thought of their children growing up rich in America. Perhaps they simply felt they had no choice. They were starving and the smugglers were waving money before their eyes. In less than a week, all the baby girls were gone.

The shantytown throbbed with the ache of loss, and those who had not sold babies because they had none to sell seethed with anger and refused to speak to those who had, calling them traitors of the worst possible kind— worse than the Catholics and the selfish cowards who had fled south.

A good nine months of silence passed before the tension began to ease. New baby girls were born, and many of these new arrivals were named after their sisters who were growing up rich in America.

Hưng has only once seen an American, at least someone he was sure was an American, and even that was from a distance. This man was lying on the shore of Trúc Bạch Lake draped in parachute silk. He'd been dragged to shore by men just like Hưng, poor men fishing farther along the shore, fishing despite the danger, because when bombs fell, fish rose—dead, not always intact, but in good numbers nevertheless.

Now, having met Miss Maggie, Hưng is able to picture who one of those babies of the shantytown might have become. A strong, educated young woman with a good job who speaks with confidence and does not lower her eyes when she meets a stranger. He thinks of all those babies, women now, their *áo dài*s flapping in American winds, and he wonders if they still know the Vietnamese language, if they have married American men, if they eat phở for breakfast, if they even know the taste of home. He must ask Miss Maggie if America still suffers the deprivation of phở. He wonders how many young women like her are haunted by questions about the past, their homeland. And how many old men like him might have some answers.

If only he had not been so careless with his memories. Carelessness has cost him dearly in the past: shouldn't he have learned when his papers were taken from his shack? He was too angry at the time to think of it, but he should have dedicated himself to his memories then. He should have worked hard to preserve all that he could, because soon there will be nothing of them left.

Maggie can't sleep. She's remembering that winter morning with her mother in Minneapolis when they lost all contact with Vietnam. The snowbanks were the size of elephants that day, the sky bright, flakes swirling around them as if they were figures in a shaken snow globe. Maggie's feet were sliding around in her boots as they trudged up the street because even though she was only ten, her mother had bought her ladies' boots so that they would last a few winters.

They passed Phở Việt Anh, where they usually stopped for lunch, because although Mrs. Trang made the best *phở bắc* in Minneapolis, Nhi wasn't in the mood for the lady's gossip. They pulled open the door of the new Vietnamese restaurant down the street instead, bells tinkling overhead as they walked in.

The place was thick with cigarette smoke and the noisy clatter of dominoes on Formica tabletops. Maggie's mother nudged her into a booth and took a seat beside her on the red vinyl bench.

"Nghiêm Nhi?" asked the man who came to take their order, his mouth and eyebrows almost cartoon-like in their expression of surprise. He stared at Nhi, not closing his mouth.

Her mother squinted. "Do I know you?"

"I'm Paul," he said, his finger to his chest. "Paul Nguyễn. Văn Hai's colleague from Saigon. Photojournalist. Associated Press."

She raised her eyebrows in recognition.

"I'm very very sorry about Văn Hai," Paul Nguyễn said.

"Ma?" Maggie prodded.

Her mother rose from the booth. She walked back into the kitchen with Paul Nguyễn, leaving Maggie alone at the table. She returned a few minutes later with a glass bowl of vanilla ice cream.

"Daddy didn't make it out of Vietnam," Nhi said to the tabletop once she sat down.

They both sat and stared at the bowl of ice cream. Maggie thought of the figure eights she'd learned to make on ice that winter wearing borrowed skates. She remembered the sensation of gliding backward.

"Daddy's not coming?" Maggie said after a few minutes of silence—voicing something she had perhaps known for years.

"No, Daddy's not coming."

"But where is he?" she asked.

"Oh, Maggie," said her mother, burying her face in her hands. "I'm sorry." She shook her head. "He's left us for the next life."

Because we left him, Maggie thought to herself, we left him standing on the tarmac at the air base.

"Maybe his next life will be in Minneapolis," Maggie finally said, trying to comfort first her mother, then herself— a pattern that, in retrospect, had already become entrenched.

It wasn't until she was older that Maggie learned the details that had surfaced that day. At sixteen, she sought out Paul Nguyễn, discovering he now worked at Abbott

Northwestern Hospital as a lab technician. They sat on stools in a dimly lit room, Paul wearing his lab coat and twisting a piece of paper in his hands.

"So your mother never told you," he said. "I suppose you were too young. The fact is, your father and I waited too long to leave."

"But why did you wait?" Maggie asked.

"It was important to continue getting the stories out. I think we assumed that as long as there were still Americans in Saigon we would be okay. But then the city was surrounded, under attack from all sides.

"Your father and I fled to the American Embassy. There were thousands of people already there, desperate, crawling over the walls. The embassy was getting people out as quickly as it could. When it was our turn, your father and I waited up on the roof in a terrible thunderstorm. But the next helicopter never came. We waited for hours and I remember your father finally saying, 'It's over.'

"I knew he was right," said Paul, throwing the twisted piece of paper into the trash can. "We went and hid in the bomb shelter. Hundreds of us crammed into this hot, dark tunnel. We had no plan, Maggie, just prayers. Within a few hours the soldiers stormed in and shone their lights into our faces. When they reached your father and put a gun to his head, he just held up his hands and said, 'I'm done. I'm old and you have already taken my hands. My wife and daughter are safe in America.'"

Why had her father given up when he had so much left to fight for? Paul Nguyễn had survived; he even had his hands despite being taken from that bomb shelter to a re-education camp where he'd been imprisoned for four years.

Maggie slid off the stool and reached for her knapsack.

"Listen, he'd been through a camp once before," Paul pleaded. "I just don't think he could face it again. You have to understand, Maggie, re-education makes it sound so much more benign than it was—it's the remaking of the individual, destroying him in order to rebuild."

But Maggie didn't understand, she was angry. She couldn't imagine what could be so bad that he would give up his life, his family, a future. But then perhaps this was why he had ensured their passage to America. So that she could be spared ever having to know.

The Quiet Inside

In the absence of Old Man Hưng this morning, Tư and his father are forced to settle for an inferior bowl. The broth at Phở Hong Việt on Mã Mây Street is passable and the beef should be good because it is supplied by Tư's mother, but still, they would feel disloyal if they said this phở was anywhere close in quality to Old Man Hưng's. Whenever they are forced to come here then, they make a point of complaining.

"Not enough pepper, eh, Tư?"

"And he can't have trimmed the fat, do you see this oily film on the surface?"

"I think it's because he's buying the cheap cuts again. It's not Anh's fault he's cheap."

"Can you taste any star anise? I think he's reusing the pods, because I don't taste it at all."

"There's hardly any heat in this chili paste."

"He cooked the noodles for too long. They're like glue now."

"Dad? What is this?" Tư says, pinching a bean sprout between his thumb and forefinger. "Some kind of Saigon invasion!"

"Thank you, Bình and son," the proprietor interrupts. "I'll be happy to charge you double today for your enjoyment of so many insults."

Tư is slurping his broth and watching a cockroach dart across the wall when his cellphone rings. The cockroach skips over the lip of the skirting board and falls to the floor. Friends in high places, he thinks, looking at the phone number as he lifts his feet.

"Cao Mạnh Tư at your service," he answers loudly in English.

"Good morning," says Miss Maggie Lý, sounding so American he has trouble picturing her Vietnamese face. "I was just wondering, Tư—yesterday, when you said if I ever needed the services of a tour guide? Well, I just might. Any chance you could stop by the hotel today?"

Yes, okay, Miss Maggie's request is a little bit inconvenient, but you do not say no to a request from the Metropole, as he says to his boss in a subsequent call. And how can he resist the intrigue? This is a chance to figure out just who this lady is and solve the mystery of her relationship to Old Man Hưng.

"The hotel contacts you directly now?" Tư's father says, raising his eyebrows, impressed.

Tư feels meeting Miss Maggie Lý was somehow fated. That life is about to improve measurably.

The lobby of the Metropole is so quiet by comparison with the street that it takes a few moments for Tư's ears to adjust. He stands and inhales the smells of burnt toast and coffee before making his way down a hotel corridor in search of Miss Maggie's office. He checks to make sure his fly is pulled up, then knocks three times for luck on the door.

So much art is stacked against the walls of Miss Maggie's office that she can't open the door the whole way. Tư is forced to squeeze past her as she holds the door open, his thigh brushing against hers, causing him to look down with some embarrassment.

"I had no idea the hotel had so much art," says Tư, finally casting his eyes about the room.

"Everyone was surprised," Miss Maggie says. "It's my job to make sense of it all. It's taken almost a year, but I'm close. Listen, how's the old man doing? Did you get him home all right?"

"He's okay," says Tư. "He did at least agree to take this morning off, but I'm sure he'll be back to selling phở tomorrow."

"That's good news," Miss Maggie says, sitting down. "Listen, I really appreciate you coming. Here's what I wanted to talk to you about. More and more hotel guests are being referred to me because they're interested in contemporary

Vietnamese art. I don't really have the time to take them around the city and show them the various galleries and studios; I'd never get my work done if I did. It would be really useful if I had a guide I could call when these situations arise, and I thought you might be just the man for the job."

Tư cannot imagine the basis upon which she has reached such a conclusion, but then why question something so flattering? And look at that smile, so warm and inviting he can feel it in the pit of his stomach. Perhaps it is the Americanness of her direct gaze, but no girl has ever looked at him in such a way, as if she is in need of something only he can deliver.

"Certainly," he says, straightening up in his chair, though he's not certain of anything at all.

"Great," she says, pulling out a map. "I assume you're familiar with the Museum of Fine Arts, so I thought we could start by visiting some of the major galleries in the Old Quarter—I haven't even been to all of them myself yet."

Tư picks up the map. None of the locations she has marked are familiar to him; his expertise is in relation to the more common tourist destinations. Still, he will do his best to serve Miss Maggie Lý and earn the possibility of more flattery in future.

Miss Maggie stands up, shuffles around the table and behind Tư's chair, reaching for her purse. "Ready?" she says, touching his shoulder.

Tư's whole arm radiates with warmth. He feels something in his lower body as well, something he is quite sure he shouldn't, but it's not every day that a lady touches your shoulder. He springs to his feet and follows her down the corridor, her black heels clickety-clacking on the tiled floor.

As soon as they have stepped onto the street, Tư starts making conversation of the sort he learned during his first week in tourism college. "Hot today, isn't it? Soon the rainy season will be upon us and sweep some of this humidity away. You've been here long in Vietnam? Where in the U.S. are you from exactly? Nice weather there?"

"Midwest," says Maggie, two steps behind him now, "lots of snow."

Tư is forced to conjure the map of the U.S. in his head. He thinks *west* as in wild west—Texas, mostly—but he's not entirely sure about the *mid*.

"Minneapolis," she says, "Minnesota."

"Ahh. So you are a fan of the Minnesota Vikings?" Tư says, hoping to impress her with this knowledge, turning round to confirm the look of astonishment on her face.

Maggie laughs. "Not really my thing," she says. "But how do you even know that? Isn't it all about soccer here?"

"I just like to study facts, particularly about foreign countries. Do you know that football originated from the sport of rugby?"

"Really," says Miss Maggie in that way Phương is always warning Tư about.

Miss Maggie follows Tư down the narrow path of sidewalk, squeezing between a wall of motorbikes to their right and a string of red plastic tables to their left. Tư would like to recite to her the rest of the names of the American football teams he knows, but his voice would be lost in the collective roar.

Tourists always ask him, How can you think with all this noise? But truthfully? This is where he finds himself meditating. The more crowded the better. In Vietnam you are with family from childhood to death—and when family and neighbours are not watching, you can rest assured the government is.

Twice each day the district report is broadcast over the loudspeaker, listing those who have committed crimes and infractions. Once Tư heard Phương named among those who were late in their payments for motorbike licence renewal, and he felt very ashamed for him.

"You don't honestly listen to that propaganda, do you?" he'd asked Tư. "We're a city of three and a half million. How many Nguyễn Phươngs do you think there are in our district alone?"

Phương was right; no one is paying very close attention to the report anymore. You don't need to spy on your neighbour now and envy his brand new television and suspect him of accepting some bribe, perhaps from a foreigner, or of having some Việt Kiều traitors in his family sending him money from the U.S. Now, instead of reporting you to the district council, your neighbour will say, Friend, help me split this television cable, will you? Hey, friend, why don't we pool our resources to buy a satellite dish?

Tư steps off the sidewalk and onto the road. "Wait," Maggie calls out. "We're not going to cross here, are we?" She is pointing across the river of traffic between them and Hoàn Kiếm Lake. "Can't we just walk to the top and cross up there?"

"But this way is much quicker. Do you never come to the lake?"

Maggie shakes her head.

"You never cross the road?"

"Not this one," she says.

"How do you come and go from the hotel?"

"I take a taxi."

"Every day?"

"At least twice a day."

"*Ôi z̃ôi ôi*," says Tư.

He guides Miss Maggie into the street by the elbow. It's almost like floating, like walking on water. "Look straight ahead," he says, "and whatever you do, don't hesitate. You need to find the quiet inside."

Inside Tư's quiet, he finds the girl of last Christmas in her fuzzy red-and-white outfit. Her lips like a butterfly, her skin dewy like a newly peeled potato. He doesn't hear the traffic as he crosses the road, he hears her whispering in his ear instead: *You can kiss me, you can touch me, if you'd like.* Those same words slip out from between Miss Maggie's perfect teeth just before he reaches the sidewalk.

"Wow. My God," says Miss Maggie. She holds her stomach for a moment, and Tư wonders if she's about to be sick. Never mind, the lake air will refresh her. Hoàn Kiếm is at its most beautiful in the morning, and its most romantic, when young men sit with their girlfriends under the banyan trees while Tư envies them and the mist slowly dissipates into a chalky sky.

"It's beautiful," she says, looking at the surface of the lake.

It strikes Tư as very sad that Miss Maggie is only realizing this after a whole year in Hanoi. For all the changes that are happening in the city, the lake remains constant and still.

"According to local legend, six centuries ago the turtle god rose from the water to relieve Emperor Lê Lợi of the magic sword he used to defeat the Chinese Ming. The city was born from this lake and so, in some ways, are its people. The lake is the city's liquid heart." Good line! Tư commends himself. Perhaps he should try that one out on the old man, admirer of poetry that he is.

Tư and Miss Maggie walk side by side along the paved path that circles the lake while young couples share secrets on benches, men lean in over chessboards, an old married couple plays badminton, racquets in each hand, and middle-aged men and women march past them swinging their arms in the air like propellers. They are too late for the early morning legions who practise tai chi.

Tư is relaying the history of the decisive battle that freed the Vietnamese from the Chinese in the fifteenth century as he and Miss Maggie walk past the Bridge of the Rising Sun. An old woman with baskets slung from a bamboo pole across her shoulders approaches and smiles at Tư with black and gold teeth. "Help an old woman and buy from me," she says to him.

Tư waves her away, keen to carry on with this important story, only to realize he is now talking to himself.

"What is she selling?" Miss Maggie calls out from where she has stopped.

"Sticky rice in banana leaf," Tư says, walking back to join her. "With quail egg inside."

"I don't sell to Việt Kiều," says the woman with a country accent so muddy thick it is unintelligible to Miss Maggie. "Neither should you," she says to Tư, sucking her blackened teeth.

"She's not buying in any case," Tư tells the old woman, waving her away.

"What did she say?" Miss Maggie asks, staring after the woman as she shuffles off.

"She hopes you are very happy in Hanoi."

Tư is explaining the way the old guild system worked as they walk into the narrow, congested streets of the Old Quarter. Miss Maggie seems less interested in history, though, than in what is immediately in front of them. What's that? she asks. What's this?

Tư wonders how it is that she looks so Vietnamese yet has such questions. Where has she been living for the past year? Does she never leave the hotel?

"This is it," Miss Maggie says, stopping in front of a building much wider than any other on Hàng Bồ Street. Tư double-checks the map. The gallery is bright white and stands out in marked contrast to the tube houses that flank it. He pulls open the carved wooden doors, revealing a vast space with high ceilings.

As soon as they step across the threshold, they are greeted in English by a team of immaculate girls, hair parted in the middle and slicked back tightly, all dressed alike in white, long-flowing traditional *áo dài*s. The woman in charge, European with a thick accent, stands behind an ornate gilt-edged desk and clasps her hand over the mouthpiece of her cellphone to say she'd be happy to answer any questions they might have once she's done with her call.

"Please wander," she says with a wave.

Tư has never seen so much art in one place, except in the museum. He moves around silently, eyeing the paintings. Girl in *áo dài*. Water buffalo. Woman working in rice paddy. Pagoda. Bamboo bridge over river. Mist over mountain. Schoolgirl in *áo dài*. Boat on Halong Bay. Water buffalo . . . They look like postcards to Tư, the kind that tourists hand to him at the end of their trips, saying, "Would you mind sending these for me? I didn't get a chance to buy stamps," and pressing a ten-dollar bill into his hand.

"It's all a bit romantic, isn't it," Miss Maggie says in English. "And kind of innocuous."

Tư doesn't know the word. Like inoculation? A shot in the arm?

The owner waves apologetically and rolls her eyes. *Sotheby's*, she mouths at Miss Maggie.

Tư and Miss Maggie wander in opposite directions around the room, the blur of images becoming wallpaper, until Tư spies something familiar. A painting of the Old Quarter by Bùi Xuân Phái. Tư recognizes it immediately because there are several of Phái's paintings on the walls of Café Võ, which his father used to take him to see as a boy. Mr. Võ has the most extensive collection of Phái's work because the artist paid for all his years of coffees with paintings.

Tư's father even has one of Bùi Xuân Phái's drawings

at home. It was a gift from the artist himself to Grandfather
Đạo, which Grandmother Amie somehow managed to hold
on to. It's an ink drawing on brown paper of a lady, just the
black outline of her body, and apart from showing it to Tư,
his father has always kept it rolled up—the nude was too
naked for the Party, not to mention too bourgeois—though
since Đổi mới he has not felt the need to keep it locked up in
the bedroom chest.

Tư picks up a photocopied sheet of paper. The prices of
the paintings are listed in dollars and have a great many
zeros. But how can this be? Bùi Xuân Phái died in desperate
poverty—the man didn't even own a bicycle, just the canes
on which he used to hobble about—but this painting is on
sale for thousands of dollars.

The owner is still on the phone by the time they finish
their circuit of the room.

The second gallery is only two streets away and the
owner of this one is not on the phone. He greets Miss
Maggie in a familiar way, then engages her in a conversation about a group of artists in Singapore, leaving Tư to
wander about the room. More of the same. Girls in white
*áo dài*s returning home from school. Woman in rice paddy.
Sunrise over Halong Bay. Lady with lotus flower, boat on
Perfume River, different lady with lotus flower.

"It has a timelessness to it," says Miss Maggie, coming
to stand at his side. "An almost conspicuous avoidance of
history."

Tư is looking at a pretty but by now familiar scene of a
village depicted through a gauze-like veil of rain. He's not

sure what Miss Maggie means. Sure, these are images you see in the countryside, but you also see highways, factories, ports, manufacturing facilities, mines, airports, industrial parks and resorts being built along the coast. And what about the cities? These artists don't seem to paint the cities. He worries that if this is all foreigners see, lazy rivers and poor people ploughing fields by hand, they will think Vietnam a backward country.

"What do you think?" Miss Maggie asks. "Would you ever have a painting like this in your home?"

"But these are not for a Vietnamese home," Tư says.

"You're right about that," says Miss Maggie. "Ninety-eight per cent of the contemporary art produced here leaves the country."

Tư, who likes a statistic, says he's not at all surprised. He checks the photocopied piece of paper for the price of this piece, which is a heart-attack-making eight thousand dollars. Wait until he tells Phương. They could eat 11,428 and a half bowls of phở for that amount of money. They could eat phở every day for thirty-one years and three months. Even for a more-than-average-earning Vietnamese person to make that kind of money it would take close to twenty years. Twenty years without eating or a roof over one's head or a motorbike or a change of clothes. But Tư doesn't know any Vietnamese who would buy such a thing, in any case. If you had eight thousand dollars to spend you might rent a shop for a year or invest in a business or buy a better motorbike and some land or pay for a wedding or a funeral.

Something's not right with this business. Someone is getting very very rich.

The woman who lives next door to Phương's family is whacking crab claws on the sidewalk with a mallet. She passes a thin pink sliver over her shoulder into the eager mouth of the toddler standing behind her. Tư high-fives the toddler before slipping down the alleyway and turning right into a courtyard. Phương's bedroom light beams through the bars of his window above.

Tư bounds up the stairs, nearly knocking over Phương's sister on the landing.

"He won't talk to any of us," she says. "He won't even come down for dinner. You talk to him. It's probably some stupid thing about a girl."

Tư pushes open his friend's bedroom door. He finds Phương lying on his mattress, wearing nothing but a pair of boxer shorts covered in red hearts—a birthday gift from his last girlfriend. Phương has had many admirers and many dates, but not actually many girlfriends, none he's ever introduced to his family, in any case.

The fan creaks each time it reverses direction, pushing perfumed waves of incense in Phương's direction. He doesn't seem to hear Tư come in; he's wearing his headphones and Tư can hear the tinny treble all the way from the doorway. Phương is staring at the ceiling, a bottle of *rượu*, rice whisky, a small jug of *nước mắm* and a bowl of hardened rice on the floor within reach of him on the mattress.

Tư has never seen his friend like this, even over a girl; Phương dismisses girls after the initial flirtation, using American expressions like she was "dirt cheap" and "crumpling my style." Music will always come first in his life, which worries his parents and sometimes Tư as well. Family is always first in Vietnam; why does Phương have to be so contrary?

Tư nudges Phương's foot, which is hanging over the end of his bed.

"Mmm?" Phương moans, raising his head. He immediately collapses back onto the mattress.

"Phương," Tư says, lifting the headphones off his friend's ears. "What's wrong?" He sits down on the edge of the mattress. "What are you listening to?"

"Sex Pistols," says Phương.

"What does that mean?"

Phương shrugs. Even if he knows, he's not in the mood to talk. He wants to get high.

They climb up the stairs to the third floor and, with a quick nod to the ancestors' altar, ascend the metal stairs to the roof. Two of Phương's father's shirts have been left to dry on the line, the chickens are quietly clucking in their cages and the dog they are fattening up for Tet is licking his balls. The smells of kerosene and cooking oil float up from the street.

Phương uses the light that spills from the neighbour's roof to help him roll a joint. The man they always use for cyclo tours in the Old Quarter supplies him. Tư is not one for this mood-altering practice himself; he prefers the predictability of good and cheap old-fashioned *bia hơi* at happy hour, which can sometimes make you tired or fill your stomach too much to eat dinner and make your mother angry, but most times it just makes you happy with an urge to sing karaoke.

It is wrong to be smoking marijuana overtop of the ancestors, you certainly wouldn't swear or have sex on top of them either, but it does at least get Phương talking.

"Have you ever noticed how many promises foreigners seem to make?" he says, exhaling to the clouds.

"What are you talking about, Phương?"

"How many times has some tourist said to you, Give me your e-mail address, let's stay in touch. There's a CD or a DVD or a book I'm going to send to you when I get home. Or even, Hey, you should really come and visit me in New York or Berlin or wherever."

Sometimes there is a brief exchange of e-mails in the first month, but when that stops, as it inevitably does, Tư no longer really takes it personally.

"Do you remember that Australian?" Phương asks.

How could Tư forget? Tư had found him very aggressive, both in manner and body. His neck was thick as a tree trunk and a blue vein in his forehead throbbed like it had a heart of its own. He'd caused Tư a great deal of embarrassment at Hồ Chí Minh's mausoleum with his short pants and rude voice and his mocking laughter at the fact that Uncle Hồ is sent to Russia every year for a bit of preservation, but Tư had to save face for Phương's sake—the guy said his sister was a music producer in Sydney.

"That asshole didn't even take my CD, Tư. You heard him—he said he was going to give it to his sister, but then when I was cleaning out the van the other day? I found the CD jammed between the seats. I've wasted all this time thinking that this might be my big break, I even went to the consulate to look into getting an Australian visa, when this guy just abandoned the CD in the van like it was some piece of shit."

Phương's little sister pops her head through the door in the roof just then. Phương stubs the joint out in a pot of coriander. She sniffs the air and asks if they want some food. She is carrying the leftovers from dinner on a tray. She crouches down on her knees and lays pieces of fatty-skinned broiled fish onto the rice in two bowls. She has just washed her hair and it hangs damp around her shoulders, turning her loose white shirt translucent. Tư cannot help but stare at her nipples, more grape seeds than the raisins of the girl dressed as Santa's helper.

Tư turns the conversation to the subject of the last couple of days, news he is by now *desperate* to share. He tells his friend about Hưng's accident and Miss Maggie Lý, the Việt Kiều who has now called the agency and booked his services for the rest of the week.

"Can you believe it?" Tư asks, his whole body a question mark.

"No," says Phương, deadpan.

"I don't know what this lady's story is, but she's got some kind of connection to Hưng," says Tư.

"But how does Hưng know a Việt Kiều?" Phương says. "Especially one working at a place like that. I mean, we don't even know any Việt Kiều, Tư."

"I don't know," says Tư. "Maybe you can help me figure it out."

"Yeah, okay," says Phương.

Hah! Tư feels he has very cleverly led Phương back into the daylight. And hopefully back to work. Now all that is needed is a bowl of Old Man Hưng's phở in the morning and Phương's balance will be truly restored. They will be back to normal, the A-team smiling with the New Dawn.

An Inverted World

Hưng can see the sheen at the bottom of the kidney as he pushes his cart onto the hotel construction site in the dark before dawn. Absent for just a day and they've begun to fill the pool with water. He has faced the inevitable need to move on for so many decades that he is resigned to it. Other things are more worrying. The price of meat, for instance, which just continues to rise. He has dealt with the meagrest of rations, crops lost to weather or war, the indignities of bullying, bribery and black markets over the years, but somehow the inflation that came with Đổi mới is proving the toughest challenge of all.

Hưng is spared some expenses living as he does, collecting his own wood and not having an "official" residence or place of business. Still, the gang leader who claims to be policing the shantytown demands protection money every month, threatening to have their names added to some register that would otherwise recognize their shacks as residences and tax them accordingly.

Hưng knows how much worse it is for people in the countryside, especially the farmers, when fuel is so expensive and taxes are so high. Often the only other people awake when Hưng pushes his cart through the city before dawn are groups of children traipsing in from the countryside, children whose families cannot afford to keep them in school, who must come and shine shoes or sell peanuts or worse in order to keep their parents and siblings clothed and fed. Those children whose homes are far away might rent a room, ten or twelve of them together, sleeping in shifts, peeing in a bucket, lice jumping from one head to the next.

Hưng can recognize them at a distance, almost see himself in them. How lucky he was to have had an Uncle Chiến. What indignities and deprivation it must have spared him.

When Hưng arrived home in the village for the first time after being sent to his uncle in the city, his father had openly embraced him. A gentle but nervous man, Trong Tri had always quietly loved and pitied his ninth child, privately telling Hưng he was the one most like him. But his love for Hưng was no match for his wife's ire, for her attachment to superstition and village gossip; his love for his son was a lonely beacon.

Hưng's father wiped the celebration off his face and focused his attention on the sheer weight of the plump sack of coins Hưng had deposited onto the table as soon as he entered the house. "So business is good," he said with admiration.

"Uncle Chiến has many many customers. The shop is always very busy," said Hưng.

"Well, I know you are a great help to him," his father said, making Hưng feel unusually proud.

His mother swooped in then and scooped the sack off the table. She tossed it in the air, catching it with alternate hands. "My, my," she said. "What a rich new world you inhabit."

Hưng's father quietly advised him to keep his birthmarked cheek to the wall when he greeted his mother in future, and Hưng found that when he did so on subsequent visits, his mother even managed to smile at him, suggesting he might want to bathe or lie down after his long journey—*after* he unburdened himself of his heavy sack of coins. He would spend one night with his family before making the three-day return journey, a night when his mother would cook something good and tell him news of the village, treating him like the visiting relative from the city he had quickly become.

Hưng's father would whisper to him upon his departure, "I am proud of you, my son. But I would be proud of you without the coins. Please believe that."

And Hưng did believe that. He returned to the city each time with the satisfaction of knowing he was helping his family.

The respect Hưng had for his father mutated into pity as he got older, pity for a man bullied by his wife's small-mindedness, a man who could have had much more from life if circumstances had allowed. Ironically, his father had created for his blemished son a chance of a far better life than any Hưng ever would have led in the village.

Later, after Uncle Chiến became sick, it became impossible for Hưng to leave the shop and return home to his family's village. His uncle spent more and more time resting in the backroom, but the rest seemed to age rather than heal him. Just a few days before he died, Uncle Chiến reached out and touched the mole on his nephew's cheek. "You've been a blessing to me," he said, "not a curse."

Hưng's parents periodically sent one of his brothers to the city to collect the money from him after Uncle Chiến's passing. This brother never did stay for breakfast, despite Hưng's insistence, or offer more than the barest news. Throughout the winter of 1954, in the months after liberation, his brother failed to appear. Hưng socked away a portion of his rapidly declining proceeds for his family each month and worried about them more and more.

Land reform was now underway in the countryside, and although Uncle Hồ had promised this would liberate the peasantry, it was the peasantry who were proving most resistant to the idea—with good reason.

"You can't just impose the Russian model on a country like Vietnam," Đạo kept repeating. "We simply don't have the vast tracts of arable land that it would take to create these large collective farms."

Hưng thought through the implications for his village. He certainly couldn't imagine wealthy families like the Changs ever relinquishing their land. What would it take to revolutionize his village—any village for that matter? What would it take beyond theory?

"They would have to merge hundreds of small farms," Hưng said over Đạo's shoulder as he leaned in to replenish the small jar of fish sauce on the table.

"That's what worries me," Đạo said. "It would take charging every one of those small landholders as a class enemy if they showed any resistance at all."

The need to get the sum of money he had amassed over the months into his parents' hands became more urgent as a consequence of this conversation. The next day, for the first morning in twenty-five years, the last eleven under Hưng's ownership, Phở Chiến (& Hưng) was closed for business. Rather than straining the oxtail bones, peppering his silken broth with cloves, drinking a fortifying tea of ginseng just before the early-morning rush, Hưng was on a motorbike, gripping the broad back of a man he had paid to transport him back to his village.

The ravages of war with the French were evident along much of the three day journey south of Hanoi, but for the most part, the driver avoided the pockmarked and battle-scarred roads and travelled along rural tracks, which made for a bumpy 320 kilometres. At the port city of Vinh, however, the devastating evidence of recent history was unavoidable. The city had been virtually flattened: the French had even bombed their own factories; sea, land, and sky were the colour of ash.

The driver would take Hưng no farther than Vinh, blaming impossible tracks muddied by autumn rains. Hưng was thus forced to travel the last and most familiar kilometres on foot. As a boy, he had cycled the nineteen kilometres on his rickety Chinese bicycle to the industrial port every morning to attend school, pedalling the distance back to his village every afternoon. But the landscape displayed an alien nakedness now. Quyết Mountain stood bald, without its crown of cooling pines. The terrain was a lonely grey, devoid of shadows.

Hưng walked along the buffalo track by the Lam River as it snaked its way through the tentative new growth rising from the scorched earth. This was troubled land at the best of times: Uncle Hồ country. Hưng could understand the great man's desire for revolution because he too came from this poor place where the farmers were engaged in ongoing and often losing battles with the chalky soil, the hot, dry Laotian winds, the storms that tore inland from the Gulf of Tonkin, not to mention the landlords constantly driving peasants to produce more despite the mercilessness of the environment.

While Hưng believed it was time for the humbling of people like the wealthy Changs with their orchid-white skin, gold teeth, cruel taunts, vast acreage and team of beleaguered workers, he was genuinely worried about the fate of smaller landowners in the village like Widow Nguyệt. After Hưng's parents had laboured for fifteen years in her fields, Widow Nguyệt had felt moved to grant them a plot exclusively for their own use. His parents had erected a shrine in her honour in that field as if she were their own ancestor. It was from that plot that they'd been able to earn the money for the shared use of a water buffalo and to have school uniforms made for the last of the boys—Hưng, despite the curse upon his cheek, included.

Hưng had continued to wear that school uniform long after he was sent to Uncle Chiến in Hanoi. While Hưng felt proud of the implication that he had had some education, Uncle Chiến's chief dishwasher called him over one day and asked if he knew how ridiculous he looked—like an oversized, provincial schoolboy who'd been expelled from school years ago but didn't have the heart to tell his parents.

Hưng burned with shame. He didn't have any other clothes, certainly nothing respectable enough to wear while serving in a restaurant in the city.

"Give the uniform to me," the dishwasher said more gently. "I'll make you a shirt from it. Ask your Uncle Chiến for plenty of đồng and I'll buy the material to make you a pair of trousers as well."

As if to ward off any further expectation of kindness, she looked at his birthmark and quickly added, "Shame we can't cover up that mud stain on your future."

Hưng raised his hand to his face as he walked the last kilometre toward his family's village. He caressed the soft fur of the auspicious mole with the tips of his fingers, a sensation that often gave him comfort.

He could see no water buffalo in the fields, no conical hats floating above the green paddies, no women moving down the track carrying buckets of water balanced on either end of bamboo poles. Only the dead ancestors in their marble tombs remained in the rice paddies. Nothing but the frogs that croaked at night was audible, as if day and night had been reversed.

He was relieved to see the rise of the pagoda just ahead,

the landmark at the edge of the village. A thin stream of incense, woody and sweet, reached his nose.

Hưng carried more than a month's worth of earnings in his pockets. He stuffed a fifth of that total into the wooden box at the foot of the pagoda, reached up to rub the toe of the gleaming white Buddha, bowed his head and raised his hands. Mid-recitation, he heard someone grunt to his left. An old woman was shuffling down the path, head bent, firewood weighing down her shoulders, feet gnarled and splayed.

"Grandmother," Hưng faltered, dropping his hands in abandoned prayer.

She did not look up, simply waved him aside as if to speak or alter her gait would cause her to lose the balance of wood upon her shoulders.

"Grandmother," he repeated. "It's Hưng."

She slowed and whispered, "Go back," through teeth stained sepia by betel nut. She tilted slightly to the left, and Hưng reached out, pushing the wood sliding off her shoulder to the middle of her back so that she could right her balance. The wood was smooth, lacquered red, no ordinary firewood. He moved aside to let her pass.

The temple, he realized, as he watched her hobble away. She was carrying wooden beams from the temple on the other side of the village. What would drive an old woman to such desecration?

Hưng lingered with a sense of dread behind the bamboo hedge that surrounded the village, in that hidden place where he had first discovered what it was that made him a boy. He looked to the sky for the courage to step through and onto the village road, a road built by bricks given by men from elsewhere who had married and taken village women away.

He held his breath in the silence, one foot following another until, approaching the ochre-walled *đình*, the communal hall and home of the village spirit, he heard laughter from inside. He drew back at the sight of the row of soldiers' boots at the entrance. He stood by the communal well. The stretch of wall to the left of the entrance to the *đình* was pockmarked by gunfire. Below that riddled surface a cloud of flies swarmed above a dog licking sticky bloodied ground.

Suddenly he could smell it—the tinny scent of fresh blood, and beyond it, the older stench of decaying bodies. He could smell it so acutely that he could taste it, like rust in the mouth. He broke into a run, loping toward the other end of the village, past buildings with collapsed mud walls, houses whose thatched roofs had gone up in flames, past the charcoal-stump residue of trees that used to offer nuts and bark and shade.

The Chang family house was nothing more than a scorched outline. His own family's house, though without its roof, at least remained. He pushed the front door open with his foot and stepped onto the dirt floor. The squat stools were tucked under the wooden table, the blankets were all neatly stored away in the chest, everything in the room lay in order—covered in a fine black dust, but otherwise as if ready for a new day. In the pantry beyond the main room, pots and bowls sat stacked on the wooden shelf and a fistful of fragrant herbs hung from the ceiling.

The bowl of shrivelled fruit and the maggots in the rice pot hinted at a lengthy absence, as did a certain smell his nose refused to interpret.

Hưng lifted the photo of his grandfather from the ancestral shrine but then thought better of it. He put the photo back in place, then closed the door quietly, as if people lay sleeping and he wished to disappear forever from their lives.

He exhaled on the threshold, then broke into a run down the track, past Widow Nguyệt's beaten, collapsing house, toward the house of the postmistress who had showed him rare kindness when he was a boy.

He burst through her front door, tearing through cobwebs, wanting to scream, and threw himself down upon the dark, wooden planks of the floor. He inhaled the smell of rot in the village while a bird beat itself senseless in the rafters overhead. He thought of birds he'd called friends as a boy in lieu of human companionship. He thought of tadpoles and lotuses, things he used to wade through water to collect. He remembered the flute he'd once carved from a piece of bamboo and how he'd tried to communicate with the birds through its whistle.

Then, between heaving breaths, he heard a muffled thump below the floorboards. He sprang upright, ran back outside the house and pulled up the door to the root cellar, casting alien light upon a face he knew from his boyhood, wizened now, crumpled and petrified.

The postmistress raised her hands so as not to have to see her executioner, but when the blow did not come, she peeked from between her gnarled knuckles and cried, "Oh my God, Hưng. Hưng!"

He reached his arm out to her, but she would not take it.

"Please leave me, Hưng," she said, her voice vestigial, fading. "I am old. It is better if you just leave me. Everyone is gone."

But where had everyone gone? He clambered inside the root cellar, pulling the door shut behind him, encasing them together in the dark. He begged the old woman to speak.

She spoke without euphemism because she had nothing left to lose; what would it matter now if she were killed for denouncing the soldiers who had come to liberate the village?

"They filled the air with speeches about our revolutionary duty, saying it was our responsibility to help them root out all class enemies—only then would we live in the glorious new light envisioned by the great father.

"The Chang family knew they would be the first accused. They ran and barricaded themselves inside their house and the soldiers just took a torch and burned the house down. You could hear them screaming, Hưng, but the soldiers just said, 'Burn, you bastards, and let this be a lesson to the rest of you. We will turn all landlords, notables and reactionaries into ashes, into dust; we will cleanse this place of greed.' Hưng, anyone with a patch of dirt to call his own is an enemy in their eyes. Anyone who grows so much as a carrot for his own consumption.

"The ones who surrendered their land without resistance have been sent away for re-education, but the ones who did resist, oh, Hưng," she said, her voice breaking. "They called everyone in the village to the *đình*. They forced us to watch.

Shot them dead and left their bodies to rot in the street. Their families were too afraid to claim them."

"And my parents?" Hưng asked.

"Hưng," she said, her face in her hands now, speaking through her fingers. "There are sons of the village among those soldiers. Those sons were the ones to point fingers and say, that man has a vegetable plot, and this family owns land they have not told you about down by the river, and this man works a kiln for profit, and that one raises silk-worms for sale, and that Widow Nguyệt built her wealth on the backs of peasants, and these people here, her neighbours, are beneficiaries of that wealth."

"These people—my parents?"

"Yes," she croaked.

He could smell the mildew of starvation in her mouth; he could smell her last days.

"And my brothers were the ones to report them?"

"You will find two of them in soldiers' uniforms smoking a pipe in the *đình*."

"And my sisters?"

"I lost track of who was killed and who just ran," the old woman said, hanging her head. "I don't know where they went. Up into the mountains, perhaps, or out to sea, what does it matter now?

"Have you any plastic?" she asked, a moment later.

"But why?" said Hưng.

"Because then I can suffocate myself."

Hưng kissed her forehead, the skin as thin as rice paper, and bid her goodbye.

He reached the far end of the village. The temple was no longer standing guard between the village and the world beyond; it had been torn apart, limb by red limb, to serve the fires of the starving. He heard a nightingale sing the song of an inverted world. He inhaled the scent of a rare, night-blooming flower, a smell that would forever be associated with the village he would never return to again.

Dandy Peacocks

Tư makes his way to the Metropole on foot, his thoughts numbed by revving engines, the insistent beeping of horns, the crowing of street vendors, the racket of hammering and sawing, the spark-flying screech of metal cutting metal. "Dancing Queen" blares through giant speakers on the sidewalk of a café where schoolboys and office workers sit under a green-and-white striped awning dripping with Christmas lights, steaming bowls of phở perched on their knees.

Tư takes a moment to adjust to the hush of the Metropole, idly scanning the front page of the *Vietnam News* lying on a table in the lobby, the headlines declaring the imminent launch of the "Learn and Follow the Exemplary Morality of President Hồ Chí Minh Campaign," and the president's posthumous awarding of the Gold Star Order to two former Party officials for their effort and dedication to the cause of national liberation in the late 1940s.

He throws the paper down and walks along the corridor to Miss Maggie's office. He finds her having breakfast—a cup of black coffee and a buttery French pastry—and adding red dots to her map. At her invitation, Tư takes a seat. They visited five galleries yesterday, perhaps only a quarter of the locations she has marked on the map.

This morning she has made appointments to meet two artists at their studios. The first of these artists turns out to be one Miss Maggie represents in her gallery. He works in an old stilt house that has been lifted beam by beam from his mother's village in the North and rebuilt in the middle of a housing block near West Lake. He has old-fashioned manners and no cellphone, or wife, but given the prices of his paintings Tư wonders just how honest he is, because what the hell does he do with all that money?

Tư leads Miss Maggie to the next atelier marked on her map, turning down one of the narrowest lanes in the Old Quarter. Miss Maggie has never met this artist, though she says he is very famous, which must mean famous in the ninety-eight per cent international sense because Tư has never heard of him.

"Here's what I want us to do," she says. "Let's pretend I'm your client and you're taking me on a tour of various galleries and studios. I'm just trying to get a general over-view of the contemporary art scene, I haven't committed to buying anything yet.

"Oh," she adds, "and I don't speak a word of Vietnamese."

Tư repeats these instructions to himself as they pass through a set of iron gates. They've entered a garden full of Buddhas—two hundred or more Buddhas—laughing happy Buddhas, Buddhas with crumbling faces, bright orange, bronze and marble Buddhas, stone Buddhas covered in moss. This artist is certainly crazy for Buddhas. Or maybe he's just plain crazy, thinks Tư, because he appears in the garden wearing a flowing silk robe, more like a lady's *áo dài* than anything a normal man would wear.

"Wow," Miss Maggie says. "He's a real dandy."

Tư will look up the word *dandy* in his dictionary when he gets home. For the moment, he chooses to interpret this as "peacock." The man is like a strutting peacock, displaying his colourful plume of feathers.

"Welcome! Welcome!" the artist bellows as Miss Maggie greets him in English. "Please"—he waves his arms—"Coffee?"

It would seem he has quickly exhausted all the English he knows. "How serious is she?" the artist asks Tư quietly, still smiling.

"She has a serious interest in art," Tư replies.

"I mean as a buyer. How serious is she about buying?"

Tư fears an honest answer would cause the bellowing man in women's clothes to do something unpredictable, so he responds with what he knows in English to be called a white lie, even though for him white hardly seems an innocent adjective, symbolizing death as it does. "She takes buying very seriously," Tư says, nodding and matching the artist tooth for tooth with his New Dawn smile.

"Sit! Sit!" the artist says to Miss Maggie, once they have followed him up the stairs to his studio.

Miss Maggie sits down on a stool that swings 360 degrees, enabling her to view the art covering three walls of the rectangular room of this renovated tube house. At the far end of the room a team of workers is standing at a long table. Nine young men and women wearing splattered aprons are each working on a different painting. The last artist worked alone, but then, thinks Tư, perhaps that is because he was not so famous.

Tư begins to translate. Does the artist mind if they ask some questions?

"Yes! Yes!" the artist says, jumping up to pull a heavy black book down off a shelf. Photos of pieces currently on display in galleries in Hanoi and Saigon, Singapore and Hong Kong. Shipping to the U.S. only $150.

"Please! Please!" he says, flipping through the first few pages for them.

Tư translates Miss Maggie's questions about method and materials and themes he likes to explore and why those themes and who are his influences and why does he think contemporary Vietnamese art is receiving so much attention and what does he consider uniquely Vietnamese and what does he attribute to the French and Chinese and is the evolution in Vietnamese art different from the evolution in Chinese art and does he feel his expression restricted today by Party concerns and what about his own journey to becoming an artist?

"Please! Please!" he says, flipping some more pages of

his black book for them. To Tư, he says, "Why so many questions? She is exhausting my creative energy. Please, enough."

"He wonders if you would like to see the pieces he is working on now," Tư says, pointing to the long table at the back of the room.

The artist jumps up with relief and gestures for them to follow.

Miss Maggie looks over the shoulders of the young artists, watching them work. The paintings seem very similar to the ones they saw in the galleries yesterday.

"Excellent!" the artist says, picking up a paintbrush. He adds his initials in black to the corner of a newly completed piece of work.

A young woman with hair cut short like a boy places a tray of coffee on a corner of the long table. Tư would like to ask her why she has cut her hair, because she will never get a husband looking like that. He hopes for her sake that she is not married to the artist, who may have insisted she maim her appearance in this way so that no other man will look at her. Imagine all that flesh hovering above you. Tư shudders, repulsing himself with the thought—as oppressive as China pushing its weight down upon Vietnam.

While Miss Maggie waits for the black drip of her coffee to finish, she moves around the room studying the work on the walls.

"Bill Clinton!" says the artist, pointing at a painting at eye level.

"Ah, so this is the one," says Miss Maggie.

"Bill Clinton bought this painting?" Tư asks, very impressed.

"Well, he bought one just like it. They now call it Bill Clinton style. Isn't that depressing?"

Tư isn't sure how he is supposed to respond. What is depressing about Bill Clinton? He is something of a hero to young people in Vietnam. He threw a giant burning log on the slow fire of Đổi mới when he lifted the trade embargo with the U.S., and he was the first U.S. president to visit Vietnam since the war.

Miss Maggie finishes her cup of coffee, stands up and thanks the artist for his time.

"I thought you said she was serious," the artist reprimands Tư while handing Miss Maggie his card. "But she is clearly a philistine."

Tư does not know the meaning of this word, but the artist has said it in a French way, and he thinks it must be some kind of insult because Miss Maggie has raised her eyebrows in a very American expression of doubt.

Tư is deeply embarrassed by the behaviour of this dandy peacock. It is shameful. No better than a beggar harassing a tourist in the street. From what he has seen of the contemporary art scene so far, he can only conclude it is a world of arrogance and greed.

They walk back to the Hotel Metropole together in silence as if Miss Maggie, too, has been depressed by what they have seen. Tư would like to apologize, but he's not sure exactly what he would be apologizing for.

"You did well, Tư," she says.

"Oh?"

"You protected the interests of your client. You didn't let him manipulate her with his hard sell. It can be an aggressive business. You don't want people to feel pressured into buying."

Maggie sinks into the steaming water of the bath holding a wineglass aloft. She plugs the dripping tap with her big toe, and listens to the wind rattling a pane of glass in the reception room. She smells the chicken Mrs. Viên down the hall must have cooked for dinner; she hears the monotone drone of a radio in the distance.

Perhaps it was the rare treat of company all day, but Maggie feels lonelier than usual this evening. These are the hours that should be spent with family and friends, sharing food and news of the day. Maggie wonders where Tư lives, whether his mother irons his sagging hipster jeans for him, whether he has a girlfriend and if Tư's mother and the girl's mother are plotting to see their children marry.

Maggie's mother had spent years asking when she and Daniel were planning on making things proper, making her proud. Daniel was an installer at the Walker Art Center—a gentle loner a few years older than her whom she had come to know when he hung the pieces for the first exhibition she curated. Daniel had an expansive brain and an enthusiastic heart—even going so far as to spend three years studying Vietnamese in order to impress her mother—but he was also burdened with a capacity for such sadness that it could, on occasion, replace him at a table, in conversation, in bed. There were dark walls Maggie had to stroke with a delicate hand, particularly when it came to his own family.

Maggie was twenty-six when she met Daniel, thirty-five when they were driving to the wedding of a university friend of his in Ann Arbor and he suddenly divulged the fact that his father, a man he'd simply referred to as dead up to this point, had served in Vietnam. Had served but in some ways never returned. The body yes, but not the rest of him.

It ended right there, really, on the road to Ann Arbor, Maggie staring out the window at a salt-stained world, realizing that Daniel's attraction to her was obviously so much more complicated than she had ever known and in some ways had nothing to do with her.

She couldn't bring herself to talk about it initially, especially with her mother. As betrayed as she felt, she saw herself a failure. That somehow, she should have known. It cast doubt on all her relationships, forcing her to wonder what she represented to other people, whether people saw her at all.

"Another girl?" her mother eventually had asked.

Maggie nodded, an easy way out.

"American?"

"What's that got to do with it?" Maggie snapped.

"Better to stick with your own kind," said her mother. "Better for the children."

Maggie realized in that moment what her mother and Daniel shared. Their feelings always dominated. And she catered to them both.

The relationship with Daniel had broken down almost

three years ago now, and apart from two dates with a man who evoked no great feeling in her but whom she slept with nevertheless, Maggie has retreated from the possibility of love. Since her mother died two years ago, finding a connection to the past has seemed of more fundamental importance. She needs an anchor to weigh her down, a sense of place and belonging. To be grounded before she begins anew.

As far as Maggie knows, her mother never entertained the possibility of another romance in her own life, though she does remember a particular look of longing Mrs. Trang's husband used to give her mother whenever she and Maggie came into their restaurant. It was as if he were an animal in a shelter in need of a new home. Perhaps that was enough flattery to keep her mother going.

Her mother was such a beautiful woman, so elegant and refined, it had pained Maggie to see how often people dismissed her as just another immigrant—a cleaning lady with little English, someone just off the boat, that Chinese lady, an anonymous and slightly sad woman pulling a bundle buggy full of vegetables bought in Chinatown down the street, yanking her heavy load up the steps onto the bus, searching for her bus pass, the driver shouting at her or over-enunciating as if he thought she were deaf or of little intelligence.

Nhi had worked diligently for years as a cleaner at the hospital, and while she'd seen her pay increase steadily and had gained more responsibility over time, language always held her back. She only ever mastered the most basic of phrases, never had a bank account or a credit card, and she spoke more Cantonese than English in the end, thanks to the ladies with whom she played mah-jong.

Maggie paid her mother's bills, renewed her bus pass, filed a tax return on her behalf. Twice a year she took her to Target and J.C. Penney to replenish her wardrobe. Maggie was her mother's bridge to America and without that bridge, Nghiêm Nhi stayed rooted on immigrant shores.

Maggie remembers how her mother used to sit at the vanity with the oval mirror in her room every night, silver-backed brushes and jars of Korean whitening and anti-aging creams lined up upon it. She would remove her impeccable makeup with cotton balls, unpin her chignon and brush her long hair. She still looked elegant stripped of her makeup, just less able to conceal the disappointment that showed in the lines around her mouth.

Every time Maggie looks in the mirror she fears seeing evidence of that same disappointment. It's both a surprise and a relief to see her father's eyes reflected back at her. A glow of obsidian. Animated and alive.

Propaganda and Political Education

Hưng stacks firewood between the foot of his mattress and the wall in preparation for breakfast tomorrow. He had hoped to distract himself with chores this evening, but that devastating trip home to his village that is no longer a village has been replaying itself over and over again in his mind.

The memory of it had begun as he stared at the water pouring into the pool this morning. It accompanied him as he pushed his cart over to the TV tube factory in Bưởi, where the workers are on strike. Happy as he was when his customers eventually turned up, seeing them reminded him of returning to his shop after that trip home all those years ago, of trying to go on, to serve breakfast as usual despite the song of helplessness and devastation ringing in his head.

Back then, his customers had berated him for his disappearance. They did not ask where he'd been for a week,
did not notice Hưng had turned inward; they simply wanted
the assurance of breakfast every morning. They wanted him
to do his job.

Only little Bình and his father paid Hưng any attention.
Bình eagerly relayed the news of the alleyway: the pink
flower that had sprouted up between the rocks beside the
back door, a spider's web with fifty rings, the rumour of a
man who was said to be sleeping in the alley at night. Đạo,
meanwhile, lingered after breakfast asking for Hưng's
input on a play he had begun working on in Hưng's absence.

"What might you say if you were a peasant who owned
a rice paddy across the river from your village and a Party
official told you that from now on you'd be working for a
share of the harvest on a collective on your side of the river,
only that farm was fifty kilometres away? I just need a few
lines. Something that sounds natural. Realistic."

Hưng felt his intestines tighten. His parents *were* peasants
who owned a rice paddy and they had nothing but that rice
paddy and the one water buffalo they shared with another
family, and it would appear they had been killed because of it.
Did Đạo really have no idea what it was like to be a poor
peasant? For all his talk about equality across class, his invita-
tions to Hưng to share his point of view, Đạo was still, in the
end, an educated young man of Hanoi, schooled in the western
way, who had never done manual labour or gone hungry. Đạo
could feel outraged by things in the abstract that he would
obviously never feel in his bones.

Hưng walked away from Đạo in lieu of replying, marching through his bedroom and out the back door into the alley to check how much water remained in the rain barrel. He was flapping flies out of his hair and berating a young man urinating against the side of the building when he heard Đạo speak his name.

"Hưng," said Đạo, touching his elbow. "What happened to you? Where did you disappear to last week?"

Hưng turned to face the man who had taught him so much yet knew so little of the real world. "You'll forgive me," he began.

"You're a Hanoian, Hưng, you should free yourself of that country habit," said Đạo.

"These problems with land reform that you have been addressing?" Hưng continued. "They are not just theoretical. They affect real people in real ways."

"Which is why we need real people like you to tell us what you have seen with your own eyes," said Đạo.

But Hưng could not speak of the horror he had just witnessed. He refused, furthermore, to be treated as Đạo's token friend from the country. He did not say that words could never capture the devastation. That he believed a knife through the stomach would more effectively communicate the pain than anything one could produce with a pen. Hưng could not say such things to a man still so resolutely optimistic that words could change the world.

"What is it, Hưng?" Đạo asked, his eyebrows knitted in confusion.

"That is the question," Hưng said cryptically. "For nothing is as it seems."

Đạo opened his mouth as if to speak but then closed it. He turned away and stepped through the door, returning to join the other men in the shop.

Đạo's faith in words remained unshaken. Over the next couple of weeks, under Đạo's direction and the keen editorial eye of an aging revolutionary named Phan Khôi, the men in the shop committed themselves to producing a literary journal they would publish and distribute.

When *Fine Works of Spring* was released later that month, it immediately drew to Hưng's shop the officers of the newly created Department of Propaganda and Political Education. Like flies to feces, Hưng couldn't help but think as he watched the men in uniform descend upon copies of the journal lying open on the low tables.

They confiscated everything they could: sketchbooks, notebooks, newspaper. They stroked the shafts of their guns. They spoke in a language at odds with the threat of their presence, smiling as they stressed the importance to the revolution of having men like Đạo and his colleagues join their ranks as ideological educators. They needed artists—as illustrators, sloganeers, balladeers.

"And you are just the type of man we need to lead the new Literary Association for National Salvation," they said, pointing at Đạo.

Hưng, standing firmly rooted with his hands on Bình's shoulders, watched the men in the shop watching Đạo. Đạo stared at the wall just beyond the officers' heads, his jaw firmly set. He remained silent until the officers were out the door.

"What is art if its creation is dictated?" he said angrily to the men who surrounded him. "What is art if the critical eye turns blind, if we can no longer use it to comment independently on the state of the world?"

The same officers appeared the next morning and every morning after that. They promised status within the Party and priority in government housing to those who would fulfill their revolutionary duty by submitting themselves for re-education.

Hưng did not close his doors that day until the men had exhausted themselves with debate, and for Bình's sake he did his best to radiate a calm he did not feel. The boy had already proven himself a capable assistant—ducking beneath gesticulating arms and the plumes of smoke that billowed from nostrils and mouths in order to slip empty bowls off the tables—but when the officers began to turn up, Hưng gave Bình additional jobs to distract him— refilling water glasses, collecting clean chopsticks from the dishwasher in the alleyway, the same woman who, decades before, had sewn Hưng his first decent shirt.

The men in the shop appeared taciturn and unmoved, only ever erupting once the officers had departed. Debate had never threatened their solidarity, but over the days Hưng could see the circle around Đạo develop the pointed ends of an ovoid.

"Might it not be in our interests, ultimately, to co-operate?" asked a young poet named Trúc. "Give them this for now, leave us free to pursue our own work later?"

"Right," said a balding calligrapher. "We temporarily set our own pursuits aside."

"Weak, weak!" Đạo shouted, pointing at each of them in turn. "If you give these things up, they will never be returned to you! Do you even hear yourselves? The Party celebrates its liberation of the peasantry while it devastates the countryside. How can you believe anything they promise?"

The next day, Hưng saw the ovoid that surrounded Đạo collapse into a straight line.

"You're a coward," Đạo spat at the calligrapher.

"And you are a hypocrite," the calligrapher shouted back, jabbing his fist in Đạo's face, "a self-serving anti-revolutionary."

Hưng was not the only one in the room who gasped. He immediately sent Bình to collect bowls from the dishwasher in the alleyway. He wondered how much Bình understood. Of events both in the room and the wider world. Hưng walked to the back door and stood on the threshold while a disembodied voice spewed propaganda through a megaphone.

"Who are the people?" he heard Bình ask of the dishwasher. "Every day he talks about 'the people.'"

"Well, we are," said the woman. "All of us."

"But why is he so angry at all of us?" Bình asked.

The woman shrugged, unable to offer the boy an answer.

The following morning, the ninth day of the officers' appearance, the young poet Trúc rose, crossed the floor and reported himself for duty. On the tenth day, the calligrapher and his cousin followed.

"There are many different ways of fulfilling our revolutionary duties, comrades," Đạo pleaded with those who remained. He then turned to the officers, addressing them directly for the first time. "Why not allow us the freedom to develop a national literature? How better might we serve the revolution than to tell the stories of a people liberated from imperial rule after centuries of struggle?"

"And what qualifies you, a man who stubbornly refuses to do his duty, to know best?" one of the officers asked, jabbing a firm finger into Đạo's sternum.

Hưng saw the anger in Đạo's jaw. He placed his hands firmly on Bình's shoulders. The officer raised his gun and pointed it briefly at Đạo's head before nudging his new recruits out the door.

Hưng has a memory of Bình holding out a small fistful of clean chopsticks just as a man fills the doorway of his shop. The light is too dim to make out the man's face, but the row of shining medals pinned across his chest suggests he is neither an officer of the Department of Propaganda and Political Education, nor a recruiter for the Literary Association for National Salvation. He is a comrade of a different order altogether.

The men who remained allied with Đạo had released the second issue of their journal, *Fine Works of Autumn*, the day before. Hưng had found anonymous notes stuffed under the front door of the shop twenty-four hours later: *We have been waiting for this, We are hungry, You give us hope, Please continue*, read the bulk of the messages. *Your disease could be fatal unless you seek immediate help*, read a solitary note he did not pass on to Đạo.

The man in the doorway thwacked the butt of his rifle on the floor. The chopsticks cascaded from Bình's hands, clattering on the tiles. The boy's fear was enough to propel Hưng forward, but the officer simply swept Hưng aside with a steely arm, walking straight over to the men seated in the far corner of the room. Three armed men followed him in, guns held tightly to their chests.

Đạo rose, while the rest of the men remained seated, silent. Bình looked from his father's face to the officer's face, then up to Hưng's. Hưng pulled the boy toward him, pinning him against his solid thighs.

The officer stood before the men with his feet planted firmly apart, his hands stiff on his hips. He spoke with a chilly lack of inflection. "There's a particular scourge of arrogance and narcissism that seems to afflict artists and intellectuals," he began. "You've been brainwashed by foreign ideas and been made slaves to your own egos. This sickness of the self needs curing. It has already perverted your politics. Must we really wait to see what it will infect next?"

"Comrade, sir, I assure you we believe fully in the theories of Marx and Lenin," said Đạo. "We believe absolutely in communism, the most wonderful ideal of mankind, the youngest, the freshest ideal in all of history. But if a single style is imposed on all writers and artists, the day is not far off when all flowers will be turned into chrysanthemums."

Let a hundred flowers bloom; let a hundred schools of thought contend, Hưng thought to himself. Đạo was alluding to Chairman Mao's invitation to artists and intellectuals to share their criticisms in order to shape and strengthen China's new order.

But the beauty of Đạo's language was wasted on these men. They remained stone-faced, unimpressed. Two of them moved toward Đạo and lifted him up by the elbows, suspending him above the ground.

"This is a warning to you," the officer said. "If you do not cease and desist with your publications, if you do not find a way to use your energies for the revolutionary good, you will have no garden left in which to grow your stupid, ugly flowers."

Hưng felt Bình's spine twitch against his thighs as the two men dropped his father. Đạo winced as he went over on his ankle. The officer bent at the waist and swiftly spat into the bowl of phở in front of Đạo, wiping his satisfied lips on the back of his hand before departing.

Hưng loosened his grip on Bình, stepping forward to lift the sullied bowl off the table. Bình followed Hưng through the shop as he carried the bowl out through the back door, tipped the broth into the alleyway and cracked the ceramic in half against a rock.

Đạo appeared on the threshold behind his son. "Come, Bình," he said, putting his hand on the boy's shoulder. "Say goodbye to Mr. Hưng. Breakfast at home from now on."

Hưng, still holding the broken pieces of ceramic in each hand, turned around and waved goodbye to the sullen boy, knowing it best, and painfully aware that the days of Bình shadowing him were unlikely to come again. The moment was bittersweet: Đạo was finally being a father to his son, but protecting Bình meant sending him away.

The following morning, the officers were back, making a great display of throwing armfuls of confiscated copies of the journal into the burning guts of an oil barrel planted in front of Hưng's shop. Black smoke billowed in through the front door while the officers broadcast messages of condemnation over a crackling megaphone, calling *Fine Works of Autumn* the work of reactionaries and Trotskyites, the senile ravings of syphilitic minds.

The men in the shop did not speak or otherwise react; they simply carried on eating from their bowls. When Hưng suggested the men might wish to leave by the back door, Đạo said, "We will not be cowed by their theatrics. We will leave by the front door." And so they did, the eight of them who remained: in solemn and single file.

The effects of land reform soon began to be felt in the city. The baskets of country women rattled with a few bruised apples, the price of rice became impossible, the greens in the market were limp reminders of things that had once grown in abundance, the only meat available was grey and taut with age.

Hưng did without green garnish and pounded tough cuts of beef with a mallet and was simply grateful that the men did not complain, still came morning after morning to eat a soup that could not be compared to the soup of earlier times, came despite the rings of late nights beneath their eyes and the worry apparent on their faces.

They'd become a small army dedicated to thought and solemn talk. They gave up shaving, perhaps having given up returning home to bathe and sleep in their beds. They needed a faster and cheaper way to communicate with the people, a way to extend their readership and reach. They agreed to produce a tabloid-style magazine going forward, one they would call *Nhân Văn*—Humanism.

Hưng remembers inhaling the ink rising darkly from the pages of the first issue, reeling drunk from the intoxicating smell and the thrill of its daring words. Just as he was burying the issue safely beneath his mattress in his backroom, Party officers were raiding the magazine's offices, burning books and papers and shelves and damaging the press.

Đạo moved the giant press to a secret new location at the back of a communal house in his neighbourhood with the help of men in black masks. The men published the next two issues of *Nhân Văn* from here in quick succession, but they might as well have fed the magazines directly into the fire given how rapidly the copies were confiscated and destroyed.

The men were quieter than Hưng had ever known them to be, both exhausted by their efforts and wary of the potential presence of spies in their midst. Hưng was relieved that Bình was at least safe at home with his mother, Amie; he felt sure that any day now the shop itself would be set on fire, but he missed the boy like one might miss the sense of smell. The boy had never wanted ideology or politics; he wanted the simple things a man like Hưng offered: customized chopsticks, an extra dash of fish sauce, praise for a chore done well, a greeting just for him.

There were details that Hưng used to share with Bình, things that no one else noticed, things Hưng no longer saw in the boy's absence. Hưng lost track of the translucent trail left by the lizard that made its home on the wall of his backroom.

"Why does he leave a trail?" Bình had once asked. "Do you think he wants us to find him?"

The atmosphere in the shop was so tense that Hưng longed for the relief he used to feel whenever he felt his hope for Vietnam's future flagging and he looked over at Bình and was relieved of despondency or doubt.

Then suddenly, one morning as he was delivering a stack of bowls to the dishwasher in the alleyway, Hưng caught sight of the boy in an adjacent doorway. Only his ears and knees seemed to have grown in the months since he last saw him.

"Bình," Hưng said. "But what are you doing here?"

"Ma only makes rice," the boy said, shuffling over. "She never makes phở."

"Yes, well, I can understand that, Bình. It's a lot of work and she's a busy woman. But rice is not so bad, is it?"

He shrugged his small shoulders. "It's okay," he said. "Everything's just quiet."

"Ah," said Hưng. "You miss the conversation, is that it? The company?"

Bình blinked. "I miss you."

For a man who had largely gone unwanted in his life, this was a particularly unsettling thing to hear. And how did one respond to affection, particularly when expressed so nakedly? One cleared one's throat, shuffled back and forth on slippered feet and slowly recovered one's composure.

"What about this, Bình," Hưng proposed. "Ask your mother's permission to come see me at the end of the week. You wait here for me, just in that doorway where you were waiting this morning, and I will bring you a bowl of phở."

Bình did come to the alleyway behind Phở Chiến & Hưng accompanied by his mother that Friday. "Of course I gave my consent," Amie said to Hưng. "The boy is terribly fond of you. But please, you mustn't let Đạo know, he'd be furious with me. He means well, he's just trying to keep us safe."

And so they had crouched in the alleyway and eaten Hưng's phở that Friday and the next. The Friday after that, Bình came without his mother. He carried a chessboard, laid it down in the dirt, and tried to entice Hưng into a game.

"One move each," said Hưng. "That's all I have time for."

"But I don't know how to play," said Bình.

"Oh dear," said Hưng, squatting down in the dirt with the boy, the board between them. "I'm not sure that I do either." Hưng picked up a wooden piece carved with the Chinese character for elephant and laid it down.

Hưng carried on with his routine every morning, bracing himself for the day when his shop would be burned to the ground. Winter was upon them, the grey days of November, when the fourth issue of *Nhân Văn* was published. Đạo delivered a copy to Hưng after dark, knocking on the back door of the building. Hưng, heart in throat, opened the door.

"I went out into the country myself," Đạo said to the ground. He hesitated, a man of words unsure of what to say next, his uncharacteristic awkwardness silencing them both. "To my wife's village," he finally added, pressing the magazine heavily into Hưng's hands.

Hưng read the editorial that night by the weak yellow light of his lamp. There, listed plainly, were the crimes of land reform, unmasked by poetry or allegory. The Party had violated the Republic's constitution by making illegal arrests, deliberately misclassifying peasants as landowners, seizing their property, throwing them in prison, subjecting them to barbaric torture, performing executions and abandoning innocent children, leaving them to starve to death.

The editorial went on to suggest that it might be time for new leadership, since Hồ Chí Minh and the other senior Party officials seemed to have become rigid and closed-minded with age. They had now forbidden all protest—but had they not, as young men, engaged in protest themselves? How had the Party come into being in the first place? Were they now, from the comfort of their positions of power, content to stagnate, to atrophy, to close the Vietnamese mind?

Hưng was overcome by a fear of the sort that turns a mortal heart into concrete. He wished with every fibre of his being that Đạo had not gone so far in his attempt to compensate for his failure to empathize with the peasantry. Đạo had not merely criticized the Party's policies, he had committed the ultimate crime—insulting Uncle Hồ—for which he risked the threat of the ultimate punishment.

The next day, none of the *Nhân Văn* contributors turned up for breakfast. The room was so quiet that Hưng could hear the slow beat of his heart. After breakfast was over, the fire extinguished, the tiled floor swept, the chopsticks neatly housed, Hưng closed all the shutters, pulled the beret Đạo had given him years before down over his eyebrows and left the building by the back door.

The paranoia that had stopped the men talking in the phở shop had now infected him as well. He put his hands in his pockets and studied the ground as he walked very deliberately in the opposite direction of the *Nhân Văn* office. When he was certain he had not been followed, he doubled back and emerged at the busy eastern edge of the Old Quarter, slid into Café Võ, strode through the length of it, exchanging no more than a nod with the owner, and walked out the back door into yet another alleyway.

He turned the corner.

He smelled the burning before he saw it. This time the Party had not been content simply to destroy the contents of the office. They had razed the neighbourhood communal house, the place for meetings and worship of the ancestral spirits, at the back of which the men of the Beauty of Humanity Movement had been given sanctuary. A crowd of people stood across the street and stared at the smouldering rafters, too late to save the building or the people who might have been trapped inside.

Đạo in flames—Hưng couldn't bear to think of it. Đạo choking, gasping for air. Hưng walked away as he had walked away from his village's temple, feeling as if everything vital had been desecrated. He eventually found himself at the shores of

Hoàn Kiếm Lake. He studied the ever-calm surface of the water, willed a turtle to rise from the murk and walked across the red Bridge of the Rising Sun toward the temple on Jade Island.

A single spiral coil of incense burned inside the temple, where once, not long ago, there would have been hundreds. He raised his hands to pray, but a great listlessness overcame him and he abandoned the effort. It was communism that caused the weight in his arms. Religion is a thing of the past, the Party said, an instrument of oppression that keeps the common man in bondage.

But where he found no comfort in the temple any longer, he still prayed each night to the ancestral spirits, lifting Uncle Chiến's photo from its small altar at the back of the shop, dusting it, offering fruit. He prayed for Đạo's life, but woke each morning in certain distress, dread lodged like an egg in his throat.

Days passed without any sign of Đạo or his colleagues. Hưng found himself at the threshold of Đạo's apartment in the French Quarter. The door had been torn from its hinges. "Bình," Hưng called out, his voice echoing in the front room. "Amie?"

He knocked on the doors of the adjacent apartments to no avail. But someone must have heard him, for the next day, Đạo's wife came to see him at the shop. "He must have been sent to a re-education camp," Amie said.

Hưng failed to reply, fearing a fate far worse, having no reassuring words to offer.

"Hưng, please tell me you think he has been sent to a re-education camp," she begged.

Hưng could not imagine Đạo ever abandoning his

convictions, but then, perhaps there would be torture and brainwashing, the likes of which Hưng had read descriptions of in *Nhân Văn*.

"I will keep the broth hot in anticipation of his return," Hưng said, which became true the moment he uttered it. This would be his vigil.

"Did Đạo tell you we had another baby, Hưng?"

Hưng took a step backward, startled by the news.

"Last month. A baby brother for Bình. But the umbilical cord was wrapped around the baby's neck."

Amie's voice was one of quiet desperation, her expression one of pain. "His face was blue from lack of oxygen," she continued, "but instead of cutting the cord and freeing him, the midwife just pulled the cord tight."

"An act of mercy," Hưng said gently. "It must have been too late for the child."

"But not for the child's sake, Hưng. Not for my sake or Đạo's either. Do you know what the midwife said?" Amie's lips were trembling now. "A child like this will be of no use to the revolution," she whispered. "This is what prompted Đạo to go to the country. To finally see the devastation for himself. To be able to write of it."

Hưng suddenly felt Đạo's presence, as if they stood side by side bearing witness to the carnage of his village. Đạo now understood that the revolution would not stop short of murdering everyone who stood in its way. But they had missed the opportunity for this conversation, the moment where Đạo might have said, *Now I understand with my heart*, and Hưng might have said, *Forgiven*.

"Perhaps you should take Bình away from Hanoi for the time being," Hưng said.

"Yes," replied Amie. "We will go back to my mother's village. You'll send word to us if you hear anything, won't you?"

"Of course," said Hưng, leaning over to the rattan drawer. "And take these. They belong to Bình."

He watched Amie run down the street, her hand gripping the boy's short chopsticks, her *áo dài* flapping behind her like a struggling kite.

Shit on a Canvas

Beyond the sound of birds, there is little to suggest it is morning when Maggie strikes a match to light the gas burner. She sits down on a hard wooden chair at the table and waits for the kettle to boil. The sky outside the kitchen window is an industrial grey designed to challenge the most resilient of spirits, so unlike the blue expanse of a Minnesota morning at this time of year. She misses home—the ease and familiarity of it—though she misses fewer people than she expected. It's easy to assume colleagues as friends until you are no longer working beside them every day.

She always felt herself an alien to some degree—not at work so much, but in the wider world. It happens when people—even the most enlightened among them—can't resist asking you where you're from. It reminds you that you have no attachment to the history or geography of a place, except insofar as you are pioneering your way through it in your own lifetime, your roots buried in some faraway earth.

You don't always want to answer the question.

And the answer is not always the same.

Maggie presses the plunger into the Bodum prematurely, forcing it down with both hands. She adds a thick dollop of condensed milk to the cup and takes her first sip of coffee, pressing a fingertip to the few grains of coffee stuck to her bottom lip.

Despite the dullness of the day, she's looking forward to spending it with Tư. He showed her the lake the other day; she introduced him to some art. She wonders if he considers it a fair exchange.

Only in her last year of high school did Maggie realize she wanted a career in art. It had never occurred to her as a possibility before because she lacked artistic talent, something her father must have realized when she was just five years old. She hadn't known there were options like curation until a trip with her sociology class to see an exhibition documenting the protests in Tiananmen Square.

"But why are they placed so far apart?" she had asked her teacher.

"That was probably a curatorial decision."

"What do you mean?"

"Well, the curator takes the work and presents it in such a way as to tell a story. If you read these pieces from left to right, chronologically, you realize how much of the story is missing. All that white space. You go from thousands of people in that shot to only one person in the last shot. Maybe you're supposed to use your imagination to fill in the gaps."

When it comes to her father's story, she has exhausted her imagination. She wants the justice of facts, some hard evidence.

Hưng wakes late this morning, battling a storm of a headache. What a relief it would be to lay his head in Lan's lap as he had once done, the velvet pads of her forefingers massaging his temples in hypnotic circles. He had been working his hardest in those days, his earliest days as a roaming phở seller, seeking customers on empty streets in the mornings, making his broth and pondweed vermicelli in the afternoons, and spending his nights fashioning dung cakes and foraging for reeds for his fire and repairing the cart he had built out of random scraps.

They were sitting together in front of his shack after a late supper—Lan weaving a basket, Hưng whittling bamboo chopsticks—when he described the pounding in his head being like that of a blacksmith forging a horseshoe on an anvil.

"Come," she said, placing the partially finished basket by her side and patting her thighs. "Lay your head here."

Hưng hesitated. Whatever touch had passed between them before had been accidental, or inadvertent.

"It's all right," she said. "I used to do this for my brother when his head hurt from too much studying."

Hưng eased himself down onto his back and inched his way up so that his head finally rested in her lap.

"Relax your weight," she said. "You won't break me."

Oh, but how wrong you are, he thought to himself. He could feel his head becoming liquid, melting into her thighs as she drew those sensuous circles around his temples and pressed her fingertips between his eyebrows and on either side of the bridge of his nose.

"Close your eyes," she instructed him.

He hadn't realized they were still open.

"Tell me a story," he whispered.

"But I'm not the storyteller," she said with a quiet laugh.

"Then you are the healer," he said, feeling himself drifting off to a place too sublime to be earthly.

That memory alone is enough to part the dark clouds in his head this morning. A ray of light, however fleeting, propels him to gather his things, load up his cart and set off into the day.

On Miss Maggie's agenda today are two more ateliers. As they set off down the street, Tư prays that the dandy peacock was just an aberration and that some decency prevails in the world of contemporary art.

They are once again confronted by twenty lanes of traffic between them and the lake. "The quiet inside," Miss Maggie says of her own accord, closing her eyes for a second before stepping off the curb.

Unusually, Tư cannot find his own quiet this morning. He is worried about the old man. Hưng doesn't appear to be limping anymore, but his movements have really slowed down since his accident, and something was missing from the phở this morning: it had tasted only ninety per cent complete. Tư had also spied two neatly folded grey blankets stacked underneath the old man's cart at breakfast, leading him to wonder if Hưng might actually be sleeping at the factory, having lost the energy to travel back and forth.

With Phương being so moody and the old man out of sorts, Tư begins to wonder if the problem isn't astrological. There's not much one can do to negotiate with the planets other than breathe deeply, still the mind with some Zen practice and wait until they orbit back into alignment.

Tư's meditation tends to be of a strictly mathematical nature. He recites pi to himself as he glides across the lanes of traffic. He's at twenty decimal places by the time they reach the lake, fifty-two by the time they reach the Old Quarter.

The sun is putting in a rare appearance. Steam rises where shopkeepers have scrubbed and rinsed the pavement. Tư puts on his wraparound sunglasses, which instantly add swagger to his walk. He might not have Phương's good looks, but he knows how to look cool—he hopes Miss Maggie can appreciate this. He wonders if she's ever had a Vietnamese boyfriend. She's probably used to American-style dating: eating hamburgers before seeing a Hollywood blockbuster, maybe with Russell Crowe, and then kissing in the back seat of the guy's car. Ahh! But they do not live with their parents, so perhaps he is inviting her back into his apartment and they are getting naked while the widescreen television is blaring some hip hop on MTV.

The thought of none-of-this-waiting-until-married business stirs him up. How many men does the average thirty-
something-year-old American woman sleep with before she
is married? How many times has Miss Maggie had sex? All
that experience might actually lead her to be thoroughly dis-
appointed with a guy like him, he realizes.

They make their way down a winding back alleyway
sticky with fish guts and scales. The artist they have an
appointment to see lives at the dead end of this alley.
Curiously, he has taken the name of a Filipino island—
Mindanao, he calls himself. To change one's name is to defy
the parents and the stars; what kind of son would do such a
thing? The answer soon becomes apparent.

Against the long wall of his tube house, Mindanao has a
row of barrel-chested, straw-stuffed mannequins that must
have been left behind by the French, all topped with papier
mâché heads. A Vietnamese emperor, a legionnaire with an
opium pipe in his mouth, Presidents Bill Clinton and Hu
Jintao. The last of the mannequins is topped with the fish-
bowled head of a Russian cosmonaut.

The rest of his work is even more shocking. A series of
paintings hang on the wall, all repulsive nudes with inflamed
mouths and genitalia, one of them delivering a pig out his
anus. There are serpentine men poking each other with
their penises through what looks to be an American flag.
A mannequin with a Vietnamese face hangs from the
ceiling, suspended by ropes twisted around its clay testicles. The head lolls to one side, tongue hanging out, eyes
about to explode.

Tư is staring aghast, stunned by this creature and his disgusting art.

Mindanao is telling Miss Maggie that the Party regularly closes down his shows. This might be one of the first times in Tư's life that he thinks the Party is one hundred per cent right. "The economy might be post-communist, but the cultural climate certainly isn't," Mindanao says. "I'm constantly being charged with depicting social evils and undermining public morality, both by the Ministry of Culture and Information and other artists alike."

He carries on, boasting about getting fined, being followed by the Bureau of Social Vice Prevention and having his studio regularly ransacked. "What's saved me," he says, "is the support I get from foreign institutions, because they aren't subject to the same kind of scrutiny. But it gets exhausting. I'm considering moving to Hong Kong. It's where most of my work sells, in any case."

He leads Miss Maggie over to a series of lacquered panels perched on easels, which he says he's doing as a commission for a gallery in Singapore. He explains his technique: he has cut up old propaganda posters—"Nixon's Headache," "Greater Food Production Is the Key to Expelling the Americans," "It Looks as if Uncle Hồ Is with Us in the Happy Day"—changing the order of the words and distorting the messages, then overlaying these with the brown resin of traditional lacquer.

"I refuse to produce this benign nationalistic art the Party still encourages," he says. "All those soft pictures of girls in áo dàis, rice paddies, water buffalo and the like. It's just crap.

They all do it, virtually every one of my contemporaries. Even the ones with talent. I would rather see shit on a canvas."

"Do foreigners actually buy that man's art?" Tư whispers to Miss Maggie when Mindanao leaves her to wander around the room.

"Sure," she says. "Quite a number actually. I take it you don't like it?"

"I think it's disgusting," Tư cannot refrain from saying. "Disgusting and useless."

"Well," she says, "at least he's got a point of view. Time will be the judge in the end."

So much for Zen. The palindromic prime numbers Tư calculates as he walks over to Phương's house this evening are overrun by a torrent of words. Time will be the judge? She cannot be serious: time will only reveal a guy like that as an animal! Nationalistic art or pornography—are these really the only two artistic choices? One portrays the country as backward; the other portrays the country as perverted. Why would artists willingly engage in either if they weren't backward or sick themselves? He knows he crossed a line by expressing his disgust to Miss Maggie, but he couldn't help it. He was equally appalled by her calm reaction to that freak's work. She might look Vietnamese, but her tastes are evidently very American.

Tư takes a run at Phương's bedroom door; he cannot continue to manage all these thoughts on his own. He smashes his shoulder into the skull and crossbones, once, twice and a third time, when the door finally gives way. He collapses onto the mattress where Phương is lying in the same heart-covered boxer shorts he was wearing days ago, again with his headphones on, the bottle of rice whisky within reaching distance nearly empty.

Tư doesn't even greet his friend. He rubs his shoulder and says, "You should see some of the crap that gets passed off as art today. These deviants are getting paid thousands of dollars to shit all over canvases! I couldn't hold my tongue today, Phương. The Việt Kiều lady from the hotel was admiring this artist's work and I told her exactly what I thought of it."

Tư lies back and covers his eyes with the crook of his elbow. "I bet he comes from Saigon," he says, and they both know what *that* means—drugs and prostitution flourished there during the war, ruining the morals of one generation then the next.

Phương sits up straight on his mattress. "Put these on," he says, passing Tư the headphones. "Listen to the words."

It's some gangsta rap about a killing spree. Alleys full of dead niggas and pregnant hos.

Tư is nodding his head to the beat when Phương suddenly yanks the headphones off his friend's ears. "Ugly, no?" he says. "And violent. Very, very violent." Phương's eyebrows are flying up his forehead. "So maybe the U.S. is not just tall buildings and Disney World and movie stars. It's not all progress and pretty."

That's very true, thinks Tư. It's a world without morals and dignity. Miss Maggie's indifference to the insult and indecency of Mindanao's work tells him more than he needs to know about Americans. How can he possibly continue with this tour? His New Dawn facade has officially cracked. What if more of his opinions start leaking out? He'll be fired; perhaps his tourism licence will be revoked. Better he should make a pre-emptive move and quit this assignment, despite the request coming from so high up.

"Cheers, my friend," Phương says, reaching for the nearly empty bottle. He drains it, then burps. "Do you ever think you might not get married?"

Tư raises his eyebrows. What's this all about? Of course Tư doesn't think this; not getting married is not an option.

"Did I ever tell you how my parents met?" Phương continues.

Tư knows Phương's father was a soldier when he met his mother, a village woman. He had an awful job with the People's Army, scouting for land mines along the border with the South. Phương's father used to tell him about how he would be sent on ahead of the troops and usually find himself in some village at night, where people were obliged to feed him and give him a bed because he was one of the good soldiers fighting for the freedom of the country.

"My father was sleeping in this house one night, and he got up to go and pee outside. When he came back inside he climbed into the nearest of the son's beds. Except it wasn't their son he crawled into bed with, was it?" says Phương. "It was their daughter.

"But how was he supposed to know? All the children were bald; their heads had been shaved because of lice. The girl screamed and my dad was so terrified he slapped his hand over her mouth to quiet her. They stayed in this position all night, both of them trembling with fear.

"The next morning, the girl's father wouldn't look at either of them. He just said, 'Take her. Take her away.'

"But what was my father supposed to do? He said to this man, 'Look, I'm a soldier. My job is to locate land mines. This is the middle of the war. I sleep in a different bed every night, if I sleep at all. I can't possibly take the girl with me.'

"The girl's father said, 'Take her or I will kill her.'"

"*Ôi ʒŏi ôi*," says Tự. "That girl is your mother?"

Phương nods. "He had to take her," he says, shrugging. "He threw her over his shoulder and ordered her to stop screaming. She was only eleven years old. He had to hide her in holes and tunnels, and he left her with water and rice cakes, and he always promised to return, even though every time he went to search for land mines he thought he would be killed. She's never forgiven him."

"But they've been married forever," says Tự. "And they have you and your sister."

"Still," says Phương.

Is this why Phương can't commit to any girl? Is this why he's been depressed? Whatever Phương's reason for telling him this story, Tự finds himself pausing in the doorway of his own family's kitchen when he gets home, watching his parents play dominoes on the floor.

They defy astrology; whatever the planets are doing, his parents remain at peace with each other. It's both comforting and frustrating. Tự knows marital relations are not always so smooth. He doesn't find his parents' example particularly instructive. Divide the chores, show respect to each other, spend time together playing dominoes and drinking tea. His father cooks as much as his mother does; they both have full-time jobs and they see themselves as equals.

Tư cannot imagine romance between them, but his father once told him that his mother was the only girl at the factory who did not giggle and turn her head away when she spoke to him. She neither covered her mouth nor fluttered her eyelashes in obedience. "It was very rare for a girl to look you in the eyes back then," he said. "Very rare and very powerful."

Tư was mortified to hear this. Her direct gaze meant his mother felt passionately toward his father—and who wants to think of one's mother in this way? But he is grateful that his parents chose each other, when so many marriages of their generation were forged by arrangement or circumstance. He is particularly grateful after hearing Phương's sad story.

Tư's parents have had their struggles, but these are ordinary struggles. A difficult life was normal in the dark days before Đổi mới, when all they could afford was a room in the Old Quarter separated by a curtain from a family in the next room. Tư's father pointed out that room to him once because Tư didn't believe it when his father said that all the people in the rooms of four adjacent buildings had had to share a pit latrine and an outdoor kitchen. Their water even had to be carried from a communal pump three streets away.

Sometimes their old neighbours from those days come to visit, and Tư listens to them reminisce, making light of hard times, laughing when they say things like: Can you believe sixteen of us shared that one small pot of rice? And *ôi ʒôi ôi*, the rats, do you remember? How did the vermin get so fat when we were all so hungry? Remember the time Anh wove a hammock for the colicky babies? It cured them all completely. And then when my wife had the liver pains, Anh managed to find liquorice root.

"Sometimes I miss when the world was like this," one of Tư's father's old friends says, "when neighbours cared about neighbours, and someone would cut someone else's hair, and in return, the one with the new haircut would massage the haircutter's feet. Now, I have to say, that is a very fine television you've got there, very fine indeed. Do you have satellite?"

Tư's mother will sometimes put a stop to all the reminiscing, saying there are many chapters in a life, not all of them happy, but they are lucky to have the assurance that another chapter will come even if it is in the afterlife when the soul takes up residence in a new body.

Tư has personally not given much thought to the afterlife. A strange thought occurs to him in that moment: What if his soul were to be reborn in a Việt Kiều's body, or even that of a total foreigner? Would life be fundamentally different? It certainly would be if he could choose the particular body, because he'd opt for someone wearing football cleats, a striker who boots the winning goal in the FA Cup—*Ahhhhhhhhhhhhhhhhhhh!* the crowd going wild.

"Tư, I kept the fish warm," says his mother, pointing toward a clay pot.

Tư kneels and spoons rice and a few nice chunks of white fish and ginger in broth into a bowl, then sits down on the floor with his parents. He lifts a few grains into his mouth.

"I meant to tell you, I dropped in on the old man after work today," says his father. "He seems a bit worn down by his accident, don't you think? Did you notice the absence of coriander among the herbs this morning?

"Everything I said seemed to drag him back to the past. I suggested that perhaps I could build him a better cart. He pointed at each of the wheels, and the axle, and every single wooden board in turn and told me this long, meandering story about how he had acquired each piece."

This sounds like one of Hưng's wandering metaphors, something his father would never understand. Bình is a straightforward man who puts one foot in front of the other day after day. He is quietly resigned to what is past and he accepts most of the present. Sometimes it frustrates Tư that his father doesn't speak out, doesn't even complain when the Party introduces some ridiculous new law like the one they're proposing to force everyone to wear motorbike helmets next year.

Tư's father would have preferred to hear Hưng say, *Excellent. Thank you very much. This cart is really just a heavy piece of crap I built out of scraps forty years ago. I can't wait to replace it.*

"And then you know what, Tư?" says his father. "After he has worn me down with this very long story about his cart, after he has refused to consent to me building him another one, he suddenly says to me, 'Did I ever tell you that you had a baby brother?'"

"What?" Tư says, putting down his bowl.

"That was my reaction," says his father. "My mother apparently had another son a few years after me but he lived for less than an hour."

"But why tell you now?"

"I have no idea."

Tư hates to think it, but it sounds like Old Man Hưng is unburdening himself of secrets. His father is too close to see it.

Hưng is not one for drink, but Bình left him a bottle of rice wine, suggesting it might relieve the pain in his leg. Hưng does feel pain. Not just in his leg, but in his chest. He is lying on his straw-filled mattress, a single candle burning for Đạo, seeking comfort in the quiet babble of voices in the dark beyond his shack, sipping from a glass—strictly for medicinal purposes.

Over the years, Hưng has tried to strike a balance between painting a portrait of Đạo that gives Bình some sense of the man's importance, and apologizing for his behaviour as a father. "He was busy fathering a movement when he might have been fathering a son," he once said to Bình. How could Bình possibly understand that his father's neglect was not personal?

While Hưng has tried his best to keep Đạo's memory alive for Bình, the introspection of the past few days leads him to the sad conclusion that he has failed. What was he doing giving Bình a baby brother with one hand then taking him away with the other? The only true portrait of Đạo is one that includes his poetry, the poetry that ran like blood through him, but Hưng no longer has any of it, neither in his possession nor in his memory.

Hưng's greatest regret in a life of considerable regrets is that it never occurred to him to write Đạo's poems down while he still could. Instead, he shared them with a girl who proved herself unworthy. He was deceived into believing love mattered more than legacy. He squandered the thing that mattered most.

Our Place in Buddha's Universe

Tư and Phương are standing behind a giant potted palm in the lobby of the Metropole waiting for Miss Maggie. Tư sees his friend eyeing her up and down as she shakes the hand of a European man in a pinstriped suit before walking over to them.

"She's an important person, Phương," Tư hisses. "VIP."

"So? She's still a woman," Phương says, stuffing his hands into his pockets and fiddling with the keys at the end of the chain hooked to his belt loop. His forearms are tanned, and thick veins disappear beneath his shirtsleeves above the elbows.

For a minute, and not for the first time, Tư hates his best friend.

"Good morning, Miss Maggie," Tư says brightly. "Please let me introduce one of the finest drivers from the agency."

"Pleased to meet you," she says in English.

"Phương doesn't speak English," Tư takes some pleasure in saying. "It is why he is just the driver and I am the guide."

"So, are you ready to go?" Miss Maggie asks, switching to Vietnamese.

"Actually, Miss Maggie, I wanted to have a word with you about the current arrangement."

"Is there a problem?"

"I just don't think I am the best tour guide for your purposes."

"Sorry," she says, shaking her head, "I'm not sure what you mean."

"I would like to resign from this assignment."

"Oh," Miss Maggie says. "What's the problem exactly?"

"No problem, Miss," says Tư, desperate to escape without confrontation.

"Well, there obviously is."

Tư stammers and looks to Phương for help.

"Miss," Phương says, rallying for his friend, "Tư has found some of the art he has been exposed to over the past couple of days deeply offensive on a personal level."

"Oh," says Miss Maggie. "I'm sorry, Tư. I'm really sorry to hear that."

Tư just wants to flee. "I better get back to my regular job," he says, slinking backward.

"Can you come back at the end of the day?" she asks. "We can chat about it and settle up then, okay?"

Tư consents with a slight bow.

As he sits in a café down the road from the hotel sipping a second Coke through a pink straw, Tư wonders if he should go and visit Old Man Hưng. He, of all people, would understand why Tư could not continue with the art tour. He feels compromised: he has never quit an assignment in his life. Perhaps Hưng could offer him some kind of absolution. But Tư would feel embarrassed if his need were obvious. He needs a pretext for an unexpected visit.

I know, Tư thinks; Hưng has to walk great distances in those awful slippers every day, surely he could use a better pair of shoes. Old men don't normally wear running shoes, but then Hưng is no normal old man. Tư knows just the place to get a good knock-off pair of Nikes. He pays for his Cokes and sprints with purpose out the door.

Half an hour later, he is walking toward Hưng's shantytown, whistling while he swings a plastic bag containing a bright-white pair of size seven knock-off Nike Air Force high-tops. Walking this route only confirms the wisdom of his choice of gift for the old man. It is three kilometres southwest of the Old Quarter, at least two of them on cracked asphalt, open drains running at the edge of the roads, and oops!—that's unfortunate—there goes a small dog disappearing into a sewer without a grate.

Tư turns down the dirt track toward the pond. The old woman who slipped in the mud the other night is collecting stones from the road, dropping them into her extended apron; a young man is tugging at small tufts of grass. There's no litter along this track, not a single plastic bag or battered tin, or any dogs or cats for that matter either.

Tư finds the old man at the pond's edge, scrubbing his big pots. It's muggy here, mosquitoes circling Tư's head as he squats down beside him. He hopes Hưng no longer eats the fish from this pond—they must be radioactive with poisons from the tire factory on the other side of the railway tracks—look at that cloud shimmering over there like soy sauce in a hot pan.

"Tư," Hưng says, surprised. "You don't have work today?"

"I did," says Tư. "It's a long story."

"Come, we'll have some tea," says Hưng, turning his pots over to dry. He cups his knees and groans as he stands, then makes his way up the slight muddy incline toward his shack.

Tư ducks through the doorway, then places his palms together by way of greeting his grandfather at his altar while Hưng puts the kettle on to boil.

"Did I ever tell you how your grandfather got that scar on his cheek?" Hưng asks.

Tư shakes his head. He's always thought that line was just a shadow.

"Your grandfather made a very passionate speech, saying that if just one person read the words of their publications, if one single heart was moved, they had done their job: they had succeeded in setting the truth loose in the world.

"There was this man—he wore a beret and carried a thick book, just like they all did back then—who stepped out of the shadows in the corner of the room. He walked toward Đạo as if he were about to shake his hand and congratulate him for such inspirational words. Once he reached your grandfather, this man raised his book without a word and smashed it with two hands across his face.

"Đạo fell backward and everyone leapt to their feet. I was down on the floor with him, holding his head, when I saw that it wasn't a book the man had used to assault your grandfather but a brick wrapped in paper. Đạo coughed and spat out two of his teeth. His cheek was cut just there where you see the scar. It had been deeply serrated by the edge of the brick: his cheekbone shone like a pearl. I was thankful your father did not have to witness this.

"In the commotion of it all, the stranger slipped out the door. He was a spy, that seemed certain. But Đạo just said, 'We cannot let them intimidate us. It just makes it even more important that we carry on.'

"It was a great privilege for me to be the one who stitched his face with a needle and thread. I anaesthetized him with rice whisky and offered him a bed. He took refuge in my backroom, not wanting to alarm your grandmother or your father with his appearance. But you know, I didn't see a battered face, I saw a strong face," he says, pointing at Đạo's picture, "that strong jaw."

Tư inadvertently strokes his own chin, wondering if he would ever have such courage. Everything about his life can feel petty and selfish when he thinks of the heroism of people in the past. What value is he really adding to the world? He plays some role in introducing foreigners to Vietnam, but the thrill seems to have gone out of it for him recently. More than the thrill.

"Sometimes it's hard to feel your life has any worth by comparison," he finds himself saying out loud.

"But it is not a matter for comparison, Tư," says Hưng. "We all have our place in Buddha's universe."

Tư reaches for the plastic bag and pulls out the high-tops. "I thought maybe you could use some new shoes."

"Well," says Hưng, clearing his throat. "They're quite something. Is this the latest fashion?"

"That would probably be the Nike Air Jordans, but these are still pretty cool. Do you like them?"

"Very much," says Hưng, "thank you." He places them alongside Grandfather Đạo's portrait on the ancestral altar. "I wouldn't want to dirty them, though."

Having sent Tư on his way with a small packet of lotus seeds for his mother, Hưng worries he has made the boy feel insecure. He understands Tư's concern about the worth of one's life. What strikes him is that he hasn't heard this type of concern expressed in a great many years. Men of Đạo's circle might have wondered such things, but no one since would dare posit a question with the individual at its centre. It's the freedoms of Đổi mới, Hưng thinks. In some ways, Tư's generation shares more with their grandfathers than with their fathers.

He should have told Tư that a hero is just a man, a person who makes mistakes from time to time. It is natural when speaking of the dead that we tend to remember the heroic things rather than the flawed. Hưng has for so long been invested in giving Bình a portrait of his father as a hero that it seems he has forgotten Tư. The boy might actually be better equipped than someone of his father's generation to understand the imperfections and contradictions that characterize a man, however great.

Đạo had dedicated a poem to Hưng in the last issue of *Nhân Văn*, though Hưng had not read it until years later. He'd never been able to bring himself to turn the pages beyond the editorial that had determined Đạo's fate. It was Lan who finally pushed him to do so. Lan with her insatiable appetite, begging him for more. He turned the page of the magazine and stared.

"What is it?" Lan asked, putting her fingertips to the paper.

Hưng inhaled deeply before reading the line of dedication. "'To H who is wise in matters of soup and well beyond.'"

"H," said Lan. "Is it you?"

Hưng read aloud the poem that followed.

Đạo wrote of longing for those who had disappeared, all the innocent farmers and compromised children. He wrote in the elliptical way of a poet, without naming who was responsible. He had gone well beyond theory and found the stinging heart. Đạo had atoned through poetry, spanning the differences between their worlds, capturing the tragedy of the countryside so viscerally that Hưng could taste blood on his tongue.

Hưng stopped reading and wiped his lips.

"What's the matter?" Lan asked.

"My mouth," he said, turning toward her. "Is it bleeding?"

She put her delicate finger to his chin and said, "Open." She peered into his mouth. "There is no blood. But, Hưng," she added, "I can taste it too."

Hưng still holds that poem somewhere deep inside him. He can share stories about the Beauty of Humanity Movement with Tư, with Bình, even with a relative stranger like Miss Maggie, but he has not been able to share poetry with another soul. Not since the day he returned home from peddling his pondweed noodles to discover all his papers—the journals and the poems, every single one of them—gone.

He had torn the place apart. He had wept for years, not observably, but on the inside. The poems that he had memorized slowly bled out of him from lack of use. Is this why his chest hurts now?

He swallows a good medicinal dose of Bình's rice wine as the sun beyond his shack sinks into the ground. He toasts Đạo's picture upon the altar, framed and illuminated by a ridiculous pair of shoes.

Tư returns to the Metropole at half past five and paces the lobby while he waits for Miss Maggie. He's rehearsing a speech in his mind, one that will allow them both to save face. If she pushes, as Americans tend to push, and forces him to say something less than polite, it will be she who is at fault for not knowing the Vietnamese culture.

Miss Maggie approaches with a smile and her jacket folded over her arm. "I thought we could get out of here," she says. "Go somewhere for a drink."

"Um. Yes?" says Tư, disarmed by her informality.

"And please try to call me Maggie," she says over her shoulder as they snake their way up the sidewalk. "The Miss just makes me feel like a schoolteacher."

Maggie, Maggie, Tư repeats in his head as he follows her to a place he doesn't know even though he thought he knew almost every bar in the city. It's a funny little Russian vodka bar called Na zdorovye—"cheers"—the only Russian word Tư knows because they replaced Russian with English as the second language in schools in 1988.

Which is just fine with him. Tư finds everything Russian, apart from perestroika and glasnost, a bit sad. The crappy Minsk motorbikes and the cloudy potato vodka that makes you sick and all the stories of young Vietnamese who got scholarships from the Russian government to study in Moscow but ended up freezing to death alone in unheated apartment blocks in winter.

That whole generation of sour-faced old men now very high up in the Party got their training in Russia, men who probably fantasize about being one of the ones whose brain is sent to Moscow after they are dead to be sliced into a thousand pieces and mounted onto Plexiglas sheets revealing many things of great importance to the scientific community.

Russia is the absolute last place in the world Tư would like to visit. He might even prefer to see shit on a canvas.

The vodka bar is stuffy and windowless, full of smoke and the clash of foreign languages. They sink into a red velvet sofa, which feels a bit damp. Tư checks to make sure there aren't mushrooms growing between the cushions. Miss Maggie, *Maggie*, orders vodka for both of them, then clinks her glass against his. Tư is not used to women who drink, and he wonders what people in the bar must think of their unusual pairing. She is at least ten years older than him, certainly of an age where she should be married.

"So tell me," she says. "Your friend said you were offended by some of the art you saw."

Tư has a screed in his head about the greed and arrogance of artists like Mindanao and the one who was a dandy peacock who are only making art for money, growing bloated and arrogant in their service of the foreign market, behaving like French plantation owners and getting rich off the backs of the Vietnamese slaves who are doing the *actual* work. And what about people in positions of influence like Miss Maggie? They are no better—encouraging and indulging these artists in their crude misrepresentations of the country and presumably, like all those foreign gallery owners, getting rich in this process themselves. He expects more of someone of Vietnamese heritage, but that is the deceptive lie of her face.

He is too schooled in politeness, however, to offer anything more than, "I am simply uncomfortable with the ways in which Vietnam is being represented in many of these contemporary art galleries."

"How so?" she asks.

The subject of Mindanao's pornography is too uncomfortable to raise with a lady, even one of questionable values. "You would think we are all still pulling ploughs by hand and sleeping alongside pigs and oxen," he says.

"That's what sells, I'm afraid. A kind of timeless and romantic fantasy of Vietnam. No unpleasantness. No war."

"But we don't live like this," Tự stammers. "Where is the truth in it? In the past, there were artists and writers who would risk their lives to depict reality rather than some socialist utopia."

"I know," she says quietly. "My father was one of them."

"Seriously?"

"No joke."

"Huh," he says, cocking his head to the side to get a better look at her, a different angle. So who was her father? And if he was such a principled man, shouldn't she know better than to indulge these contemporary artists in their gross distortions of Vietnamese life? Tự's mind floods with questions, but before he has a chance to ask any of them, she slides an envelope full of money—good crisp American dollar bills, from what he can see—across the table.

"For the days you worked," she says.

Tự quickly sweeps the envelope off the table into his lap. It might look like he's taking some kind of bribe, and you never know who's watching.

"So," he says quickly, changing the subject. "Your father was from Hanoi?"

Miss Maggie nods as she stares at the bottom of her empty glass. "He was an artist here in the forties and fifties," she says.

"Ah, so this is why you have such an interest in Vietnamese art."

"Yes," she says.

"Would you like another drink?" Tư asks, intrigue now trumping anger. "*Maggie*."

"I shouldn't," she says, then pauses. "Oh, all right, then." She nods her head at the waitress and points at their empty glasses.

"I understand why you find that work offensive," she says.

"And you don't?" he asks, emboldened by the drink. "Would you rather see shit on a canvas?"

"Hah," she laughs. "You mean Mindanao. I know. I understand what he's doing, but that doesn't mean I like it and it doesn't mean he isn't an asshole."

Tư bursts out laughing and quickly slaps his palms over his mouth. He has never in his life heard a lady use such a word. Wait until he tells Phương.

"It's an issue of freedom of expression," she continues. "The artists and writers who used to frequent Old Man Hưng's restaurant? They were shut down because the Party didn't like what they had to say. You can't really defend them without extending the right to someone like Mindanao, whatever you might think of his work."

Perhaps this is what Phương was suggesting the other night when he slapped those ugly lyrics onto Tư's ears.

"Hey—did the old man know your father?" Tư asks, suddenly realizing the likely connection between them.

"He might have. It's possible he was part of that group, or at least known to them. Unfortunately the old man isn't sure."

"Your father might have known my Grandfather Đạo then."

Miss Maggie smiles. A very lovely smile that causes a ripple in Tư's stomach. He attempts to reciprocate, though he knows he cannot offer her comparable loveliness given the stains on his upper teeth. He imagines their ancestors looking down on them: beauty and the beast.

"That's a nice thought," says Miss Maggie. "Hưng said he was in good company."

"You must come again for breakfast," says Tư. "The old man's memory is a bit random. Maybe next time will be your lucky day."

The Memory of Taste

The sun has not yet risen when Maggie climbs aboard the motorbike behind Tư and wraps her arms around his middle. Tư is mortified by the erection that springs up in response to her hands. He remembers the way Phương looked her up and down as she walked toward them in the hotel lobby the other day, and his erection quickly leads to thoughts of what she might look like naked. He is forced to conjure up an unpleasant memory of the Australian who pissed off Phương in order to kill his erection before they arrive at the Chương Dương Bridge.

This is not the best of Old Man Hưng's locations, given that people use the space under the bridge as a toilet and the smell of urine is very strong. Thankfully one forgets this as soon as one raises a steaming bowl to one's nose, as Tư assures Maggie, standing in line behind his father.

"Ah," the old man says to Maggie. "You've finally come to me again. I was beginning to worry that perhaps you did not like my phở."

"She came with me," Tư says proprietarily over Maggie's shoulder.

"I'm glad to see you have become friends," says Hưng, making Tư feel self-conscious. "I'm afraid nothing has come to mind about your father."

"Actually, there was something I should have mentioned," says Maggie. "His hands. After the camp, they were like claws."

"So he could no longer paint," says Hưng.

"No, not really."

"That must have been very hard for him. It reminds me of a poet I knew who lost his tongue."

"But how did he eat?" Tư interjects, the steam rising from his bowl.

"He used his imagination," says Hưng, "his memory of taste."

Tư's father asks him to hold his bowl so he can lay his windbreaker down on the sloping concrete ground for Tư's guest to sit upon.

"That's not necessary," she says, "but thank you."

Tư wishes he had thought of this gallant gesture, but then his father is displaying rare animation this morning, obviously impressed by the new company his son is keeping. He takes his bowl from Tư and squats down between them, leaning over to suck back a few quick spoonfuls of broth. "Ah," he says, wiping his mouth on the back of his hand. "Miss Maggie," he says then, clearing his throat. "Tell me, what is it like to grow up Vietnamese in America?"

She raises her eyebrows and Tư is made uncomfortable by his father's directness. In tourism college they were taught that American notions of what constitutes a personal question are quite different from their own. Tư has learned this the hard way, through responses to questions like: And what do they pay you to be a pharmaceutical representative with GlaxoSmithKline, Mr. Clark? Is this lady your wife or your daughter? Do they have the death penalty in your state of Texas? Why are the insides of your ears so hairy?

"It was complicated," Maggie replies. "When I was young, especially, you know, in the years just after the war."

"I spent most of the war hiding in the caves at Tam Cốc," Tư's father says. He throws his head back, moves his hand up his chest and indicates rising water. He pretends to be gasping for breath.

Tư stares at his father with astonishment, so slack-jawed that he is forgetting to eat. His father is not a conversational man.

"One day my mother saw Việt Minh soldiers coming toward the caves in a sampan," Bình continues. "Thanks to my mother and a sharp stick, I was not conscripted," he says, pointing at the glass eye that eventually replaced the one his mother damaged.

Miss Maggie cringes. Tư wishes his father didn't have to be so graphic.

"You know, I saw an American soldier once," Bình carries on, sitting with his bowl now clenched between his knees. "I had been fishing in the river and I was making my way back to the village when I heard the crack of a tree branch above. I looked up and I saw an American soldier hugging the trunk. His plane must have been shot down. I remember the look in his eyes and I could see he was afraid of me—just a boy with two small fish—and so I looked away and left him to hug this tree, far away from his comrades and his country. He was gone the next day. I had been hoping to give him a fish."

Tư has never heard this story before and is beginning to feel rather excluded. "So, uh, Miss Maggie, Maggie," he interrupts. "Can you tell what is so special about Old Man Hưng's broth?"

"Maybe the way the taste evolves in your mouth?"

"That comes from years of experience," Tư's father says. "It is an indication of the strength of Hưng's commitment to his craft that even in the years we had no rice he could find a way to make noodles."

"And he doesn't get bored of making the same thing day after day?"

"It's like religion for him," Tư says.

At that moment, Phương jumps down from the bridge above, waving his arms, shaking the keys to the van. He's brought the company vehicle so that Bình can take the motorbike to work. Maggie and Tư have to move now— Phương has left the van parked on the bridge above.

Tư drains and rinses their bowls, shoves them into a plastic bag, then climbs up the bank and hops into the van.

Tư has his face plastered to the glass as he watches Maggie saying a long goodbye to his father. Bình is unusually expressive, his fingers moving in the air like they are folding origami.

Tư taps his fingernails against the glass impatiently.

"You shouldn't get so involved with foreigners," says Phương.

"I'm a tour guide, Phương; it's in the job description. Besides, she has a deeper connection to this country than you know."

Phương snorts.

"What's the matter with you?"

Miss Maggie steps inside the van just then and Phương immediately hits play on the CD player.

"This is Phương's music," Tư says in English. "What do you think?"

"It's not really the kind of music I listen to normally," she says, "but the beat, it's kind of infectious."

The booming bass accompanies them all the way to the Metropole. So does the delicate floral scent of Maggie's perfume, which floats above the mint of the Happy Toothpaste air freshener hanging from the rear-view mirror and causes Tư's nostrils to flare.

"What does *infectious* mean?" Phương asks as they watch Maggie walk up the hotel steps, both of them staring at her behind.

"I think it's something like a disease," Tư says with considerable satisfaction.

———

Maggie feels warmed through, sated but not inflated, though having been raised on the sweeter broths and abundant garnishes of America, she has to admit she finds the phở here, Hưng's included, a bit austere.

When she was a child, her mother had taken her for a bowl of phở downtown once a week. She never cooked it herself, never passed on a recipe—too hot, she said, too much work—but what she really meant was, How would I know who was marrying whom, who had lost her life savings at a casino and whose son was going to become a dentist?

It had to be the gossip that drew her, because it certainly wasn't the phở. People get lazy in the U.S., she always said. Too many ingredients and too much choice leads cooks to take shortcuts, flavouring weak broth with things from packages and jars. Beware the evil of the stock cube.

Maggie remembers the salad her mother used to make, dressed with a mixture of fish sauce, sugar, garlic and lime juice. She would peel a cucumber, then slice it very finely. She would tear mint leaves and coriander and slice tiny red shallots and a red chili. Then she would cut five niches around the edges of a carrot and produce a cascade of orange flowers with her knife.

As Maggie climbs up the hotel steps, she unzips her purse, reaching into it for the velvety reassurance of worn paper. She had brought one of her father's pictures with her to breakfast in the hope that there might be an opportunity to show it to the old man, but after hearing about the poet who lost his tongue and meeting Bình, such a gentleman, laying down his jacket for her to sit upon, a man whose own mother had caused him to lose an eye in order to save the rest of him, she couldn't pull the drawing from her purse. Everyone has a painful story. Her father's is just one of millions.

Tư is back to regular work with the agency, but despite the wide stretch of his New Dawn smile, he feels his shoulders stiffening this morning as he shakes the hand of Mr. Bob Brentwood from North Dakota. It is the man's receding hairline, the belly spilling over the belt holding up his khaki trousers and the fact that he is travelling alone that tell Tư Mr. Bob Brentwood is a vet on a war tour.

While Tư wants to offer such tourists a broader history of the city, the ancient things that existed long before the war, they are generally only interested in the story since 1965, most specifically the lake where Senator John McCain was shot down and his prison cell at the Hanoi Hilton. They have come to Vietnam to see the DMZ, China Beach, My Lai, Khe Sanh Combat Base, the Rex Hotel, the Củ Chi tunnels, imperial Huế, the Hanoi Hilton—places that make them very choked up with emotion.

If Tư said "China Beach" to an ordinary Vietnamese person, even one who had lived through the war, they would think he was talking about a beach in China. If he said, "Hanoi Hilton," they would think first of a hotel.

Tư didn't know many of these places until he'd had a full week of lessons on the subject in tourism college. He also learned the names and plots of various movies—*Apocalypse Now*, *Full Metal Jacket*, *Platoon*, *Hamburger Hill* and *Rambo:*

First Blood—all of which are banned in Vietnam, but all of which he, like all his friends, has secretly watched on pirated DVDs from Malaysia.

Tourists often tell Tư that they have every intention of going straight back to the U.S. to lobby the government to compensate the victims of Agent Orange. And how can they help the Vietnamese people here, right now? they want to know.

What can you do here? Spend your money, thinks Tư. Did you shoot a Viet Cong rifle at the Củ Chi tunnels? Play with the AK-47s the communists used against you? Sample the manioc the soldiers lived on throughout the war? Crawl into a tunnel that was widened to accommodate the very non-Vietnamese width of your behind? Excellent. I hope you had a very nice time. And if you would still like to spend some more money? Well, then you can consider giving me a very good tip.

For Mr. Bob Brentwood, Tư suggests an itinerary that would satisfy anyone on a war tour. "And for lunch I would like to recommend the favourite restaurant of Bill Clinton," he concludes with great enthusiasm.

"What about the favourite restaurant of your president?" Mr. Brentwood asks.

"Of course," Tư says because he doesn't know how else to respond.

Mr. Bob Brentwood is not displaying predictable behaviour. Rather surprisingly, he brushes Tư's proposed itinerary aside and says that he has become a Buddhist in recent years and would like to visit a temple. While Tư has met young white Buddhists before, this is his first old one. The young ones have often shaved their heads and declare they have given up meat and alcohol, and even sex in some cases, and just once he would like to ask one of them why they feel it is necessary to be so extreme to be a Buddhist.

"Which temple would you recommend?" Mr. Bob Brentwood asks.

Tư immediately thinks of his mother's favourite—that of the Trưng sisters. They have commanded an audience for two thousand years despite the Chinese defeat of their short-lived dynasty, which led the sisters to drown themselves in the river.

Inside their temple, giant spiral cones of incense hang from the ceiling. The smoke snakes and billows, and ashes fall limply to the floor. Tư leads Mr. Brentwood through the fog of incense toward the altar. Tư bows to the statues of the kneeling Trưng sisters with their copper-leaf crowns, their arms outstretched to receive their audience.

Tư admittedly finds it hard to imagine a world where such sacrifice would be necessary: today one is more likely to kill oneself because of debt or drug addiction or a broken heart than for reasons of protest or principle. He whispers a few words of prayer to ward off debt or drug addiction or a broken heart in his own life, then stares upward at the cards that hang from the burning coils of incense.

"What are the tags for?" Mr. Brentwood asks, his eyes watering.

"You give some đồng to have your name written down on a card, and then the incense carries your prayers up," says Tư.

Mr. Brentwood pulls some đồng from his pocket, and Tư gestures to a novice monk. The monk pulls the card down from the coil and passes it to Mr. Brentwood along with a pen that he pulls from his orange folds. Mr. Brentwood places the card on his thigh, bends his knee and writes down his name before saying, "How do you spell your name?"

"My name, Mr. Brentwood?" Tư stammers.

"I'd like to pray we can forgive each other."

This man is looking for forgiveness? From him? It is Tư's job to understand and respond to the needs of his clients—but forgiveness? Even when General Khải welcomed President Bill Clinton he didn't offer him forgiveness. Nor did the general demand an apology. He simply said that it is better to make up for what happened in the past with actions in the present.

Tư finds himself in a very uncomfortable position. Mr. Brentwood is looking at him with some kind of emotion on his face. Emotion is admittedly not a subject in which Tư has developed much expertise. Tact and sensitivity in the face of the foreigner's emotions, he reminds himself—rule #10. The instructors at tourism college had cautioned him about dealing with Vietnam vets and couples who are adopting babies from Vietnam, particularly the women. "Their opinions might be very different from your own," his instructors said, "but it is your job to remain neutral and friendly. Give them your best Vietnamese smile, and when in doubt? Just change the subject."

"I think it is best you put your name alone," Tư finally says. The man is trying hard to be a good person, Tư can see this, but still, he cannot give Mr. Brentwood what he wants.

The Campaign to Rectify Errors

Hưng had sensed Miss Maggie in the line this morning before he'd even seen her. Perhaps he'd smelled something sweet beyond the familiar warmth of his broth. He had not been surprised to learn of her father's mangled hands, though he wishes such a lovely girl were not familiar with this kind of suffering. The cruelest torture in the camps had often been the most deliberate, destroying the mouth of a poet, the mind of an intellectual, the will of a man of resolve.

The propaganda could lead one to believe that much of the inmate's time in a re-education camp was spent in a classroom. Lessons on Stalinism and productive socialist thinking, lectures condemning American imperialism and the puppetry of the South. But Hưng knew the truth beyond the propaganda; they all did.

Hưng had never felt such loneliness as he did those first few months after Đạo and his colleagues disappeared. Having been surrounded by their company for so many years, only to have it all taken away, was far worse than the isolation he had felt in childhood.

As much as he missed Bình, at least he could assume the boy was safe, far away in his grandmother's village. But where Đạo had been taken, if Đạo was even still alive, Hưng didn't know. The re-education camps were scattered throughout the North, inmates constantly being shuffled between them precisely so that their families could not locate them and interrupt the progress of their ideological retraining.

As he'd promised Amie, Hưng kept his shop open as if it were a lighthouse, a bright star to guide the men home. He counted their absence in months, months during which he made phở from less and less every day, marking the arrival of each new moon with a knife blade against a wall, each cut a little deeper than the last.

Independent businesses in the city had begun to close all around him. Little food reached the city anymore. Millions of hectares of farmland had been razed to remove those peasants stubborn enough to remain. Didn't the Party understand that no one who had survived the devastation of land reform would be able to forgive their brutality? They had murdered families, hundreds of thousands of them, including his own. The new collective farms were failing to produce. Who had the will for such a thing? More than a million people had fled south.

One day in late 1956, Hưng was drawn out of his shop. The streets were filled with Hồ Chí Minh's message of personal apology. The Party would now launch the Campaign to Rectify Errors: those who had been wrongfully charged as landowners were to be reclassified as "middle peasants."

But it's too late, Hưng wanted to shout. Like his parents, most of these people were already dead and gone. Gone too was Hưng's favourite butcher, gone was all the beef. Gone too was the spice man, the salt and pepper, the cinnamon and star anise. Gone were the rice sellers, the noodle makers, the fish sauce and soy peddlers. Gone were all the dogs from the streets.

And in place of all that was gone? Government shops, their shelves tragic displays of meagre produce farmed by labourers in camps that would soon kill half a million more.

Hưng bought what he could with his ration card, but he lost days to standing in line. Ten hours of waiting for chicken only to be told there was no chicken left. No option of trying a store in another district. This is the district in which you are registered. There is no chicken left, only bones. Here: there is turnip instead.

He'd boiled onions and chicken bones and lime leaves he plucked from a tree by the lake until the tree was left naked. He floated chunks of taro in water and fed five to ten faithful regulars a broth too weak to be called soup.

Then, one morning twenty-three months after Hưng had last seen Đạo and his colleagues, Phan Khôi, the aging revolutionary who had edited *Nhân Văn*, appeared at the entrance to Hưng's shop. Phan Khôi, who had always struck

Hưng as imposing, now looked as shrivelled and harmless as a one-hundred-and-ten-year-old walnut. His eyes had sunk deep into his skull. He had no teeth with which to chew and no tongue left with which to speak.

"You'll have some broth, won't you?" said Hưng, trying to encourage him to take a bowl, but Phan Khôi shook his head and waved the bowl away. It was as if he simply wanted to be seen, that was all, and when he vanished that morning as suddenly as he'd appeared, Hưng was left to wonder if he had just been visited by a ghost.

But two days later the ghost returned and so too, eventually, the fewest words.

"*This is the world after the end*," Phan Khôi struggled to say, his voice a gurgled whisper in the dark backroom of Hưng's shop. "*We are all ghosts now, Hưng. There is no more beauty. Perhaps Đạo is the luckier one in the end.*"

Hưng sank onto his mattress in despair. In keeping his shop open he had been performing a vigil, keeping hope alive. He had been wilfully naive. Đạo was gone, Phan Khôi had confirmed it. The world would never be the same.

It hardly mattered when Party officials came to requisition Hưng's shop for their own use in 1959. Hưng's remaining customers had nothing left to offer him except their tales of suffering. He had nothing left to offer them but rain and river water.

Hưng ran to the backroom and grabbed the *Nhân Văn* magazines, *Fine Works of Spring* and *Autumn*, and all the handwritten poems he had accumulated over the years, quickly stuffing them into a burlap sack. The Party officials followed, pushing him out of the backroom and into the alleyway and claiming possession of the building, saying he would be charged as bourgeoisie if he did not simply walk away.

And so he'd walked away, but not simply. He'd walked to the shores of this muddy pond. He'd caught a duck, fed his neighbours, met a girl, shared Đạo's poetry. Then he'd sent a note to Đạo's wife and son in the village on the Sông Cả River.

> Dear Mrs. Amie and young Bình,
> I am sorrier than I know how to express. I had been praying Đạo was sent to a re-education camp just like his teacher Phan Khôi. I felt sure that whatever Đạo might be forced to endure, he would one day reappear in Hanoi. Phan Khôi told me Đạo did not even make it as far as a camp. They chose not to re-educate in his case.
>
> I will honour Đạo like my own ancestor and keep a stick of incense burning in his memory for all eternity, at least all the eternity I have left since I have no descendants to continue the tradition after I am gone. I hope the countryside teaches you many things, Bình. I would welcome your visit should you ever return to Hanoi.
>
> Hưng

Maggie takes a hotel car to Đống Đa district at the concierge's insistence. "It's not a good place," he says. "Especially at night." Rikia had said much the same thing after calling her husband. "He spoke to his driver, but he is only willing to let me pass this information on to you because I told him you were setting up a charity for the poor.

"Take this at least," she said as Maggie was about to leave the kitchen, handing her a lemon meringue pie destined for the garbage because of the slightest singe to its edges. "It will make me feel like less of a liar."

Maggie needn't have worried about asking the driver to let her out before getting to the shantytown. He comes to a stop, his headlights illuminating a potholed and rocky dirt track. "You'll have to walk from here," he says. "I'm not going to lose a muffler over this."

The driver turns on his high beams and illuminates the first fifty metres of the track, but as soon as Maggie passes over a slight rise, she is plunged into darkness. As she stares ahead into the unknown, she's less convinced this is such a good idea. What if the old man resents the intrusion? What if the picture means nothing to him?

An hour ago she was in her office entering names and descriptions of pieces of art into a database. She has devoted herself to cataloguing and preserving the hotel's collection, yet her father's drawings are in terrible shape. The one she'd brought to breakfast with her this morning was lying flat on her desk. She ran her fingers down its nearly translucent creases. Leaned over and inhaled its musty smell. She can take it in with all her senses, but the meaning of this particular drawing has always eluded her.

Her father's story might be one of millions, but it is still the one that matters most to her. She reaches into her pocket for the reassurance of the paper and carries on walking in the dark, sticking to the middle of the track, listening for creatures in the verges. The air is pulsating with the night's crickets and acrid with the smell of burning kerosene. She tenses her shoulders, gripping a bottle of wine under her arm, and keeps her eyes fixed on the fires burning in the distance. She tries not to squeeze the cake box she holds in her other hand.

Maggie is close enough to the shantytown to hear voices when something flies out of the dark and smacks her on the thigh.

"Jesus!" she yelps, leaping backward.

"Money," says a boy in English, his hand outstretched.

"You scared the crap out of me."

"Money, Mister. Pencil."

"Who taught you to beg?" she reprimands in Vietnamese, causing the boy to scurry off.

"Stranger coming! Lady stranger!" she hears him shout.

So much for an unobtrusive entrance. She sees the outlines of people assembling at the end of the track.

Before Maggie has a chance to explain herself, a woman is pressing silk pillowcases against her skin. "You buy," she says in English. "Very good price."

A teenage boy waves a fan of postcards before her eyes. Someone else tries to tempt her with a bottle of Coke, tapping his fingernail against the glass.

"I've just come to visit someone," says Maggie.

"Lady," says the boy who first ran into her, "what is in the box?"

"It's a pie." She opens the lid of the box and everyone leans in to have a look.

"Ooh," says the boy, wiggling his finger toward the crust.

"Van!" a woman shouts, slapping the boy's wrist.

"Who are you coming to visit?" a pockmarked man asks.

"Old Man Hưng," she says. "Can you tell me where I might find him?"

"He lives beside the spinster Lan," says the woman who just slapped Van's wrist.

"I'll show you," says the boy.

"Here," Maggie says, holding out the cake box to the group. "Please, you can share this. It's very good."

"Hưng first," says the pockmarked man, pulling Van away from the box.

Van natters away as Maggie follows him, re-enacting some pivotal moment from a soccer game that is lost on her while they weave between shacks, through hanging laundry, past people huddled around small fires. The boy hoofs an imaginary ball into the air, jumps up to meet it with his head, adds a karate kick for good measure, then segues into the plot of a Bruce Lee movie he says he saw projected onto the side of a building last year during Tet.

He stops in front of a row of shacks facing a pond and bellows through the doorway of one of them: "Foreign lady for Mr. Hưng!"

Maggie winces. Old Man Hưng pokes his head through the doorway. His hair is sticking up off his head and he is wearing a tattered grey undershirt.

"What are you yelling about, Van? I'm not deaf."

"A lady is here to see you."

"I'm very sorry to disturb you, Mr. Hưng."

"Miss Maggie?" The old man squints and pats his chest as if looking for a pair of glasses. "Is something wrong?"

"I just wanted to talk to you, if that's okay. I didn't get a chance this morning."

"Come." He beckons her into his shack. "Off you go, Van."

"But Old Man Hưng—"

"Yes?"

"There is a cake," the boy whispers.

Maggie offers the old man the box and opens the lid for him.

"From your room service?" he asks.

"From the restaurant," she assures him. "The chef is excellent."

The old man peers inside the box and inhales. "I smell lemon, but what is this on top?"

"That's meringue," says Maggie. "They beat the egg whites with sugar until they're stiff and then bake the whole thing at a low heat."

"Huh," says the old man. "I've never seen such a thing."

"I will get you a knife, Mr. Hưng," says the expectant boy, bounding off, shouting, "Ma! Ma! Get a knife!"

Maggie follows the old man into his shack. His few belongings are stacked neatly on wooden crates, but the space is narrow and cramped, with nowhere to sit down really except upon his mattress.

Van pokes his head through the door of Hưng's shack a minute later. He holds a crude knife with a roughly serrated edge that looks like it could skin the hide off an animal. Hưng takes it from the boy and slices the pie in half. "There's plenty enough there to share, Van," says Hưng, as the boy receives half the pie with grateful hands and a gleeful yelp and disappears into the night.

"I brought you some wine as well," says Maggie, handing Old Man Hưng the bottle she has held clamped under her arm.

"That's very generous of you," he says, turning the bottle around in his hands. "Is this the kind they make from grapes?"

"It is." She nods. "French."

"Đạo will enjoy this," he says, rising to place the bottle in front of a candlelit altar. "Bình's father. Tư's grandfather. He was a man of European tastes despite himself."

Hưng places the bottle and a slice of the pie alongside an orange, a banana and some grains of rice positioned in front of a framed picture. Maggie doesn't know what to make of the very white pair of basketball shoes also parked there.

Hưng stares at the picture, the face of a man, for some time. His lips move as if he is reciting a prayer, and Maggie feels as if she is interrupting a private moment. She's not even sure the old man remembers she's there.

"Mr. Hưng?" she prompts gently.

Hưng looks at Maggie for a few seconds as if trying to place her. "They slit Đạo's throat," he says. "The very day that they came to arrest him."

Maggie doesn't know what to say. "I'm so sorry," she eventually utters.

"You know," he says, turning away from the altar, back toward her, "that story of your father's escape from a camp raises the question of whether it's possible any of the men I knew might have managed to escape."

Maggie takes this as her cue. She pulls her father's drawing from her jacket pocket. "I wanted to show you this," she says nervously, laying it down on Hưng's mattress. She's worried he'll think it clumsy. That he'll dismiss it as insignificant or unintelligible.

"My father drew several like it for me when I was a child," she says.

Hưng leans over the drawing then picks it up, holding it to the weak light. He reaches for a pair of glasses. They are thick-rimmed and don't have the elegance of the previous pair. They don't seem to be the right strength for him either. He holds them like a magnifying glass rather than putting them on.

"It's a bit blurry," Maggie says. "Smudged."

"Cats," Hưng remarks. "In a fight. 'Once we were Siamese,'" he says, reading the bubble of text that floats halfway up the page.

"I've never fully understood it."

"The North and South. The country was ripped apart by the partition in '54." Hưng slowly raises his finger. "'The skin of a fruit, discarded; a skinless fruit,'" he says.

His mouth hangs open. His pupils float toward the corrugated tin ceiling, his finger still poised in the air. He looks like a man watching stars fall to earth. Mesmerized, Hưng begins to whisper to himself, barely audible. He sways back and forth like a child.

Maggie hears something about a homeless man. The line, "Your fruit is a feast for maggots."

Hưng coughs and raises his hand to his chest. He continues to cough, then splutter.

Maggie reaches out to touch the old man's back. "Did you ever have that X-ray, Mr. Hưng?"

The old man closes his eyes and leans his head back against the wall of his shack. His bottom lip quivers and tears pool in the corner of his eyes. "It's not that," he whispers. "I thought it was gone. I didn't think I could remember anything beyond the first line."

Maggie's perfume still lingers, or is it the cake that is in fact a pie that he smells? Hưng cannot be sure. His senses are as confused as his emotions. Something in him has been rattled loose. Perhaps this is what the release of tears does to you; having so little experience with the phenomenon, he really doesn't know.

Hưng has only shed tears once before in his adult life— at the sight of Bình returning twenty-five years after his mother took him away.

One unremarkable day in the years after the war, a man of Đạo's likeness arrived in the shantytown on a bicycle. "Uncle Hưng," the man had said.

Hưng pulled Bình—now a grown man—into his shack and showed him the ancestral shrine he'd built in Đạo's honour.

"I apologize for the fact that the drawing is not a perfect likeness," he said, but Bình had already closed his eyes.

Hưng joined the man in prayer. When Hưng opened his eyes some minutes later, water was dripping from his chin onto the front of his shirt. It had taken him a moment to understand the source.

In all these years since their reunion Hưng has never been able to recite any of Đạo's poetry. The last person to hear the poems was Lan, the girl who had sat beside him under weak moonlight decades ago, repeating back to him those lines that pleased her most.

A feast of flowers breeds butterflies of a thousand hues.
The angels of revolution float on gossamer wings.
Her lips were like cherry blossom, new and pink in spring.

Lan's lips *had* been like cherry blossom. He had even dared to put his finger to the centre of her plump bottom lip as she delivered that line, speaking it as if she had written it herself. She had paused, not breathing, then touched the delicate tip of her tongue to the rough tip of his finger, transforming him from a solid into a liquid. She had closed her lips around the tip of his finger and sucked, taking in the entire liquid being of him as if through a straw.

Hưng can taste the salt of Đạo's words in his mouth when he wakes. He yearns for something sweet. He pulls the paper box perched on the crate that holds his clothes toward him and sticks his fingers into Maggie's lemon meringue pie.

The Real Vietnam

To see the old man smile at Maggie when he sees her again this morning, to see the gleam of his new dentures, affirms Tư's own positive assessment of her.

Tư's father had also smiled at her when she emerged from her apartment building. He'd even attempted some English. "Good morning, Miss Maggie," he said as she climbed onto the back of the Honda Dream II, the three of them riding together to breakfast.

Tư felt a bit embarrassed; his father pronounced his vowels like a deaf man. "Have you been reading my English phrase book?" he yelled into his father's ear as they lunged into traffic.

Bình laughed and said he was just doing a bit of mental calisthenics; good to exercise the brain with a new challenge once in a while.

His father thinks English is a language only for the young.
It's Russian he knows as a second language.

"I was wondering, Maggie, is there phở in America?"
Hưng asks over Tư's shoulder this morning. "Have the Việt
Kiều managed to keep the recipe alive?"

Maggie clearly enjoys the question. Her eyebrows do a
little dance as she says, "Every major city has its little Saigon,
and even in small towns you often find a couple of Vietnamese
restaurants, usually in a row."

Tư has met plenty of Americans familiar with the taste of
phở, but her description paints a new culinary picture of the
U.S. in his mind. He tends to think of uninterrupted kilometres
of hamburger chains and Kentucky Fried Chickens. The latter
came to Saigon last year, the first and only one of the American
fast-food chains allowed into Vietnam, and while Tư has never
tasted Kentucky Fried Chicken, there are people eating phở on
the streets of New York. And maybe even in smaller towns like
Little Rock, Arkansas, home of Bill Clinton. Perhaps while the
Vietnamese are becoming more Americanized, America is
becoming more Vietnamesized!

"I am very glad to hear there is phở in America, even if
it has to be Saigon phở," says Old Man Hưng. "For all its
riches, America would be a very poor place without it."

Tư's father is once again being a gentleman, laying his
windbreaker down on the ground for Maggie. Oh, thank
you. Are you sure? That's so kind of you. What about
you?—too much fuss and too many thank-yous, just like a
typical American.

Steam rises from their bowls, dissipating in the air.

"So how's work?" Maggie asks Tư. "No more encounters with offensive art and artists, I hope."

"No more art or artists," he says. "Just Americans and their obsession with the war."

"It runs very deep in the American psyche," says Maggie.

If the Vietnamese were so obsessed, if they didn't get over the war and allowed themselves to be haunted or just lay down like dogs, where would they be today? In the South they'd be speaking Khmer; in the North they'd be speaking Mandarin. The Vietnamese would be yet another ethnic minority being kicked about like a football by the big boots in Beijing.

"Sometimes I feel it is all about them, not really about Vietnam at all," Tư finds himself saying rather boldly. "Even among those who say they are here to learn about the country, *me* still seems to be their favourite word."

"But it *is* all about them, isn't it? It's the business of tourism."

Has Tư been naive in thinking his job has something to do with introducing people to Vietnam? But then, come to think of it, how can they possibly see anything beyond stereotypes when the tourism industry gives them war tours and movie tours and romance of Indochina tours, and a hotel like the Metropole drives them about town in a '53 Citroën, perhaps taking them to a gallery where they can purchase a souvenir in the form of a three-thousand-dollar painting of a lady in an *áo dài* riding a bicycle alongside a lazy river?

Tư feels quite unsettled. "Don't you think they want to see the real Vietnam?" he asks.

"But what's the real Vietnam, Tư? This is a country that erases its own history. Anything that goes against the Party. Your grandfather. My father. Millions of people. And if people aren't being censored? They're busy hiding anyway. Desperately trying to save face."

Tư's father looks uncomfortable and puts down his bowl. A few people on either side of them do the same. Tư regrets taking liberties. She is angry and she shouldn't be speaking about any of this in public, which proves her point, he supposes, but still doesn't make her behaviour any less embarrassing.

More buildings seem to have gone up along the highway since Tư last made the trip out to the airport. Kilometres of construction. Apartment blocks rising from rice paddies. Buildings emerging from swamps, a lonely university campus, shopping malls, new factories.

Why don't any of those contemporary artists paint this? Tư wonders. Vietnam is not standing still, not moving at the pace of a buffalo pulling a plough. Foreigners seem to think backwardness is romantic, whereas for Tư, nothing could be more romantic than the estimate that twenty billion foreign dollars will be invested in the country this year alone. Figures like that can make you swoon.

Tư is distracted by these thoughts on the drive back into the city, paying less attention to the French family seated in the back than he should. They have paid for the super-deluxe service, after all, and offering them informative and lively conversation as he escorts them back to the Metropole in the super-deluxe Mercedes van with the leather seats and seat belts and the multi-disc CD player is part of the package. Unfortunately, only the most senior driver at the agency is allowed to drive this van—a guy Tư calls Karl Marx because he studied German in Germany and came back with a beard, which is not only impossible to grow, but a very dirty thing in his opinion—Phương will be thoroughly annoyed.

Tư stops by his friend's house in the evening hoping to share some of his thoughts, but Phương's mother says he has gone to the library. Tư, finding this very hard to believe, makes his way straight to the bar they started frequenting while in tourism college, having some happy hour *bia hơi* after classes before going home for dinner or, depending on how much they had to drink, perhaps not going home for dinner at all and doing karaoke instead. But there is no sign of Phương here either. Tư orders a glass of beer and is once again reminded that happy hour is depressing without his best friend.

Fortunately Phương walks in just in time to prevent Tư from sliding into a funk. And he really has been to the library. Phương is carrying a collection of traditional songs, meaning songs approved by the Ministry of Culture and Information.

"What are you doing with this?" Tư asks, flipping through the pages. There is nothing but songs in praise of agricultural productivity, the Party, the workers, Stalin, Hồ Chí Minh, the revolution.

"Research," Phương says. "What's it to you?"

"Are you pissed off with me for some reason?"

"How could I be?" says Phương, throwing half a glass of beer down his throat. He burps and slams his glass down. "I barely see you anymore."

"Hey. You're the one who spent a week in bed."

Phương's nostrils flare. He holds up his empty glass and flags the waiter. "You're the one who's lusting for the Việt Kiều," he says out of the corner of his mouth.

"What are you talking about?"

Phương rolls his eyes, turning his attention back to his book.

Okay, yes, maybe Tư has pictured Maggie naked once (okay, more than once), but what man doesn't imagine a woman naked? Surely Phương was doing exactly that when he looked Miss Maggie's entire body up and down in the hotel lobby the day Tư introduced them. Why does Phương have to cheapen it?

"She's my friend, Phương," Tư says, anger hardening his jaw.

He knows it sounds strange: *friend*. It's not a word often used between men and women, but Tư doesn't know how else to describe this new relationship. He doesn't care what Phương thinks. He will prove himself worthy of Maggie's friendship. And if she happens to fall completely in love with him in the process and say, *You are the hero of my life?* Well, it wouldn't be his fault then, would it? He could turn to Phương and say, *I'm afraid you are mistaken. It is not me lusting for Miss Maggie. Miss Maggie is lusting for me.*

Tư slaps some đồng on the table and stomps out of the bar. His feet know where he's headed before his brain does. Tư marches straight over to the eastern edge of the Old Quarter. If anyone knew Maggie's father, it would be Mr. Võ. All the old artists took their coffee at his café—Võ is to coffee what Hưng is to phở—but unlike Hưng, Võ has managed to hold on to his shop, keeping his doors open throughout the decades, even during the years when his weekly rations allowed him fewer beans than he would use today to make a single cup, even during the years when the government stores carried no coffee and he had to reuse and reuse old grinds.

Tư has not visited the café since he was a child, but he finds it exactly as he remembers it. Mr. Võ has few customers at this hour, just a couple of men using a tabletop as the board for a game of cờ tướng, Chinese chess, cigarettes hanging from the corners of their mouths, squinting through the smoke as they calculate their next moves.

Tư admires the Bùi Xuân Phái paintings he remembers—the three street scenes hanging on the cracked part of the south wall. Phái's pictures of the streets of Hanoi look so very different from the streets today. They are empty and grey, without food stalls or motorcycles or markets or shops displaying shiny items or windows draped with red lanterns and colourful fabric.

"Was it really like this?" Tư remembers asking his father when he saw these paintings for the first time.

"This is the Hanoi I knew," he had said.

The Hanoi Tư's father knew looked dead.

They say Bùi Xuân Phái was so poor that he had to pull the gold caps off his teeth in order to pay the rent. Now his work is being sold to foreigners for thousands and thousands of dollars. Tư wonders if Mr. Võ has any idea how much the works on his walls would be sold for in one of those fancy new galleries. But Mr. Võ would never sell the pieces; he would not get rich off the backs of friends who died in poverty.

Mr. Võ shuffles forth from the kitchen. "I'm sorry," he says, "but I'm not serving any more today, son."

Tư has to remind him of who he is—Đạo's grandson, Bình's son.

"Ah. Yes, of course," says Mr. Võ. "I don't think I've seen you since you were a boy. How is your father? I hear he is doing very well as a carpenter. And what are you up to these days?"

Tư pulls a card from his back pocket and hands it to Mr. Võ.

"Very impressive," says Mr. Võ as he reads it.

Mr. Võ leads Tư on a clockwise turn around the room, recalling the names of the artists, many of their works unsigned. The names are as well known to him as *quốc ngữ*, the letters of the alphabet, but none of these is Maggie's father, Lý Văn Hai.

"Do you still have that big chest in the back?" Tư asks.

"I've never had the space to display all the art," says Mr. Võ.

"Do you think you could show it to me?"

"Come," says Mr. Võ, leading him to the living quarters at the back—just a mattress on the floor and the wooden chest, his ancestral altar perched upon it.

Mr. Võ moves the photo, the fruit and the incense holder aside so that he can open the chest. Tư kneels down beside the old man, who is lifting out sheets of newspaper stamped with woodblock prints, oil paintings on cracked canvases, delicate paintings on dyed silk, charcoal drawings on brown paper, ink drawings and pencil sketches done on rough paper and torn cardboard and strips of bark.

There must be a hundred pieces here, Tư thinks, as he scans them for names and dates. Portraits, street scenes, sketches of birds and animals, paintings of very nude ladies and still lifes of empty bowls. About half the works are unsigned, but Mr. Võ still remembers most of the artists' names. Tư wishes Hưng's memory were half this good.

Toward the bottom of the pile lies a series of four intricate drawings of tigers. The last of the four is a particularly gory sketch of two tigers mauling each other in a cave. Tư picks it up to study the detail. The weak light through the doorway suggests there is something written on the other side. He turns the piece of paper over and his heart begins to pound. There's an inscription on the back that reads *For Tan Võ from Lý Văn Hai.*

"Hah!" Tư exclaims, flapping the drawing in his hand. "I knew it! This is exactly what I was looking for. I know this woman who works at the Metropole, Mr. Võ, she's his daughter."

"I'm afraid I don't remember him," Mr. Võ says, rubbing his eye with the ball of his palm. "So much dust," he mutters.

"But, Mr. Võ," says Tư, shaking the piece of paper, "Lý Văn Hai dedicated this picture to you."

Mr. Võ shrugs and reaches for the sketch. He looks at it blankly. "I've been open for sixty-seven years, Tư. I've seen a lot of people come and go through my door."

He gestures at the pile of work on the floor. "Time for me to close up shop."

As soon as Maggie turns off the shower, she hears a knock at her apartment door. Mrs. Viên must have blown a fuse again. She steps out of the soapy puddle around her feet and wraps a towel around her hair. She pulls on her robe, kicking her abandoned shoes out of the foyer and into the bedroom.

But it's not her neighbour. It's Tư. "Is everything okay?" she asks. "Is it Hưng?"

"It's about your father," says Tư, his black eyes darting across her face.

"My father?" Maggie stares at him in confusion.

"Do you have a minute?"

"Of course I do. Come." She gestures, leading him down the hall. Maggie sits down at the kitchen table and wraps her arms around her waist, bracing herself for whatever Tư has to say.

Tư leans forward in his chair, places his hands between his knees and says, "I found some of your father's drawings at Café Võ."

Maggie feels as if she has been punched in the stomach. "But I went there a few months ago," she stammers. "I had a careful look at all the art—not every piece was signed, but I did ask him whether he had any of Lý Văn Hai's work. He said he must have been one of Hưng's customers. That's how I found Hưng in the first place."

"The sketches were in the chest Mr. Võ keeps in his back-room," says Tư. "Your father even inscribed one of them to Mr. Võ, but he claims to have no recollection of him."

"None at all?" she says. How is it that in the face of concrete evidence her father still remains invisible?

"The drawings are of tigers," says Tư, "big, very mus-cular. In the last one, two of them are attacking each other—kind of tangled up together like a puzzle."

Maggie stands up and rushes out of the room to retrieve her father's drawings. She returns to the kitchen and unfolds them on the table in front of Tư, smoothing her palms across them.

"He always did animals," she says. "Did they look anything like these?"

Tư studies the sketches for a moment. "But these ones look like they were done by a child."

"He did them after they destroyed his hands," says Maggie.

Tư sees only lumpen shapes, thick, clumsy lines. She sees vitality and animation, humour and heroic effort. *They could not touch him inside*, Maggie reminds herself—the last words she had heard her mother speak. They had broken his hands, but not his spirit. That did not come until later.

"What happened to him in the camp?" Maggie had asked her mother as she lay in the hospital bed after her first stroke.

"They made him dig pit latrines, Maggie, can you imagine? The indignity of it. Hundreds of them. His only consolation was the time he spent alone underground. He liked the silence and he would carve pictures of animals into the mud walls down there, pictures no one would ever see—pictures that would soon be covered in people's waste.

"After a year there was a new guard assigned to watch over the men digging the latrines. A scary one, very rigid, he carried an iron rod he would beat against his hand. One day he hopped down into a pit with your father and held a torch up to the walls.

"'You did these?' the guard asked. What could your father say?

"'But they're brilliant,' said the guard, 'Was this your job before?'

"Your father shrugged.

"And then you know what he did, Maggie? This new guard who everyone was afraid of? He began to smuggle bits of paper to your father. Dozens of little pieces. And pencils. Your father hid the paper underneath his overalls and kept the pencils under a floorboard in the little wooden hut he shared with the other diggers.

"One day he was returning to the hut when he was suddenly ambushed. Two senior guards knocked him to the ground and stripped off his clothes. They found a pencil and two drawings and demanded to know where he got the pencil and paper. But he wasn't going to betray the guard. The two senior guards dragged your father, still naked, over to the barracks where the guard who oversaw work on the pit latrines lived. They dumped your father at this man's feet. They put one brick on the ground and one in the guard's hands. And then they ordered the guard to break your father's fingers one by one.

"'But he's my best digger,' the guard said.

"'And just as good an artist as you said he was.'"

So this guard had set her father up and reported him? "But why would he do that?" Maggie had asked her mother.

"I don't know. They called me in to clean up the mess afterward. I was just a nurse, only twenty; I knew nothing about setting bones. His hands had been completely shattered. As if they were made of glass. The best I could do was wrap them in bandages. He didn't complain; he even thanked me. I loved him more than I knew it was possible to love."

Tự looks up at Maggie. "I'm sorry," he says, "I didn't mean—"

"It's okay," she says, "it's okay."

A Proper Friend

As Hưng loads up his cart this morning, he finds himself glancing back over his shoulder. Lan's shack is in darkness. He returns to his own shack, opens the paper box and cuts what remains of Maggie's lemon meringue pie in half. It is a small piece, days old now, but still a lovely yellow topped with a cheerful burst of cloud. He wraps the slice of pie in banana leaf, piercing it closed with a twig whittled into a toothpick. He loops a piece of string under the twig and ties a knot.

He makes his way over to Lan's shack, where he hangs the packet from a beam that extends over her front door, well out of reach of rats. He remembers how he used to do this during the war, but back then it was not fancy pies from the Metropole, it was pondweed and frogs' legs. Mung beans and larvae and brown bark for tea.

Hưng returns to his waiting cart, plants his feet firmly, shoulder-width apart, and grasps the handlebars. He inhales and braces himself, then exhales with a grunt as he thrusts his load up the slight incline. What an effort; he really is getting old. If he doesn't keep moving, the spirits of silence will soon be upon him.

As he rights his cart on the dirt track he can smell the moment just before the sun rises in the air. He is late getting started, but he did not oversleep. How long had he stood upon Lan's threshold? Perhaps a good deal longer than it had felt.

When Hưng returns home from breakfast duty a few hours later, he finds the banana leaf washed and laid flat to dry upon the threshold of his shack. He glances to his left. She is sitting on a stool sorting through a basket of rice. Picking out small stones and dried insects. She wears a kerchief in her hair like a woman from the country, and she wipes her brow with the back of her hand. She is concentrating on her task. She does not look up.

When her grandmother died some years after the war, Hưng had followed the small, sad procession to the temple to pay his respects. Lan turned around in her great, black mourning cape and looked directly at him. He turned his head and slinked away. It was the last time their eyes had met.

He wishes he could share what is in his heart in this moment. *I remember some of Đạo's poetry*, he would tell her.

I remember some of Đạo's poetry because of a girl who reminds me of you.

Maggie follows Tư up the street, motorbikes moving like purring cats beside them, navigating the distance by means of invisible whiskers. It is the dinner hour and people have thrown the wooden doors of their houses open to the streets; the guts are fluorescent-lit, on full display, revealing cracked linoleum tiles and blaring televisions. Motorbikes are parked in front rooms and women are crouched on the pavement boiling rice over charcoal fires, frying beef and onions, pouring bubbled dishwater into the street.

At Café Võ two men are slapping down backgammon pieces with a loud clack on a wooden board and flicking their cigarette ashes over their shoulders, while Mr. Võ swishes a broom over the oily cracked tiles and a fan overhead creaks with each laboured revolution. The place is otherwise empty.

"Tư," Mr. Võ says, as he looks up from the floor. "I don't see you for years, and then I see you two times in a week? Listen, I'm closing up now."

"This lady," Tư says, gesturing at Maggie, "I think you've met. This is Maggie Lý, Lý Văn Hai's daughter."

"Who?"

"The artist who did those drawings of tigers you have in the back."

"Look, Tư, I told you last time—you can't expect me to remember every single person who has ever drunk a cup of coffee in my establishment."

"I'd like to show them to Miss Maggie."

"Not today, Tư."

"Just very quickly."

"It's not convenient right now."

"But—"

"My wife, Tư, please, she's not well," says Mr. Võ, his hands shaking now. "She's had an operation. She's resting in the back."

"It's okay, Tư," says Maggie, putting her hand on his wrist. "We'll come back another time. Sorry to disturb you, Mr. Võ. I hope your wife feels better soon."

Maggie tugs Tư by the shirtsleeve, leading him back out to the sidewalk. "These things take time, Tư," she says. "Believe me. After the past year, I know."

"But we were so close," says Tư, leaning his shoulder against the building.

"We're still close," Maggie says.

"I don't know," says Tư. "Something didn't seem right."

"It's probably the fact that I'm a foreigner."

Tư had actually been wondering the same thing.

"Listen, do you want to get something to eat?" she asks.

Tư brightens. "Have you ever had *chả cá*?"

Maggie shakes her head.

Tư points down an alleyway to their left, taking them deeper into the Old Quarter. When they reach Chả Cá Street, they climb up a narrow staircase to a cramped room on the second floor of an old building. They shuffle past rows of people crammed side by side on wooden benches and sit opposite each other at the end of a long crowded table. As soon as they sit down, the waitress leans in over Tư's shoulder, lights a burner and slams a pan of oil down upon it. Tư orders beer for both of them and the woman promptly drops two bottles onto the table over Tư's head before thwacking down plastic plates of cubes of fish and various herbs.

The oil begins to bubble and Tư throws the cubes of fish into the pan. He tosses in the dill and stirs it with his chopsticks until it wilts, then lifts the fish onto a bed of vermicelli and dresses it with peanuts and coriander.

"Taste," he says, presenting it to her.

The fish is soft and buttery with oil, earthy with turmeric and collapses perfectly in the mouth.

"Good?"

"Delicious," says Maggie, wiping a drop of oil from her bottom lip. "You know what, Tư? You're my first proper Vietnamese friend," she says in English, as if it's the only language suitable for such words.

"I'm not so proper," he replies shyly.

The Walls

Hưng owns no land, but by claiming an inch each year, he has come to consider a small rectangular patch in front of his shack as his own. He grows long beans and peppers and onions under chicken wire to prevent feasting by the foraging creatures of night.

This year he has been blessed with an extravagant addition to his garden, a thing he would not have dared display just a few years ago. It is a flower, some type of orchid with petals like pale pink tongues. He'd come across it while pushing his cart to work one morning. He'd been suspended in an early morning dream of himself and Bình aboard a sampan, Hưng pedalling the oars with the thick soles of his feet while Bình dragged aboard net after net teeming with fish. He could still see the floor of the sampan shimmering like liquid mercury when he heaved his cart over the dirt lip of a building site, taking a shortcut through the old Soviet spark plug factory slated for demolition.

He followed the track through the dirt, stopping short of a mound that the bulldozer had clearly missed. But the shape of the mound was deliberate, he realized, a perfect circle framing this unlikely pink flower. It caused him to exclaim aloud.

He knelt and freed the flower from imminent death. He replanted her later that day, crowning her queen of a small country of vegetables.

The symbolism is not lost on him. Lan was once such a queen.

Hưng is surprised she never married. Surprised she never went in search of somewhere or something better. Her beauty has not faded in all these decades, and even though he has avoided gazing upon it, he has, on occasion, felt it shine upon his back like a warming sun.

Hưng walks down to the pond this afternoon, consciously avoiding glancing over his shoulder. He asks Thuy Doc if he might borrow his sampan for an hour. He feels he has grown stronger in the days since Maggie's visit; remembering a few lines of poetry, he feels renewed. He's in the mood to cook something special this evening, and he's thinking of the delicate warmth of an eel and mushroom soup. He leaves his slippers on the shore and pushes the wooden boat into the water, pulling his muddy feet aboard last. The bottom of the boat is a velvety green, the oars worn smooth by years of sweat and repetitive motion. He rows himself to the centre of the pond, equidistant from the shantytown and the tire factory. The water is as opaque as wood, the sky above, leaden. We are not so adventurous as the other animals, Hưng thinks, inhabiting just this narrow band between earth and water, earth and sky.

He drifts toward the western edge of the pond, dragging a net through the reeds. He looks toward home: his shack and hers, only a metre between them. He'd suggested joining their shacks once, bridging that metre with some combination of wood and bamboo and corrugated tin. It was just after Lan had taken his finger into her mouth. A wall between them had collapsed. He'd felt the urge to tear the rest of them down.

"If we took out this wall, we would have another room entirely," he said, leading her into his spare shack.

She looked around admiringly, acquainting herself with its contents. Where he slept, kept his few clothes, his cooking utensils and his stash of precious magazines.

She stood so close to him that he could smell the wild garlic on her breath. It made his mouth water, as if in anticipation of a great meal.

"I'm sure my grandmother would like it very much," she said. "But, Hưng, if we did live together, where would we all sleep?"

He cleared his throat and said nervously, "Well, that would depend."

"On what would it depend?"

"On whether I am like an uncle to you or more like a husband."

"A husband," she responded, but he could not interpret her tone.

Did this shock her or appeal to her, or was it just a simple statement of fact? Had he destroyed everything with one word or set it free?

Tư has waited a week at Maggie's insistence, but he can't stand to wait any longer. He makes his way to Café Võ alone after work one night, a camera stuffed in his back pocket. It is just before 7 p.m. and he stands in the doorway, a sick lump rising from his stomach to his throat. The tables and chairs are stacked in the centre of the room. All the paintings have been taken down; the walls are montages of tobacco-coloured outlines. Sloppy white stripes of fresh paint run from the ceiling to the floor of the south wall, where Mr. Võ is supervising a kid with a paint roller attached to a broom handle. Tư hopes to God this is nothing more than a renovation.

"Mr. Võ," says Tư, "I see you are making some changes."

"I must prepare for what is to come," he says sullenly.

"What is to come, Mr. Võ?"

"It's time for me to sell the shop and take my wife back to our village, where she can spend her last days in peace."

"I'm sorry to hear your wife is no better," says Tư, though he is not so sorry that he refrains from asking about the art. "You're taking it all with you?"

"I'm selling it," Mr. Võ says matter-of-factly.

"Everything? Even the stuff in the back?"

"Everything. Life is a circle—just as we are born with nothing so we shall die."

The room feels terribly hot to Tư all of a sudden, the air close and chemical. "But who are you selling it to?"

"One of those dealers," says Mr. Võ with a dismissive wave. "They've been after me for years. I will soon have to pay for a funeral. I already owe the money for my wife's operation. Everything costs too much money these days. Đổi mới does not make everybody rich, you know. Some of us it just makes poorer."

Tư leaves without another word—his hands clenched, his nails cutting into his palms. He punches the frame of the door as he passes through it, then pounds his way down random streets, his heart and mind competing for most agitated. He chews on some negative integers and finally, nearly an hour later, calms down. He takes shelter from the rain in a crumbling doorway on Tạ Hiến Street and spies a tiny bar across the road. He darts between the lanes of traffic and crouches through the door of the bar. The room glows red from the light of paper lanterns, the operative language appears to be Englamese and the music is the kind of rock that old white men like. Places like this make Tư feel like a tourist in his own town.

He orders a beer from a very pretty waitress who tells him there is no *bia hơi* in this place, only bottles from Germany and places like that. Tư sips his expensive beer and wonders to whom Mr. Võ might have sold his collection. He's determined to find out—he doesn't care how long it takes or whom he annoys along the way. Mr. Võ might need the money, but doesn't he realize he has just given their history away? What if it all ends up in foreign hands, lost to Vietnam forever?

Tư pulls his pen and notebook from the inside pocket of his jacket and flips through lists of new English words until he reaches a blank page. He draws a line down the middle of the page, making two columns. On the left-hand side he begins to write the names of all the artists he can remember, on the right-hand side, descriptions of the pieces of artwork he can recall hanging on the walls of Café Võ.

He makes his way counter-clockwise around the room in his mind, starting with the three Bùi Xuân Pháis. He moves on to what he remembers seeing in Mr. Võ's chest, the more dramatic works coming most readily to mind—not just Lý Văn Hai's tigers, but Nguyễn Diệp's *Requiem for Uncle Hồ*, where a face made of bricks is demolished by a sledgehammer. He remembers a painting of a Russian cosmonaut landing in a rice paddy, several portraits of men with stony faces and bleeding eyes, and a good number of naked ladies.

He taps his temple with his pen, commending himself for his memorization skills. A communist education has its benefits.

Tư's mother opens the door for Maggie. Anh is slight and feminine but strong, with prominent veins in her forearms. A single streak of grey begins at her temple and runs the length of her hair, but apart from that suggestion of maturity, she looks barely older than Tư.

Maggie follows Anh across a fragrant green courtyard into a modern kitchen on the far side. The appliances gleam under the bright fluorescent light and a woven mat covers part of the linoleum floor, evidence of a game of dominoes underway upon it. The Honda Dream II rests on its kickstand in the corner of the room, a faithful member of the family.

Tư is standing by the table examining his knuckles. He'd sounded very upset on the phone. "I went back to Café Võ," he says. "Mr. Võ's wife is dying and he has decided to sell the shop so they can go back to their village."

"And the art? Is he taking it with him?"

"He sold it all to a dealer."

Maggie closes her eyes for a second. Her eyelids flutter, those thin membranes struggling to conceal her disappointment. She places her palms on the table to steady herself. "Did he tell you the name of the dealer?"

"He was very vague about the whole thing," says Tư. "But, Maggie, I had an idea. I think my father might be able to draw some likeness of one of your father's pictures if I could describe it to him." Tư places his hands on his father's shoulders, his expression one of mild desperation.

Bình smiles weakly, with humility. "I generally stick to objects," he says. "Things without movement or expression. But I would be very happy to try."

Maggie swallows the lump in her throat and takes a seat on a hard wooden chair across the table from Bình. He apologizes for the fact that he has only graph paper. He holds his pencil, ready to interpret his son's words, but Tư has some difficulty getting started.

"They live in the mountains, don't they?" his father prompts. "Not at the very top, but in the woodland areas."

"They were in a dark cave," says Tư. "Maybe it was a cave in a mountain but you couldn't see the mountain. It was more close up."

"What shape was the cave?" Bình asks.

"The shape of an eye," says Tư. "The tigers are just to the left of the pupil."

Bình makes a few bold strokes with his pencil.

"How big were they?" Bình asks.

"I don't know," says Tư, shrugging. "Tiger size. They were strong: tearing into each other, their muscles rippling, blood gushing from the neck of the one on the right."

The concentration on Bình's face feels familiar to Maggie. The way his eyes dart across the page, his pencil turned horizontally as he assesses proportion. Her father used to do exactly this as he knelt on the floor of their room in Saigon and distracted her from the realities of a war, her arms draped around his neck as he brought a water buffalo to life.

"Now what do you think he wants to eat for dinner?" she remembers her father asking as he leaned back on his heels.

"Dog," she had said over his shoulder.

"But buffalo don't like meat, Maggie. You really are an urban girl, aren't you."

"What does that mean?"

"From the city. I should teach you about the country. Show you where the things we eat come from. When the war is over we'll go into the countryside and stay at a farm for a few days. Would you like that?"

That promise alone had made Maggie pray for an end to the war.

"Huh," Bình finally says, putting down his pencil and holding the graph paper at arms' length.

Maggie steps round to his side of the table.

"I don't really know how one captures the emotions of things," Bình says.

"What do you think it means?" Maggie asks.

"If I knew, I would probably be able to do a much better job for you."

Tư examines the page and lists all the things he had neglected to communicate to his father.

Bình tears the top sheet of graph paper off his pad, ready to begin again.

This time, Tư is more descriptive. He uses his hands to illustrate the degree of the tigers' entanglement, his face to indicate the width of the one tiger's open mouth. He describes stalagmites and shadows. Bình's second attempt is a good deal more detailed as a result.

"I wonder if they ever escape the cave," Maggie says as they stare at the drawing lying flat on the table.

"I'm going to recover those pictures for you," says Tư.

Maggie looks at him and wonders if this is what it might feel like to have a brother. She reaches out to him; he flinches. She reaches out again, grabbing and squeezing his good hand.

Hưng's eel and mushroom soup has just the right consistency and heat. He waits until Lan wanders off to the latrine in the dark before ladling some into a wooden-lidded bowl. He leaves the bowl on the stool that sits on her threshold, making sure it is illuminated by the light of her kerosene lamp.

He sits down in the dark on his own threshold and awaits her return. He hears the scratch of stiff fabric as she bends to pick up the bowl, her exhalation as she sits down, the clack of the wooden lid being shifted and set aside, the dull tap of the spoon against the bowl, her swallow, her contented sigh, the quiet words—is it true? Does he really hear them?—*Thank you, Hùng*.

An Emotional Vocabulary

Tư is standing at Maggie's office door wishing that the cuffs of his jeans were not so dirty and that he had thought to splash on some aftershave. "Can I help you?" some guy in uniform had asked as he walked through the lobby. "I have an appointment with Miss Maggie," Tư had replied defensively. "She's expecting me."

This was not exactly true, but he felt justified in saying it given the urgency of the search for her father's missing pictures.

"Tư," says Maggie, surprised to see him. "Do you have clients at the hotel today?"

"I was just coming to ask whether you have had any luck identifying the dealer."

"Not yet, Tư. It's only been a day. I contacted a professor at the Hanoi University of Fine Arts who specializes in Bùi

Xuân Phái's work. I thought he might be able to help narrow the search down—there are hundreds of dealers throughout Southeast Asia who could be interested in that collection."

"But, Maggie, this is something of an emergency. I think we need to act now. All the pistons firing. That collection is full of national treasures." He reaches into his jacket pocket and pulls out his notebook. He points to the eleven names listed there, including Maggie's father and Bùi Xuân Phái, and the brief descriptions he has written of more than two dozen pieces of art. "These are the ones I could remember off the top of my head," he says.

"Tư," Maggie says, her eyes twinkling as she draws the notebook toward her. "This is brilliant. Can I make a copy? I'd like to give it to Professor Devereux at the university. I think it could help."

Tư hesitates, suddenly feeling territorial. Isn't the point to keep this work out of foreign hands? "This professor," he says, "he is not Vietnamese?"

"Việt Kiều," says Maggie.

"Like you," says Tư, feeling deflated.

"Not exactly," she says. "He sounds very French."

Tư stares idly at a painting propped up on the arms of a chair. A man looks out a window, a faint reflection of his face in the glass, a grey sea beyond.

"Do you like that?" Maggie asks.

"I don't know," says Tư, shrugging.

"Well, how does it make you feel?"

The confusion must show on his face. "What's your

instinctive reaction?" she asks. "What does your gut say?"

Tư's gut doesn't really speak except when it's hungry or interested in a girl. His instinct makes suggestions occasionally, but he largely ignores them. "Kind of lonely?" he ventures.

"That's interesting," she says with a glimmer of a smile that Tư doesn't know how to interpret.

"Am I right?" he asks tentatively.

"It's not a question of right or wrong, Tư. It's subjective."

Subjectivity is a dangerous business: the party certainly doesn't encourage anyone to have an independent opinion. But has he not just put his hand into subjectivity's fire? Does he see loneliness where she sees hope?

"What is your subjective opinion?" he asks.

"It's like he has lost something or perhaps someone at sea, or maybe he wishes he could be on the other side where he imagines a better life for himself. Whatever the case, something is more compelling out there in that empty space than in the world that surrounds him. You feel his alienation, and yes, it is lonely," she says.

Hah! thinks Tư, so I am both subjective *and* right.

"I know that feeling," she says. "We probably all do. That's the power of art. Do you?"

Ôi zồi ôi, he thinks, what a question. He clears his throat before answering. "Sometimes by Hoàn Kiếm Lake you can have thoughts about, you know, life, feeling small, why we are here on earth. It doesn't matter if all that traffic is honking at your back."

"Is that loneliness, or existentialism?" she asks.

He opts for loneliness, not knowing the other word. "It's lonely because these are thoughts you cannot share with anyone."

"But you have just shared them with me."

Hưng has nodded off while sitting on the grass mat outside his shack, listening to Lan appreciate his soup for a third night in a row, her delicate swallow, her contented sigh. He has slipped into a dream of floating on water. He is lying on his back, the sun high in the sky, dragonflies roosting on his stomach.

"Foreign lady for Mr. Hưng!" Van shouts, tearing Hưng from his pleasant reverie.

"Goodness gracious, Van!"

"I'm sorry to disturb you again," says a figure in the dark.

He knows her voice but her face is in shadow. "Come inside, dear, so I can see you," he says. "If anyone has disturbed me it is this one here. The dim-witted boy thinks I'm deaf."

Van ignores this, fixated on the box in Maggie's hands.

"Ah, a lemon meringue pie," Hưng says, nodding at the box himself.

"Not today," she says, kneeling down beside him and peeling back the lid.

The old man picks up a brown lump between his thumb and forefinger. "It looks very much like a fungus." He turns the lump around and sniffs it. "Or an animal dropping. Off you go, Van," Hưng says, putting the lump into the boy's hands and pulling another one from the box.

"It's called a truffle," Maggie says. "Try it."

Hưng pulls his lips back and clasps the thing between his dentures, which sink into its molten centre.

"Tastes like neither a fungus nor a turd," he says, pulling the truffle away from his mouth to examine its interior. "Quite unusual."

"Have you ever had chocolate?"

"Ah," he says. "That's what it is. Not since the French days."

Maggie reaches into her purse and pulls out a sheet of paper. She unfolds it and lays it across the top of the cake box. "I wanted to ask a favour," she says.

Hưng sucks the chocolate stuck to the roof of his mouth and picks up the flimsy piece of paper. He pats his chest, then says, "Fetch my glasses for me, would you? They're just inside the door on the little table to your right."

"Bình drew this for me," Maggie says, handing Hưng his glasses. "Based on a description of a piece of my father's work."

Hưng raises the picture to his good eye, holding his glasses as if examining a diamond through a magnifying glass. "Huh. He's good," says Hưng.

"I know. And he says he's not an artist. Does the drawing mean anything to you?"

"It's a couple of Indochinese tigers attacking each other in a cave," Hưng says. "Is it in the tiger's nature to turn on his brother? I don't know. Perhaps they are too hungry to care, perhaps there has been some betrayal. I would venture that it might be a metaphor. Perhaps we, the Vietnamese, are the tigers, and this is the war we fought amongst ourselves once we were rid of the colonial enemy."

Hưng drops the paper onto his chest. He removes his glasses and rubs his eyes.

"Your father obviously did very sophisticated work," he says. "I would have liked to know such a man. As I'm sure you would have."

Hưng wishes he could offer Maggie something more. He has the sense that it is not an interpretation of the art that she is really after, but rather an interpretation of the artist, the man.

He remains on his stoop after she wanders off in the dark to her waiting taxi. He stares out at the blinking lights on the other side of the pond. "If only I could remember him," he says aloud.

"The illustrator," says a disembodied voice in the dark.

He's not sure if he's heard this correctly. For decades he has trained himself not to hear her voice, to block out its register. "The illustrator," he says, reclaiming the word from the ether, taking possession of it just in case.

Hưng falls asleep with the word in his mouth, waking to wonder if Lý Văn Hai might have been the one who populated the pages of *Fine Works of Spring* with bold caricatures and allegorical drawings, pictures Lan used to admire, touching them with the tips of her fingers, inadvertently leaning her back into Hưng's chest as she did so, him not-so-inadvertently inhaling her hair.

But how can he possibly prove the illustrator was Lý Văn Hai in the absence of the journal?

As he pushes his cart home later that morning, he thinks about a poem published in that spring volume. "When you find yourself upon the threshold of the door to your new home," Đạo had written during the brief but euphoric blush that followed the '54 revolution. He remembers an illustration of a house, its door open, a welcoming hearth in the room. Hưng repeats the words to himself, generating speed, hoping to take a verbal run at that door, skip over the threshold, find the rest of the poem waiting inside.

"When you find yourself upon the threshold of the door to your new home," he says aloud, dropping his hands from his cart, coming to an abrupt halt in the middle of the road. Damn. Nothing. Motorcycles honk and veer around him. He leans against his cart, putting his elbows upon it, closing and rubbing his eyes. Perhaps his sudden recall is limited only to that particular poem he was able to share with Maggie. He had been hopeful of a broader recovery.

Hưng arrives home and parks his cart behind his shack, hauling his pots down to the bank of the pond. He stacks them there, abandoning them for a moment while he returns to his shack. He riffles through the piles of paper he collects to feed his fires, some of them a metre high, looking for *Fine Works of Spring*. He catches himself midway through the second pile and smacks his forehead with his palm. What is he *doing?* The journal is long gone. Every single one of his papers was gone by the time the Party's vice squad overturned his shack in the spring of 1964.

His breathing had slowed as he caught sight of the Minsk motorbikes parked in front of his shack that morning. They were throwing his few belongings out the front door. His clothes flew across the threshold, his tea canister rolled down the slope; bits of straw from his mattress filled the air.

Hưng parked his cart and dared to approach his shack. "Sirs, what is it you are looking for?" he asked through the doorway.

"Are you Hưng?" an officer shouted.

"No, sir."

"Well, this Hưng is harbouring anti-revolutionary literature. You can tell him when you next see him that the Party is well informed of his traitorous connections. If he's harbouring the evidence, we'll find it."

But you're too late, he could have told them. You'll find nothing to implicate the man. Those papers are already gone. In fact, the man you are after—keeper of poetry and believer in the beauty of humanity—that Hưng is gone.

He proceeded to carry his pots down to the pond and scrub them in its brown water. He lingered over the task, not turning around again until he heard the revving of motorbike engines. He caught a glimpse of movement in the doorway to Lan's shack. She was hiding, keeping watch. He refused to acknowledge her.

One of the officers tossed a burning rag through the door of his shack as he drove away on his motorbike. Smoke billowed through the doorway; the interior burst into flame. Hưng quickly plunged the largest of his pots into the pond and filled it with water. He ran awkwardly up the muddy slope, water sloshing from side to side, and heaved the contents of the pot through his front door. He did this over and over until the flames relented. The guts of his shack were charred, but the structure remained.

———

Hưng eases himself down onto his straw mattress. He runs his fingers over his few strands of hair. He lies back and listens to the belch of an obstinate water buffalo somewhere in the middle distance. He hears the ruffle of a duck shaking water off its back, the blip of a fish gulping a spider off the surface of the pond, the whir of a dragonfly's wings. A crow lands on his roof; he hears the tick tack tick of its nails across the tin surface.

He caresses the soft mole on his cheek for comfort as he used to do as a child. It is the colour of asphalt, the texture of moss. A birthmark, a simple birthmark, as his Uncle Chiến had assured him long ago, not a curse at all.

Where Hưng had hoped to be able to offer Bình and Tư a poem by Đạo in celebration of the upcoming Mid-Autumn Festival, he will prepare a special lunch for the family instead. Cooking is something no one can steal from him—not poverty nor the Party, not a war, not a girl, not age. Since Tư shows no signs of getting married, this might be the last opportunity Hưng ever has to prepare a feast for him and his family. He will invite the lovely Maggie as well.

He will roast a whole pig on a spit. He has done this only once before, years ago for a wedding banquet in the shanty-town, fashioning a spit out of an axle and digging an oblong pit for a great fire that three young men had to feed for twelve hours. He did not ask where that pig had come from. How could he blame people who had been hungry for so long, particularly on an occasion of such celebration?

Hưng will pay for this pig himself. He will speak to Anh, perhaps travel to the countryside on Saturday in search of a discount; he will barter like the expert he is. He will dig another oblong pit, spreading the coals unevenly so that the fire will be hotter near the shoulders and cooler by the back and loins. He will make sure to cover the ears and the penis so that they do not char and crumble away—an oversight on his part the last time.

Bright Star

The old man has specially decorated his shack today. Tư thinks the red streamers fluttering from his roof are a bit excessive; this isn't a wedding, after all. Hưng greets them robustly with two-handed handshakes. He has dressed up for the occasion, wearing his Metropole trousers, the ones that make him look like a trumpet player in a military band, topped with an old jacket of Bình's, the sleeves rolled up, a red silk handkerchief tucked into the breast pocket.

Hưng brings out a jug of rice wine as soon as they arrive. Phương is the first and last to fill his glass. They recline on grass mats and straw-stuffed pillows the old man has laid down on the ground in front of his shack, and chew some betel nut at his insistence, a practice Tư's mother normally disapproves of but is willing to ignore on this occasion.

Tư chomps down hard on a leaf wrapped around slivers of betel. He is pulling bitter red fibres off his tongue when Maggie finally arrives out of breath, apologizing for being late.

She is Maggie but no longer Maggie. She is wearing an indigo-blue *áo dài* embroidered with golden cranes that hugs the perfect peaches of her breasts and skims her narrow waist, her hips. Her hair is pulled back, her skin glows and Tư wishes he could bury his face in her neck and run his hands up and down her silk-covered body.

"What does your name mean?" he finds himself asking as soon as his breath returns.

"My name?" she says, shaking her head and kneeling down beside him. "I don't know. I was named after a Scottish woman my father boarded with when he was at school in the U.S. It's short for Margaret."

"You should have a Vietnamese name," Tư says. "To match your *áo dài*."

Tư can smell the pepper sweet of lavender emanating from her skin. Show some respect, he silently berates his penis, folding his hands in his lap. He turns his head to the left to admire the pig, the whole roasted pig that Hưng is tending just metres away from them. It is a lavish and very expensive thing the old man has done: threading the entire animal on a spit and turning and roasting it for hours and hours until it has reached this glowing perfection.

Hưng's neighbours have begun to line up with their bowls. The old man has special power—he is the heart of this place, was the heart of the Beauty of Humanity Movement—he brings people together, keeps them fed.

Once thirty people have wandered off happy with their bowls of pork and rice, it is finally the family's turn to eat. Tư cannot wait to taste that pig, but first his father, not normally a speech maker, stands and offers thanks to Hưng, for all he gives to them in his role as adopted patriarch, for the care he has offered three generations of their family.

"You don't know this story, Maggie," Tư's father says, "perhaps you've never heard it either, Phương, but let me tell you about the happy day Hưng and I were reunited."

Tư wonders why his father has chosen to speak of this. It sounds like the kind of speech you would make if reminiscing about the dead.

"When the war ended, I came back to Hanoi after years in the countryside in search of a job," his father begins. "I worked as a candle maker until the Russians set up a Ping-Pong factory that paid much better wages. And that is where I met Anh," he says, glancing at Tư's mother. "We were lucky to find each other, but times were difficult. There was no rice for months, no meat. The real sadness for us, though, was that a child was slow to come. We went to visit herbalists and fortune tellers whom we could pay only with ration cards, which left us with even less to eat, and still no child.

"I began to wonder if this could be because my ancestors felt neglected. We had never built a shrine for my father, Đạo, you see: my mother and I spent the first years praying for his return, and the next years having to defend him against my mother's relatives, who blamed my father for our misfortune.

"It was Hưng who sent word to us in the village. I was nine or ten at the time, playing outside in the courtyard, when a man on a motorbike arrived at the house and, for no apparent reason, pressed a coconut into my hands. It was so light I was sure it was hollow. My mother shook it, then smashed it with a mallet, and there among the pieces of shell was a small folded piece of paper. It was a letter from Hưng with the sad news of my father's death and a promise to honour him for the rest of his life.

"I knew I had to find Hưng. Eventually I found my way here, where he had kept the incense burning for my father. I do not quite know how to put the feeling into words, but it was like arriving at the place where a river finally floods into the sea.

"And what do you think happened then?" Bình says, leaning into his toes. "Destiny finally smiled upon us. That is why we called him Tư, our bright star. The one who heralded the arrival of Đổi mới."

Tư's father turns to the old man to thank him for having been there to celebrate every occasion of Tư's life. From his birth to every Tet holiday to his graduation, to the betrothal that Tư's father says he is sure must not be long off for his son, to the marriage and fatherhood that will follow, the birth of a fourth generation who will be blessed to have a patriarch in Hưng.

Tư blushes and hangs his head.

"I fear I will not be here to see that happy day," says Hưng.

No pressure! thinks Tư, looking over at Phương—twenty-nine and not married—for help. But Phương is beyond helping: he is boozy-eyed and useless already, lying on his side, leaning on his elbow, his head slumping toward his shoulder.

Tư is about to beg for a change of subject, when thankfully Hưng says, "Let us eat."

They begin with a mild soup with pig tail and crunchy lotus root, followed by some shredded cabbage and sausage stuffing pulled from inside the roasted pig's mouth, and then the pork itself, which melts in their mouths, all its fatty parts, its salted crispy skin, balanced with clean rice and water spinach sautéed with garlic, and finally a crunchy salad of diced pig ears and bamboo shoots. Every time Tư tastes Old Man Hưng's cooking he feels as if his mouth learns something new.

Unfortunately it starts to rain just then, forcing them all to pick up their bowls and follow the old man into his cramped quarters. It is close and cozy inside Hưng's shack with the rain clattering down on the corrugated tin. Tư and his father sit on the edge of the mattress, where a drunken Phương is now lying down, and Maggie kneels on the rattan mat on the floor beside Tư's mother, the old man beside her, pouring cups of tea.

"Would you like to greet my grandfather?" Tư asks Maggie.

Hưng gestures. "Over here, my dear."

Tư has a slight feeling of resentment, as if the old man is competing with him for Maggie's attention. He notices a full bowl of pork and rice sitting on top of Hưng's unlit kerosene stove. "You've left Đạo's bowl here," Tư says, reaching toward it.

"No," says Hưng, waving his hand as he shuffles toward the altar, "I have already given Đạo his bowl."

"Who is this for, then?"

"That? For no one."

Hưng raises his hand in the air once he reaches the altar. He clears his throat and silences the room. "When you find yourself upon the threshold of the door to your new home, fear not, because you will find me there, on the other side, awaiting you, making ready the fire," he says in a measured and silken voice.

Anh reaches for Bình's hand, a gesture of affection between his parents that Tư has never witnessed before. Old Man Hưng is reciting verse. Is this Grandfather Đạo's poetry? But where has he suddenly found the words? Tư is about to ask the old man to continue, but the moment appears to have passed, and with it his memory. Hưng turns away from the altar, the spark within him extinguished.

Hưng has no energy to get undressed, drained by the effort of those words. Do words come before footsteps or is it the reverse? Does the order in which you acquire them dictate which you'll first lose? Hưng sleeps like a baby now, new to the world. He is at a loss to name the shapes and shadows that appear in his dreams. He is a blank slate upon which history will write its story. But he will wake before the story's end, he is sure of it. He will counter the lies written there. He will fill in the gaps that remain.

The Lady Next Door

The sky is heavy and grey, and Maggie sits behind Tư and his father on the Honda Dream II, riding like a Vietnamese lady with her jacket on backward and a mask over her mouth. She seems more and more Vietnamese each time Tư sees her. She now eats her noodles noisily in the way that makes them taste best, and much to his relief she does not grip him around the middle anymore when she sits behind him on the motorbike—she has developed her motorbike muscles.

Arriving at the bank of the river this morning, they find several of Hưng's other regular customers but no sign of the old man himself. He must have been forced to move to a new location. Usually they would have had news of this through the network of mouths in the Old Quarter. When the others see Bình pulling up, they know not to take the situation personally. They simply shrug and get back onto their motorbikes and seek some alternative place to start the day.

But Tư and his father both worry about Hưng's absence. Was the celebration the other day too much for him? Could he be unwell? That evening, after dinner at home, they climb aboard the motorbike and make their way to the shantytown. The dirt road down to the pond punishes Tư's behind, forcing him to stand for the last stretch as if he were riding a horse.

Bình parks the bike by Hưng's shack, which appears to be secured with a chain and padlock. The lady next door, sitting on her threshold weaving a basket from river grasses by the light of a spitting fire, tells them she has not seen the old man in a couple of days.

Hưng's cart and brazier are gone, so he must have set off with the intention of serving breakfast. Did she see him that morning? Was there anything unusual? Did he seem well enough? Might he have had a flu?

She had not seen him that morning. He leaves hours before she wakes up. "He did leave a bowl of pork and rice on my doorstep after your party, but he has not spoken to me for over forty years."

That is a lifetime of silence between neighbours, almost two of Tư's lifetimes, and yes, thinks Tư, she is never here at Tet, and even the day of the Mid-Autumn Festival she was not among the thirty people who lined up with their bowls, despite being his closest neighbour.

"Why has he not spoken to you?" Tư's father asks, rare astonishment in his voice. Hưng is not a man who has enemies.

The woman looks to the ground as if ashamed of the answer. She raises her eyes sheepishly and stares at Bình.

"Ahh," says Tư's father.

Tư looks between them, confused. Bình nods at the old woman and turns away.

"What is it?" Tư asks his father as they set off on foot toward the river. "Why does he not speak to her?"

"Did you see the regret in her eyes? The pain? My guess is that long ago she broke our Hưng's heart."

Tư feels rather chastened: he has never thought of the old man as having a love life, and it must have been something of a dramatic love life to take him from the light of loving this woman all the way to the dark of not speaking to her. Tư thinks about this as he and his father push the motorbike along the route that the old man is most likely to take into the Old Quarter given the size and awkwardness of his cart. It is three kilometres to the bridge where he last served breakfast. They peer into dark alleyways and call out Hưng's name, but apart from a drunk and a mangy dog, no one responds to their cries.

Tư and his father sit down when they reach the bank of the river and watch the struggling moon. "We're lucky to have each other," says Bình. "I was never able to help my father." A man's worth is principally his worth as a son, and this is something Tư recognizes his father has been denied.

Bình carries on talking, reminiscing about his boyhood, telling Tư how he'd felt a stranger growing up in a household of women in his mother's village. It was only in being reacquainted with Hưng all those years later that the feeling abated. He came to see himself as part of a lineage, Hưng the bridge between his own small life and a much longer and greater story. "And that was your fault, wasn't it," he says, slapping his son's thigh. "Your stubborn refusal to join me on this earth until I discovered that bridge to the past."

Tư thinks of Maggie, faced with much the same predicament. Is it that she feels a stranger in the world in the absence of a family history? Unattached? Without a bridge? Family is everything in Vietnam.

Bình leans forward and uses the cuff of his shirt to wipe dirt off the toe of his shoe. "You know, there were times after learning of his death that my mother would get so angry at my father," he says. "She would pace back and forth cursing him. Đạo could be very stubborn and arrogant. She blamed him for arousing the anger of the Party, for denying her a husband and me a father."

This is the first time Tư has heard anyone suggest that his grandfather was anything less than a hero.

"We always have a very romantic view of those we lose, especially a martyr," his father says. "We forget a martyr is just a man, a man who dared for his principles, but a man nonetheless—a less-than-perfect human being."

It's something of a relief to Tư to hear this. It is impossible to consider yourself a worthy person when there are only heroes to measure yourself against.

The following night, after another morning without breakfast, they multiply their efforts. Maggie brings a map, which makes it easy to rule out the alleyways that are too narrow for Old Man Hưng's cart. They can rule out the busiest roads as well, unless of course Hưng had another spasm of desire to seek out Maggie at the Metropole. If not, that leaves six, possibly seven routes Hưng might have taken between the shantytown and the bridge. Bình traces these onto the map with one of his soft blue drafting pencils.

They set out for the shantytown just after 9 p.m., Maggie riding the Honda Dream II with Tư's parents, Tư, Phương and his little sister on Phương's bike close behind. They cut their engines on the rise just before the shantytown, flicking the kickstands down and leaning the bikes into the dirt.

A boy suddenly appears out of the dark. "How much you pay for that bike, Mister?" he asks Tư's father of the Honda Dream II.

"Hey, I know you," says Maggie.

"Did you bring a cake?" the boy asks her.

"Not this time," she says. "Listen, have you seen Old Man Hưng?"

"No," says the boy.

What is Maggie doing bringing cakes to the shantytown? Tư wonders.

"Do you want to watch these bikes for us?" his father asks.

"Five thousand đồng," says the boy.

"Five hundred," says Tư's father.

The boy stuffs his hands into his pockets and kicks the dirt.

"And I'll bring you some cake next time," Maggie says.

"Yes, sir," the boy says in English, transformed by this sweet promise.

———

Tư feels exhilarated by the slight menace of the quiet night, a tension heightened by volunteering for the route that covers the most dangerous streets and the presence of Maggie by his side. They call out the old man's name every few steps, looking in doorways and peering down alleyways and seeing more than a few homeless people wrapped in cardboard along the way. A dog lunges toward them and growls, forcing Maggie to retreat, and in one street a woman shouts from above: "It's late, you drunks. Go home!"

On another street there are shameful things going on, though thankfully it is not bright enough for them to see anything more than the outline of a woman on her knees.

Maggie clings to Tư's arm and says, "I didn't know Hanoi could be so depressing."

"Imagine Saigon," Tư replies—but oh the delicate grip of her hand, the sweet smell of her skin reaching through the briny mist of the crayfish they had for dinner. He wishes he could reach out and squeeze her neck, that sacred place where the spirit resides. He'd inch his hand up and touch her hair, which he imagines being as silken as the feather back of a dove.

"I wonder if this is what it feels like to have a brother," she says, and the sudden swell of romance within him subsides.

It is well after midnight by the time they finally reach the bridge. They are trailed now by three drunk young men who spilled out of a hidden bar in an alleyway half a kilometre ago and have been mimicking them ever since. "Hưng! Oh,

Mr. Hưng! Where are you, Old Man Hưng?" they drunk-
enly mock.

The moonlight is beaming down through the clouds.
They can hear Phương singing under the bridge. They listen
to him filling the space with a tenor voice so glorious that it
even silences the drunks. This is no rap but a ballad, blooming petal by petal until it explodes into flower, at which point
Phương belts out a chorus of rising words. He lands on a
single note so pure it should cause the trucks on the bridge
above to kill their engines. He holds the note for a full
breathless minute, at which point the drunks, in their enthusiasm, resume shouting.

Phương stops singing and emerges from underneath the
bridge. "Who the hell are these guys?" he shouts.

"We can't get rid of them!" Tư yells. One of the drunks
burps and slumps to the ground. The other two collapse in
a laughing heap beside him.

"Phương," says Maggie, "that was beautiful."

Phương snorts. "I thought you didn't like my singing.
You said it was like a disease."

"What?"

"That day in the van. You said my rap was 'infectious.'"

"But I meant it in a good way," she says. "Like something that takes you over, possesses you. Honestly, I could
listen to you for hours."

"Huh," says Phương, sneering at Tư.

"What was that song?" Maggie asks.

"The one I'm doing for my audition."

"What audition?" asks Tư.

"For *Vietnam Idol*."

How could Tư not have known about this? He hadn't realized just how far apart he and Phương had grown in recent weeks. "But what about Hanoi Poison?"

"Dead for the time being. Got to make it past the censors. But after that? Once everyone's listening? Hanoi Poison will be back," he says with a wicked laugh.

They all turn their heads at the sound of footsteps. Tư's father is running toward them. Out of breath, he stops, bends at the waist and clutches his kneecaps.

"We found him," he says, pressing a fist into his lower back as he straightens up. "He's not far, but he's been hurt. He can't walk. Anh is with him. Who are these guys?" he asks of the drunks in a heap. "Oh, who cares. Can they help?"

Hưng's leg is throbbing as if his heart has decided to relocate; his throat feels as if he has just drunk a bucketful of sand. He opens his eyes and blinks at the blur of lights out a window. It would appear he is lying in the back seat of a taxi, his head in Bình's lap as if he were a child, though not any child he remembers being.

What the hell is happening? he wonders. Please tell me I haven't been in another accident. He remembers heading over to the Metropole with news for Maggie a couple of days ago, the rain so torrential that he abandoned his cart by Hàng Da Market, paying the bird seller a good amount of đồng to keep an eye on it. After that he remembers very little: a great wave of water rolling over his shoulder, the sound of skidding cars, being bounced against a fender, flying through fog, the great pain in his body from the waist down as he lay twisted in a muddy ditch, one of his feet facing an improbable direction, drifting in and out of sleep.

Bình is saying something about going to the hospital, which causes a surge of panic in Hưng's chest. "No no," he cries out, "not the hospital. It's full of dead people."

"What's he talking about?" Tư asks.

"Perhaps he hit his head. He seems to be confused about the year."

Confused about the year, thinks Hưng, but the year that the Americans bombed Bach Mai Hospital was a year of confusion. He just wants to go home to his shack. "Bình," he says. "Are you taking me home?"

"No."

"Not the hospital," Hưng repeats.

"You'll come to our house. We'll send for a doctor."

"But my flower," says Hưng.

"Don't worry about your flower," says Bình. "I'll go and check on all your plants tomorrow."

"*Lan*," says Hưng. "I mean the orchid."

"Yes, I know," he hears Bình reassure him as he closes his eyes.

The Rainbow That Fell to Earth

Old Man Hưng's body is broken, but there is more energy in his voice than Tư has ever heard. He is yelling something from Tư's bed, where he has been resting for nearly a week now, his leg tied to a splint Bình made in his carpentry workshop.

Hưng was hit by a car, but he doesn't remember what the vehicle looked like; the rain was heavy that day, the fog thick. Tư just wishes he could tell them something about the vehicle because he'd find that car and make the driver pay.

In his confusion, the old man's stories are frequent and revealing, and Tư wonders if he might get him to talk about the lady who lives in the shack next to his.

Tư's bedroom smells musty with woody teas and ointments and general old-manness. Tư feels guilty every time he comes in here, ashamed by the thought of Old Man Hưng lying on a mattress that has absorbed thousands of Tư's fantasies, a good percentage of which lately have involved Maggie. He absolves his guilt by thinking of these nocturnal acts as practice for married life. He needs to develop lasting power and can only do so by training the muscles. Thus far he can't manage to hold on for more than two and a half minutes, and only then when he deliberately conjures up someone ugly.

The old man groans, rousing from sleep, as Tư rests a bucket of soapy water on the floor and sits down on the edge of his mattress. Tư peels back the bedcovers and unties the straps of Hưng's splint. It looks awful: a purple bruise runs all the way up his leg past his knee, the foot is so swollen the skin is stretched taut and the ankle is slightly twisted.

Tư squeezes excess water from the sponge. "We spoke to the lady who lives next door to you the other day," he ventures, as he washes soap from between the old man's toes.

Old Man Hưng sighs. "She sings to herself sometimes. When she's bent over washing her pots in the pond, I can hear her. She'll turn around and smile for a moment, a smile just for me. It really is the most beautiful thing a man can see."

"She said you have not spoken to her in some time."

The old man raises his head and looks at Tư through his milky eyes. "Đạo?"

"Yes, Hưng?" says Tư.

"She was so beautiful, but not like your Amie," he says, sinking back into his pillow. "Her beauty was only on the outside and I was fooled into believing it was something deeper.

"She could not read herself, but I read to her, I read everything you wrote and she drank in your words and she used to say that maybe one day I would have a restaurant again, and there you would be, surrounded by the men who so admired you, and she would work for me and all would be as it had once been, only even better because you would be free to write and the girl would always be beside me. And then she shattered this most perfect dream.

"It was my fault," Hưng continues. "I failed you."

How could Hưng, the one who has acted as patriarch of their family, guardian of the ancestral shrine, possibly have failed Đạo? Tư has seen him do nothing but protect and keep alive the memory of his grandfather.

"You did not fail me, Hưng," says Tư.

"Đạo?" Hưng says with less certainty this time, the clouds in his head parting.

Hưng arrived home that fateful morning after peddling his pondweed noodles. Just a few days before, he'd dared suggest to Lan that they might join their shacks, and he was preoccupied and pained by his inability to read her reaction. He wondered if she was quietly deliberating or discussing it with her grandmother. He would simply have to wait the agonizing wait until she spoke her mind, though he could not resist embarking on a certain amount of reorganization inside his shack in anticipation.

It had been such a fine day, not a cloud or a plane in the sky, he felt giddy returning home with a new trowel thanks

to a customer who was a blacksmith. He parked his cart
and made his way down to the pond with the first two of
his pots. As he was squatting on the muddy bank rinsing
the second pot, something caught his eye—a sudden flash
of light, a display of colour, as if a rainbow had just fallen
to earth.

He turned his head to see Lan, standing such that from
where he was squatting, her head blocked out the sun, standing as if her head *were* the sun. He raised his hand to his
brow so that he might take in the full length of her beauty.
He gasped at the sight of her in a luxurious *áo dài*, just like
the one he'd always imagined she should wear. She was
wrapped in sky-blue silk embroidered with gold thread, perfectly tailored to hug her small breasts, her narrow waist, the
slight curve of her hips.

"You always said I deserved it," she said.

He was speechless, enraptured, beaming with a happiness unlike any he had ever experienced before. He felt it
burn through every inch of him.

But as she stepped aside, her head no longer blocking the
sun, her face became visible. His smile faded. Had she given
herself away to a man? Had she been lured into prostitution?

"Who bought this for you?" he asked tentatively.

"I bought it myself," she said.

"But however did you get the money?"

He watched her grow uncertain. She batted her eyelashes, then quickly glanced away, just long enough for a
terrible gaping hole to open up in his stomach. He turned
and stared through the doorway of his shack.

"Hưng," she said, reaching for his forearm, but he shook off her hand, marching stiffly toward his shack.

He stood on the threshold and cast his eyes about the room. He scanned the ceiling and the walls. He fell to his knees and rifled through the piles of his few clothes and belongings, then lifted the corner of the mattress. He crawled under the mattress, suspending it on his back.

His papers were gone. The journals, every issue of the magazine, every poem Đạo had ever written out for him or Hưng himself had copied down.

Hưng threw down the mattress. She'd taken the words of these men, taken all that was left of them and sold them to a stranger? And then clothed herself in silk?

"Who did you sell them to?" he shouted through the door of his shack.

"The man who sells firewood," Lan said, stepping backward, beginning to cry.

Hưng's eyes darted left and right as he considered running in search of the man and retrieving those papers before they fed someone's fire, but the truth was *she* was the fire. She would set light to whatever she needed to keep her flame burning. She had been using him in much the same way.

"Get out," was all he said. "Get out."

A week later he found four pillows on his doorstep— four plump, sky-blue silk pillows stuffed with duck down. But Hưng could not forgive her. He could not forgive himself. He could not even acknowledge the pillows, leaving them to weather on his threshold, bleached by the sun, drenched by the rain until they were mildewed beyond recovery, much like his heart.

How had he begun speaking of the girl next door? Here he is with Bình now, propped up against the wall, telling the man who is like a son to him about the moment when he felt the last of humanity's goodness slip away. With the loss of those papers he gave up hope, spending years in silence, wondering whether anything left in the world mattered. It was only with Bình's appearance in the shantytown all those years later that he had recovered the sense that anything did.

"I was such a fool, Bình," says Hưng. "I lost everything because of a foolish heart. Am I dying? Why else would I even consider regret?"

"Shh, Hưng, it is not your time yet," Bình says, passing him a bowl of pickled eggplant, the only thing Hưng has had any appetite for since his accident.

Hưng raises his chopsticks to his mouth.

Old Man Hưng is revealing secrets. He is teaching Tư exactly how to make his phở. It is late at night, and he is yelling the instructions from Tư's bed, the words floating down the staircase to the kitchen.

"I can smell the caramel!" the old man yells. "Those onions are done."

Tư pulls the first batch of browned onions and ginger away from the heat. He is beginning to see that this is not simply a cooking exercise, but one in patience. For a truly superior broth you need to boil the beef and bones gently for hours, skimming the grey film off the surface of the water before adding the lightly browned onions and ginger, carrot and radish, cinnamon, cloves and star anise, then returning it to a soft boil for several more hours before straining the broth and adding a pungent splash of *nước mắm*. But why has the old man ordered Tư's mother and father out of the kitchen? It is as if Hưng has decided to skip a generation and pass this legacy directly on to him.

Old Man Hưng wakes Tư for the final preparations well before sunrise, banging a cane against the floor above. Tư rises stiffly from the table where he had fallen asleep, the air dewy like a spring morning after heavy rains, and removes the broth from the heat over which it has been simmering all night. He strains it bowl by bowl through a sieve. He skims off the fat that rises to the surface as it cools, and when he sees no more evidence of shine, he adds salt and fish sauce, testing it for taste. He chops the herbs, slices the beef thinly across the grain, and places a handful of fresh rice noodles in a sieve, ready to be immersed in boiling water.

"Lastly, prepare a cup of ginseng and say a few words of prayer," the old man instructs from above. "If you have any doubts, ask Bình to taste the broth. He will tell you the truth."

Tư's father peers into the pot and inhales. He studies the surface before dipping in his spoon. He stares at the broth on the spoon from all angles, examining it for clarity and colour, making sure no fat is visible as it cools, then finally slides it into his mouth. He savours it, then inhales through an open mouth to see how long the flavour lingers.

"Good," he declares.

Does he mean okay, good enough, or really good? Where on the spectrum of good does it land?

There's no time to adjust it in any case. They hear the footsteps of the first customers in the courtyard. Word has travelled throughout the Old Quarter: the sun has only just lifted over the lip of the coast and a lineup has already begun to form right out into the alley, the familiar faces of people carrying the bowls, spoons and chopsticks they have brought from home.

"Hah," they say when they see Tư in the kitchen, trying to conceal their looks of disappointment, "the apprentice."

"Temporary situation," he assures them as he deposits the noodles into their bowls and ladles in the broth. He lays down the slices of beef then adds a sprinkle of chopped green herbs, trying to perform this gesture with the same dramatic flourish as Old Man Hưng, though in his first few attempts more green lands on the floor than in the bowls.

It is hot and steamy in the room, a dozen people now squatting on the floor and occupying all available chairs— including the seat of the Honda Dream II—slurping and burping and chatting away to one another in Tư's family's kitchen. There's a lot of creaking overhead, as half a dozen people have carried their bowls upstairs to pay their respects to Old Man Hưng, and there are still a good number more customers lined up in the courtyard outside.

No one comments on the phở, but they empty their bowls before rinsing them. Tư can only interpret this as praise.

Maggie has just arrived, and so have Phương and his father. Tư knows Phương, at least, will give him an honest answer about the broth.

"It's good," Phương says, clearly surprised.

"What kind of good?"

"The kind of good where I would like to eat it again tomorrow."

"That is good," Tư says, smiling with relief.

Maggie climbs the stairs with her steaming bowl carefully balanced between her thumbs and middle fingers. She waits on the landing and inhales from the bowl while Hưng's visitors file out of Tư's room.

Bình sits with the old man, their bowls empty and abandoned at the side of the bed. Hưng pushes himself upright with Maggie's arrival, Bình fluffing up and repositioning the pillow behind the old man's back.

"How are you?" she asks, setting her bowl down on top of the bookshelf.

Hưng throws back the bedcovers to reveal his old man's leg. It is swollen and as purple as an eggplant. Maggie pulls the bedcovers back over his leg and smooths them across his chest. His shirt is unbuttoned and he is so thin that the skin between his ribs flutters with his heartbeat.

"You have lovely hands," says Old Man Hưng, looking mournful for a moment. But then he suddenly brightens, grabs hold of one of her hands, shakes it. He frantically pats his shirt pocket with his other hand, the bedcovers, his thighs.

"Are these the clothes I was wearing when you found me?" he asks Bình.

"Well, no," says Bình, "those have been laundered."

"Can you bring me the shirt?"

Bình rises and opens Tư's armoire and pulls out Hưng's shirt.

"Check the pocket," says Hưng.

Bình pulls out a frayed business card stamped with the insignia of the Hotel Metropole, as well as a piece of paper folded into four. He unfolds it to find Đạo's faded portrait, removed from both its frame and its place on the altar.

"Turn it over," says Hưng.

"Contributors, March 1956," Bình reads from a page with a torn edge. "Here is Đạo, listed as one of the poets, Phan Khôi as editor, and yes, look at this: Lý Văn Hai. The illustrator."

"Oh my God," says Maggie, standing up to look over Bình's shoulder. She covers her hand with her mouth. She coughs. Her eyes fill with tears. There he is: Lý Văn Hai, the artist, her father. Alive. In the company of a circle of men of great talent and courage and feeling.

Hưng pushes himself upright. "This is the reason I was coming to see you, Maggie. Rushing through the rain that day like a man possessed."

Bình turns the paper over to look again at his father's faded portrait.

"It was the only paper I had to offer the woman who drew it, Bình. It's the endpaper from *Fine Works of Spring*. You'll draw a new portrait of Đạo, a far better one. Despite your claims to the contrary, Bình, you are an artist."

"And you, my dear," says Hưng, patting Maggie's hand, "are the daughter of Lý Văn Hai, illustrator of *Fine Works of Spring*."

Community Service

Hưng chomps his dentures back into place after breakfast the following morning and reclines against the pillows of Tư's bed. He has the satisfaction of having delivered Maggie a hero, but has begun to feel diminished himself. There's something humiliating about being in this room with its posters and books and toys. It is the room of a boy. Hưng cannot imagine being such a boy, a boy of 2007. Everything in the room seems alien to him—even the Vietnamese words on the poster of a kitten clinging to a tree branch seem like they're written in a foreign language. What does this mean: "Hang in there, baby?" Don't give up? Does Tư really need this kind of mantra?

When Hưng was Tư's age, he ran a restaurant, lived alone, had not the time nor the opportunity for leisure or friendship or girlfriends. Occasionally, he might have caught sight of a girl through the window of his shop, one who moved in such a way that the fabric of her *áo dài* snaked about her hips as she turned to speak to a companion, or one with a button undone at the neck revealing a tantalizing glimpse of collarbone, but these were more like mystical visions than anything real.

Hưng put his senses to use making soup instead, as his Uncle Chiến had taught him, poking the beef rump to ascertain its freshness, inhaling the scent of star anise to ensure it was fragrant, tasting the broth each morning before anyone else.

Hưng was a man of soup; he still is. These have not been the most lucid or comfortable days, but a broken leg won't stop him. Why would it? Nothing ever has.

"Hang in there, baby," he says, saluting the mewling kitten on the wall just as Tư enters the room. He sits down on the edge of the mattress and pulls a notebook from his knapsack. "There is something I want to show you," he says, flipping to a page.

Hưng squints and peers at the page with his right eye. It's a list of names, a good number of them familiar—artists he knew either in person or by reputation in the days when he still had his shop.

"You wrote this?"

"They were customers of Mr. Võ's," says Tư. "I want to add the names of the artists you remember."

But Hưng does not want to be associated in any way with that traitor Võ. Years ago, shortly after beginning his new life as an itinerant phở seller, Hưng had been making

his way down Nguyễn Hữu Huân Street when he smelled
the weak but distinctive aroma of coffee. His reaction was
primal, as if recognizing one's illegitimate offspring in the
street. He rushed forth in recognition, abandoning his
cart, pushing his way past a man idling in the doorway of
Café Võ.

He hadn't been in there in years, and it was barely rec-
ognizable as the same place with its bare and cracked plaster
walls largely stripped of art, most of it by then hidden away.

"Võ," Hưng said, waving to the owner standing at the
back of the deserted room.

"Hưng? Hưng!"

They grabbed each other by the shoulders, greeting
each other like long-lost brothers, but then suddenly, awkwardly, they snapped apart. They had never really spoken
before, knew each other only by reputation through mutual
customers. They were rivals, in fact, and only desperate circumstances, not familiarity, had drawn them into such an
unusually affectionate embrace.

"They haven't closed you down?" asked Hưng.

Võ shrugged.

"But how is it they allow you to remain open?"

"I give them information they're looking for from time
to time," he said.

Hưng couldn't believe what he was hearing. "Võ,"
Hưng said, "you do understand, don't you? They are using
you as an informant."

"I do my revolutionary duty, that is all," said Võ,
launching into a lecture on the subject.

Hưng had turned away in disgust. He walked back to his cart and resumed pushing his load, though one considerably lighter. His brazier and pots had been stolen during those brief dispiriting moments inside the café.

Handing Tư back his notebook, Hưng says only this to the boy: "Ask yourself how it is that Mr. Võ has been able to hold on to his shop, how the place was not taken from him, how he kept his doors open through all the worst years."

"He's sold the shop now. His wife is dying. They decided to go back to their village."

The man is lying, Hưng thinks. He is quite sure Võ never had a wife.

Managing two jobs leaves Tư feeling capable and exhausted in equal measure. Only time will tell whether he will collapse or adapt to this new schedule and workload. He finds some genuine satisfaction in serving a grateful public, in filling the house and people's stomachs with warmth and good flavour and sending them off into the day—greater satisfaction, he has to admit, than he has experienced serving foreigners lately at work.

After a week he is operating like a well-oiled machine, and perhaps the phở was really only on the okay side of good in the beginning, because now people are paying compliments like: Ah, that satisfies. Ah, the old man has taught you well.

At the start of the following week, though, they have uninvited guests. People are strewn about the kitchen noisily slurping their broth when they hear a knock against the frame of the open door. Tư's customers drop their spoons into their bowls and raise their shirt collars to conceal their faces. Tư's ladle droops in his hand. His mouth hangs open.

"Do you have a licence to operate a business?" one of the officers asks without inflection.

Tư must confess, no. "We are just helping out a friend for a short time."

"Helping him run a business."

"It's more like a community service," says Tư.

"Where money changes hands." The officer shakes the tin can on the table, then tips it over, pocketing the money they are collecting to buy a new cart for the old man.

"This is a donation box, comrade," says Tư. "For our friend because he has been in an accident. For the doctor's bills."

"And who is this friend of yours?"

"Old Man Hưng," Tư says, then curses himself for having given away the old man's name.

"Of course," says the officer. "We should have known."

"Sir, you have to try this," Tư says, stepping forward with a bowl, remembering how his father had seduced the foreman of the crew at the hotel under construction on West Lake. "It will—"

The officer smacks the bowl out of Tư's hand, sending noodles and broth in the direction of some of his customers, who duck but are not, unfortunately, spared. The old man hears the crash and is thump-thumping above with his cane. "What's the matter?" he shouts from the second floor.

The officers are up the stairs before Tư has a chance to reply. The exodus of customers begins, but not before they voluntarily pay a second time for this morning's phở, stuffing coins and damp bills into Tư's hands.

Hưng stares at the yellow ticket in his hands. Three million đồng for operating a business without a licence? Hưng is tempted to screw the yellow paper up into a ball and swallow it. To delight in shitting it out the other end. Has anything really changed since the Party's bold proclamation of greater freedoms? At least he is not on his way to prison right now for calling the officer a machine rather than a man—blind to the beauty of humanity, cold to the touch. Not long ago the police would arrest you if your brother had committed a crime. They would arrest you for wearing the wrong shoes or receiving a letter from abroad. They would arrest you on suspicion of anti-revolutionary sentiment if you were heard to have complained that the rice you stood in line waiting for all day was full of maggots.

Hưng tears the yellow ticket in half lengthwise and stuffs the inky fibres into his mouth.

Tư is worrying about the fine, but also mulling over the question Old Man Hưng posed about Mr. Võ the other day. A theory forms in his mind. Was Mr. Võ really an informant? Had he made a deal with the Party so that he could keep his shop: betraying his customers, reporting their activities to the Party?

Tư tries out his theory on Maggie.

"It wouldn't be all that surprising, would it?" she says. "People have always protected their interests. It's human nature."

Tư finds this deeply disturbing. If we were ruled by human nature there would be anarchy. Everything in a communist life tells you so.

"Self-interest isn't always a bad thing," Maggie says. "It can be a great motivator. And it can be used to improve the lives of others—that's true in the best cases of capitalism. It can lift a whole country out of the mud."

"Maggie," Tư says, interrupting her lesson, "Mr. Võ remembered your father—I'm certain he did. He was afraid to admit it because he was probably the one who reported Lý Văn Hai to the Party."

"But why my father? Countless artists took their coffee at his shop."

"Your father was recruited by Hưng's crowd to help them with the journal, to do the illustrations. He left Mr. Võ's orbit."

Tư looks at Maggie, hoping she understands.

"You don't think it's a coincidence that he sold that whole collection immediately after our visit, do you," she says, casting her eyes to the floor.

Tư shakes his head, "I don't."

A Note Hangs in Mid-Air

Hưng can determine a menu through his nose. He can smell shallots being minced, ginger being shaved, the slow caramelizing of sugar over a flame. It is Tư down below making caramelized fish according to his instructions. Hưng can hear the yelp of the young man's frustration as he pours the fish sauce into the pan and the sugar crystallizes and clumps.

"Turn the heat up as high as it will go!" Hưng shouts down the stairs. "And use a whisk, not a spoon!"

He must refrain from offering further advice, but how he itches to know: Did Tư buy a very fresh fish? Did he poke it and make sure the flesh bounced back in response? Did he smell its skin, make sure its eyes were clear and protruding, its gills bright red and moist? Is it a fish with enough fat underneath its skin?

Anh arrives home from the butcher shop—Hưng can hear the thwack of a good two pounds of rump landing on the wooden cutting block. He need not worry about Tư in the kitchen any longer, Anh is a very good cook; he has been enjoying her dinners for days now. If he were at home, he would be dining on only rice, rice with a splash of fish sauce, all an old man needs, but Anh's dinners seem to be knitting the bones of his leg back together in a way that a bowl of rice each night might not accomplish so quickly.

Perhaps the pace of his healing also has something to do with the company. He does not wish to burden anyone. Since the death of Uncle Chiến more than sixty years ago, Hưng has lived alone and only once imagined it would ever be otherwise.

It suddenly occurs to Hưng that Lan might be worried by his absence, but no—did Tư not mention that he and Bình had spoken to her? She must know his whereabouts, that his stay here is not permanent, that soon he will be home. They may have been silent neighbours for decades, but he still does not like the thought of her feeling abandoned.

The smell of sesame oil wafts up the stairs, and oh, how it makes him long to get back to cooking. He worries he will lose his knack and resolves to exercise the muscles other than those in his broken leg. He can rotate his wrists and neck, bend his other knee, even attempt certain tai chi poses from his prone position.

"Don't strain yourself," he hears Tư say as he enters the room. He's carrying a small white bowl in his hands.

"Tell me if I've got the balance of flavours right," the boy says, kneeling beside the mattress and offering Hưng a spoon with which to taste his shrimp broth.

Hưng doesn't need to taste it; his nose tells him everything he needs to know. "A little more lime juice and it will be perfect."

Tư sniffs the broth. "Of course, Chef Hưng."

"Hah!" Hưng laughs. "I am nothing more than a simple country cook."

"From not such a simple country."

Hưng cocks his head to get a better look at Tư's face. It's not the face of a boy anymore. "Listen," Hưng says conspiratorially, "if you want to really enhance your broth add a pinch of ground, dried anchovy."

"But that's not very Vietnamese," Tư says, his mouth falling open.

"Not so simple, are we."

Phương arrives at their house dressed, uncharacteristically, in skinny jeans. He's trying to get used to the clothes; he'll top the skinny jeans with a white shirt, black jacket and skinny tie for his *Vietnam Idol* audition next week. "What do you think?" he asks Tư, pointing at a picture of a guy with a shaggy Korean-style haircut on a page of a magazine.

With that haircut and a pair of glasses with rectangular rims, he'll resemble the best-looking member of a very squeaky-clean Asian boy band. Girls will be waving signs that say: *I ♥ Phương*, and the government censors will think

Phương an appropriate role model for youth today and everyone will be shocked at the grand finale when Hanoi Poison shows up in his place and starts rapping about freedom of expression and respect for human rights.

Phương is going to perform his audition piece for the family this evening. He has decided to stand upon their table as if it were a stage. They have cleared away the bowls and wiped the rings of fish sauce from the wooden surface. Tư is pleased to see everyone leaning back in their chairs, contented after such a good meal.

Phương asks Tư to press play on the CD player he has brought with him—a recent purchase and a real Sony, no Chinese imitation—and the musical accompaniment begins. It is a track of synthesized violins and whispering ghostly voices. It's like being inside a temple full of ancestors. Phương's falsetto floats there among the voices and then—boom—drops an octave and takes charge with a melody that is beautiful, a tone that is rich.

He has taken a traditional song and transformed it into a modern and emotional ballad even better than the one from *Titanic* by Céline Dion. As he reaches the chorus, the old man above begins banging his cane on the floor, clattering energetically, so much so, in fact, that he is interrupting their concentration.

Maggie leaps up from where she is sitting, rushing over to the staircase, the first among them to realize that Old Man Hưng is actually banging his way down the stairs.

Phương stops singing. A note hangs in mid-air. Tư presses the stop button on the CD player and everyone rushes over to the staircase, each of them reprimanding the old man: "It's too soon for you to walk."

"Stop right there."

"Are you crazy?"

"You're only going to injure yourself."

But the old man is determined, hopping down one more step and leaning into his cane. And he is singing! Singing in a terrible, loud voice like a very drunk man doing karaoke.

Tư's father is tugging the old man's shirtsleeve: "Hưng, Hưng, let's sit you down," but the old man carries on bellowing the words, having lost track now of all tune. And then he loses control of his body, clutching his chest, gasping for breath, leaning into his cane as if he will fall over. Tư's father wraps his arms around him and together they crash to the floor.

Tư and Phương kneel beside them. "Don't move him," Bình wheezes from underneath Hưng. "Get an ambulance. I think he's had a heart attack."

Voices of the Dead

Hưng wakes thigh-deep in muddy water. He has walked kilometres from his own home to trawl a net through a giant crater where just three weeks ago some thirty thousand people lived crammed together in rows of traditional houses, and the mystique of Khâm Thiên Street was still very much alive.

He used to hear stories about the street when he was a boy serving in his Uncle Chiến's restaurant, of its bars and inns promising music, beautiful women and drink. One day, Hưng used to think, one day when I have some money. But by the time he had some money, he had no time for leisure, and by the time he could afford a night of leisure, the Party had put the bars and inns out of business, outlawing gambling and prostitution as foreign social evils.

Hưng was an innocent. He had wanted nothing more, had in fact never imagined anything more than sitting in one of these bars and, in return for a few đồng, listening to a beautiful lady sing a song just for him.

And now that he is finally visiting the street? It is under water. It is the winter of 1973 and the Americans have obliterated the entire neighbourhood. The vast majority of residents were evacuated to the countryside when the U.S. destroyed the train station a week before, but the poor, the sick and the stubborn remained behind. Some of them are now fishing alongside Hưng in the muddy crater, which quickly filled with the heavy rains. They are recovering pieces of metal: tin cans and bombshells they'll be able to use as cooking vessels; the fuel tank of an airplane, which will make a good tub for washing clothes. They lift tattered bits of cloth from the water, parachute silk and torn tarpaulin dangling like seaweed in their hands. But as Hưng quickly discovers, where there is tattered cloth there is also likely to be a body. Or a piece of body. He screams as a disembodied head bumps against his thigh, its eyes rolling loose in their sockets. He screams and retches and squeezes his own eyes shut.

He hears voices around him. Voices of the dead. A man shouting below him. But perhaps those dead—the innocents—are speaking to him from above, from heaven. He tentatively opens one eye. Someone is bathing his feet. He is lying in a bed in a room full of identical beds, moss-green paint peeling from the walls. A woman's voice says, "*Hallucinating. The painkillers will do that.*"

He recognizes that voice; it is Anh. His bed is surrounded: Anh and Bình, Tư, Maggie and Phương.

"You fell over, Hưng, do you remember? Coming down the stairs."

Bình looks wide-eyed and unlined, just like he did when he was a boy with questions in his eyes. "We were so worried," he says. "We thought you'd had a heart attack."

Hưng runs his palm over his chest. He is intact. He is not a headless torso or a disembodied head.

"It was your leg, not a heart attack," says Anh. "You must have fallen unconscious from the pain. They put in three pins and two metal plates."

So he has had an operation. He lifts the sheet and sees the length of his leg encased in solid plaster.

"We should have brought you to the hospital in the first place," says Bình. "It never would have healed properly on its own."

Bình clearly blames himself. "I am a stubborn man," says Hưng.

But Hưng is also a man afraid of this place. The Americans destroyed this hospital with their bombs, and even though it has been rebuilt, Hưng still fears the presence of ghosts. The spirits of the dead have not properly been put to rest. "Please, Bình, just tell me the people—the patients, the doctors, the nurses—"

"Everyone here is alive," says Bình. "I assure you."

The ward smells like boiled chicken, antiseptic and the dusty fog of old men's urine. An orderly in pale green taps

Hưng on the shoulder with a plastic cup of pills, an awful lot of pills, Maggie notes. Hưng reaches awkwardly, his plastered leg now held aloft by a barbaric-looking contraption, throwing the pills into his mouth and washing them back with the dregs of some weak tea.

"You should get your wife to shave you when she comes in," says the orderly.

"My wife?" Hưng says gruffly.

"That old lady. Or ask your granddaughter, then," he says, pointing at Maggie.

Hưng looks down and picks at the grey blanket.

"It's okay," Maggie says. "Do you want me to shave you?"

Hưng strokes his chin.

"I'll get you a razor," says the orderly.

Maggie lathers a bar of soap in her hands over a bowl and daubs the foam onto the old man's face. He raises his chin like a curious turtle. She draws the razor over his puckered skin with some apprehension, having never shaved a man before.

He purses his lips for her as she skims off his whiskers. He turns his head to the left, then right, so she can shave his neck.

"Do you have a camera, Maggie?" Hưng asks when she is done, running his palm over his smooth cheek while studying his reflection in the back of a spoon.

"You want me to take a picture?"

She pulls her phone from her purse while he composes his face into a frown. "A little smile?" she suggests.

"No," he replies, shaking his head. This is exactly how he wishes to be preserved.

Tư enters the ward and approaches the bed just then. "You look good," he says. "How are you feeling?"

"Trapped," says Hưng.

"I brought you a cup of coffee from outside," Tư says, handing him a paper cup and peeling back the lid.

The aroma takes Hưng right back to that day at Café Võ. The draw had been primal; the smell of coffee should no longer have existed.

"Sometimes you have to give them something, Hưng," Võ had lectured. "You didn't learn this, did you. They have taken everything from you because you didn't co-operate."

"I wasn't an informant," Hưng said blankly.

"If you'd simply stepped forward and given the Party someone, anyone, they would have commended you. You would have been able to protect the rest of them."

"Who did you give them?" Hưng demanded, gritting his teeth.

"One who'd left me, in any case," said Võ. "I don't even remember his name. They had their eyes on him already because of his education in the U.S.; they would have condemned him anyway."

Hưng feels his eyelids growing heavy, drooping like leaves after a heavy rain. He tries to fight the narcotic wave that is now overtaking him, tries to shout above the roar: *Was I the fool not to play the game? Should I have sacrificed someone to spare the rest?*

The only person Hưng could have imagined sacrificing is himself.

A Stone in His Heart

Tư is lying in the dark of his reclaimed bedroom when his cellphone rings in the pocket of his jeans, which lie in a crumpled heap at the foot of the bed. Who would be calling him in the middle of the night? Oh no, comes the dreaded thought, Hưng is dead. Tư throws his legs over the sheet and grabs his jeans.

"Maggie," he exhales with relief. "Maggie," he says again.

"I'm sorry, did I wake you?" she says, her voice quiet, faraway.

Tư flicks on the light.

"Professor Devereux tracked down Mr. Võ's collection," she says.

"Maggie! Where?"

"In Hong Kong," she says quietly.

"But, Maggie, what's the matter?"

"It's been sold to a group of Vietnamese-American businessmen," she says, hiccuping back tears.

"Maybe they'll agree to let you have your father's pictures," says Tư.

"The dealer I spoke to said the purchasers were intent on keeping the collection as a whole. Preserving its integrity."

"Well, if they believe in integrity, they will believe in you," he says.

"That's sweet of you, Tư."

"You must talk to them."

"I've got a conference call booked with them first thing in the morning. In just a couple of hours, in fact—evening there."

"I'll come and wait with you."

"Would you really?"

Tư is already stepping into his jeans. Anything for you, Maggie. Anything at all.

The drug the doctor is administering gives Hưng disturbing dreams. One time it is Party officials threatening to break his other leg unless he reveals Đạo's whereabouts. They are tearing apart the room at the back of his phở shop, looking for evidence of counter-revolutionary activity. They will find it soon enough—all six issues of *Nhân Văn* are hidden under his mattress, as well as *Fine Works of Spring* and *Autumn*, and dozens of poems written in Đạo's own hand.

Another time he is on the streets during the American War. He is hunting for cicadas and worms when he comes across a sight he has become numb to, that of a woman's arm lying in the gutter. The ring finger has been cut off, but the bracelets around her wrist remain, and Hưng realizes the only way to get that silver will be to sever the hand from the arm. He picks up the arm and shakes it, just to be sure, and the bangles clatter together at the wrist, too tight to slip free. But she will love these, he thinks, as he puts the arm down and looks around him for a piece of metal, preferably something serrated.

These dreams never come to a conclusive end, but in this case, Lan is suddenly standing before him, old Lan, but still beautiful. Her fine bones, her delicate skin, her precious jewel of a mouth.

Butterflies hatch from cocoons inside his stomach.

Is it possible? Is it possible she is here at the hospital? Bình appears to be touching her forearm. Her hands are resting on the metal bar at the end of his bed.

"Bình," Hưng croaks, soft wings caught in his throat.

"You've been calling out for her all day," he says.

Is it true? Has Bình brought her to his bedside? Or is he confusing this with a hazy memory from a few years ago? He can picture her, old like she is now, standing inside his shack at the end of his straw-filled mattress, holding a bowl of chicken broth and rice. He is sick, he has been forced to pull out some teeth, she is kneeling now by his bedside, pressing a cold wet cloth against his forehead, murmuring something to him, a poem possibly, placing a white pill on his furry tongue.

And then she is gone.

But she is here. Now.

In this moment Hưng can't remember why they have not spoken for so many years, why he has avoided her gaze, why he has carried a stone in his heart.

"I was dreaming, Lan," he says, releasing butterflies from his mouth. "I was dreaming that I was going to give you silver bracelets."

She shakes her arm and several bangles fall from her elbow to her wrist. A familiar sound. A sound as clean and clear as mountain water, something he hasn't heard since he was a child.

Henry Thanh and his colleagues have charitable intentions. They believe the collection should be returned to Hanoi, its rightful home, where they want to see it housed and displayed as a permanent collection. At the museum perhaps. They've even suggested hiring Maggie to scout for the right location, but when it comes to her father's art, they are resolute.

"What happens when someone claiming to be the great-grandson of Bùi Xuân Phái turns up?" Henry Thanh asks Maggie over the phone.

"Look, I can't prove to you that he's my father, but if I were looking to capitalize on something, I'd be the one telling you Bùi Xuân Phái was my great-grandfather."

"Fair enough," says Henry. "But if we make an exception, we'll be setting a precedent. The collection's worth is the sum of its parts. Each and every piece."

Maggie hangs up the phone and turns to an expectant Tư. She shakes her head.

"Don't give up, Maggie," he says. "Come. We need to pray."

"Pray?" Maggie doesn't consider herself a particularly spiritual person. Her mother used to take her to temple once a year when she was a child, though it seemed she had lost faith herself.

"At your father's altar."

Tư must register the look of hesitation on Maggie's face, because he reaches for her hand and squeezes it. "Maggie, do you not have an altar for your father? But who is listening to him in the afterlife? Who is feeding him?"

Maggie's mother didn't have a shrine in Lý Văn Hai's honour either, except perhaps the shoebox she kept hidden at the back of her closet. But then it's not a wife's job. A shrine is a descendant's responsibility; it's hers.

She doesn't even know where to begin.

"Clear a space," says Tư.

She looks over at the writing desk, a cherry wood antique with brass fittings that came with the apartment. The desk has served as a dumping ground for receipts, loose change, keys, the few pieces of mail that have arrived for her from her bank in Minneapolis and the IRS.

She sweeps it all aside.

"You have the pictures your father drew for you," says Tư. "And the one my father did. And the paper with his name among the contributors. Do you have incense? Some fruit?"

Maggie fetches her father's drawings and unfolds them on the desk. She places two squares of chocolate and an orange beside them. She lights a thick red stick of incense and the smoke curls upward, engulfing them both.

Maggie can feel the heat of Tư's shoulder bleeding into hers as they stand side by side and raise their hands.

Hưng dreams of the artist who has just returned from America. "Sit," Hưng says, thrusting a bowl into the man's hands. He watches the man slurp the noodles and drink the broth, his expression becoming human again. He burps, wipes his mouth on his sleeve and says, "I will not forget your kindness," then stuffs some bills into Hưng's hands.

Hưng stares at the foreign currency, knowing it is worthless to him.

"Sorry," says the artist. "Let me pay you like I do at Café Võ."

Hưng says that won't be necessary, but the man pulls a notebook from his sack and quickly sketches something with a pencil. It is a drawing of Chairman Mao with a stomach full of fish. One of those fish has the face of Hồ Chí Minh. The artist tears the piece of paper from his notebook and hands it to Hưng.

"Who was that?" Đạo asks as Hưng stares at the drawing in his left hand and the foreign bills in his right.

"An artist who just came back from America."

"That must be Lý Văn Hai," says Đạo. "Everyone used to hate him because he got a scholarship and left. They used to hate him because they wished they could be

him. How long do you think it will be before he is punished for that American education?"

Đạo takes the drawing from Hưng's hand to get a better
look. "Wow. He's not afraid of anything," says Đạo. "I wonder
if we could convince him to join us. He could do illustrations for the journal."

Đạo looks at the money Hưng is clutching in his hand.
"Hưng," he says, "he paid you in American dollars. That's
a small fortune. You better hide it."

Hưng pats his shirt pocket.

"What are you looking for?"

He turns his head. It is Lan, old but still beautiful Lan,
sitting by his bedside.

"The dollars," he says. "I must remember to tell the girl."

"What girl is that, Hưng?" she asks, reaching for his hand.

"The Việt Kiều," he says, but as soon as it comes out of
his mouth he doubts her existence. She must be another one
of those imaginary creatures who keeps appearing in his
dreams. People known becoming unknown, faces dissolving
into clouds, voices disembodied. His dreams are crowded
with such illusions.

"Never mind," he says.

"You mean Lý Văn Hai's daughter?"

"You know her?" Hưng wheezes.

"There is only a metre between our shacks, Hưng.
Sometimes I can even hear you sighing in bed. That night
the girl brought the chocolate fungus—after she left, you
asked yourself aloud who her father might be, so I told
you. The illustrator."

Hưng is still in shock when Lan pulls a small glass vial by a string out from underneath her blouse and holds it before his face, twisting it round so he can admire it from all angles. It is a collection of precious MSG crystals, most expensive and cherished of all spices, impossible to find in the decades after independence. She is proud to tell him she has collected it grain by grain over the years as payment for embroidering pillowcases. She has kept the vial nestled between her breasts, close to her heart.

Not since colonial days has Hưng been able to afford this magic powder that makes one's food burst with flavour and colour. "There's a fortune in there," he says.

She lays the vial down on his chest.

"But surely this is not for me."

"I have been collecting it for you," Lan says. "In any case, it is not so expensive these days. You can now find it everywhere."

"But still—"

"And you are the cook."

"Was the cook. Will be. If I ever get out of here," he says, tapping his plaster cast.

"It won't be long, Hưng."

"Tell me, how is everybody in the shantytown? I worry about them when I'm not there to cook."

"Times are better now, Hưng. No one is going hungry."

"So they don't need me anymore."

"It doesn't mean they aren't all wondering when they will next taste your food. I hear them reminiscing about their favourites. Your spring rolls, your roast duck, that pig's ear salad."

"What about Phúc Li?" Hưng asks of the legless man who lives on the other side of him. "His mother told me she was teaching him to sew labels into shirts so he could work in a factory."

"I don't know, Hưng. She doesn't talk to me. None of them do."

"But why?"

"Because of *you*, Hưng," she says as if he is dim-witted. "Because they are loyal to you."

It is true, she has no visitors, no apparent friends; she has lived without conversation or companionship for years. But what is a life if you cannot say to another: Grey sky today, isn't it? Did that thunder keep you up last night? How's your cousin, your bunion, your mushroom-hunting, your game of chess? How she must suffer in isolation, must question her entire existence.

A great rush of feeling overcomes him. "You weren't literate," he says, "you didn't know the worth of those papers." He bites the tremor that now afflicts his bottom lip.

"But I should have understood, Hưng. I could see what the words meant to you. I was very young. It was foolish of me. I honestly thought I could protect you."

"Protect me? How?"

"I feared they would come and find those papers."

"They did come," says Hưng, his mouth hanging open. "They set fire to my shack."

"I panicked, Hưng. I didn't want to lose you." Lan hangs her head, her chin falling into her chest.

They arrived too late and found nothing. They did not

charge him with any crime. They did not drag him away or kill him. Take away his eyes, tongue or hands. They left him to his life on the shore of a muddy pond, to live in silence beside a beautiful girl named Lan. A girl who had tried to save him, but in so doing had lost him.

Provenance

It's a brooding early morning with a sagging sky, creating a mood that Tư would find despairing even if they were not faced with the prospect of eating an inferior bowl for breakfast every day for the indeterminate future. The phở at the end of Mã Mây Street seems particularly inferior now that Tư has had his own experience of cooking. He thinks the problem is less the cook's failure to trim enough fat from the meat than it is his laziness in not skimming off the grease that rises to the surface of the broth before he reboils it.

"If that were his only problem, it would not be so bad," says his father, turning his spoon over unenthusiastically. "Hưng would never be so lazy."

"Never," Tư and Maggie say in unison.

"If Hưng had his own shop again, it would certainly be

cleaner than this," he continues. "Can you smell the toilet?"
He pinches the bridge of his nose.

"Imagine it," Bình says, drawing an imaginary banner of
a bright, lucky red sign through the air, the words *Phở Hưng*
hanging on a building on a popular street in the Old Quarter,
a shop with big, clean glass windows and an open door inviting customers to take seats on proper wooden chairs inside
rather than at plastic stools on the greasy pavement.

Tư sees a gleaming, stainless steel counter. Perhaps a
gas stovetop, which would reduce the need for wood. Bright
new linoleum, easy to clean. A refrigerator to keep the meat
fresh and the herbs from wilting. Shelving for a stack of
new, white ceramic bowls and large lidded pots.

"There's a closet full of unused dishes at the hotel,"
says Maggie.

Tư's father adds a sink with hot and cold running water.
An indoor toilet and perhaps a room at the back where the
old man could live.

"This is crazy," says Tư, putting an end to this fantasiz-
ing. They could never hope to save the kind of money this
would take. Even if Tư and his father were men who gambled
at the cockfights, no number of wins could amount to that
kind of money.

"What if we formed an association?" says his father.

"You're serious about this," Tư says, pushing his bowl to
the centre of the table and abandoning his soup altogether.

"Well, he can't carry on as before. And he's never going
to retire. We have to find a way to make it easier for him."

"What do you mean by an association?" Maggie asks.

"Like a *ho*," says Bình.

"It's a fund you can turn to when you need a big sum of money fast," Tư explains. "Like for a wedding or a funeral or to build a house. Usually the association is between relatives, everyone contributing a certain amount—you keep it small and close so that everyone remains honest and has his turn at the lot."

"We could invite Hưng's regular customers to participate," says Bình.

Maggie asks how much everyone would need to contribute, perhaps calculating her own savings, but this raises the bigger question of how much it would cost to get such a shop up and running to the point where it could turn enough of a profit to sustain itself.

Tư jerks his notebook out of the inside pocket of his jacket. He's just the man for this job. Rents have soared in the past couple of years, but he thinks it might still be possible to lease the ground floor of a building in the Old Quarter for the equivalent of about eight hundred U.S. dollars a month. And then, of course, there are the taxes and licensing fees, the equipment and supplies, and the bribes that must be paid to the police. Finally, the tables and chairs and kitchen equipment and ingredients.

Tư estimates the various costs with his father's help, converts this from đồng to dollars, then rounds off the number. "Twelve thousand dollars," he says, underlining the zeros roughly. "Three hundred dollars each if the roughly forty people who are his regular customers were to contribute."

Tư's father shakes his head. "That's far too many people.

You could be dead before it was ever your turn. And it is far too much money to ask anyone to contribute, in any case."

"That's less than people spend for one night at the Metropole," says Maggie.

"What do they charge for a bowl of phở there?" Tư's father asks.

"About seven dollars."

Tư's father coughs like a cat bringing up a furball. They've never paid more than seventy cents for a bowl of phở. "Do they import the beef from France?" he says. "*Ôi zồi ôi.*"

Hưng has been waiting all morning to see someone from the kitchen. He is impatient and agitated by the time a young man, just a boy really, finally comes to the ward to speak with him. The boy hovers at the end of the bed, looking like a dog used to being kicked. Hưng struggles to begin with a compliment: "The phở has a warm fragrance," he says, "but did you taste the broth? Did it really seem sweet enough?"

"We don't taste it, Grandfather," says the young man.

What terrible teeth the boy has. Hưng leans back on his pillow. "But how can you know if the balance is right, if it is seasoned sufficiently, if you don't taste it?"

"It is because we are a hospital. We have so many to serve, we do not have the time to check and adjust."

Hưng can hear the embarrassment in the boy's voice; he clearly knows the shame in this. "But even a factory must check and adjust," he says. "If even the tiniest mechanism is out of alignment, the whole outcome is compromised, is it not?"

"Yes, Grandfather," says the boy.

"Did your mother not teach you the way?" Hưng asks with all the kindness he possesses.

"She died when I was very small."

Hưng aches for the boy, just as he once did for Bình. "I tell you what," he says, drawing the boy toward him, touching his forearm, extracting his name. "When I am better, when this damn leg is healed, I will teach you. Now, which bones do you use for the stock?"

"The cheap ones. From the neck."

"But no no no," Hưng says, cringing. "It's all about the marrow. You want knuckle bones, leg bones, tail. And you can get these cheap if you have a relationship with the right butcher.

"Beyond that, it's largely about the time of year—how much rain has there been, has there been enough grass for the cows, how is the soil where your onions and ginger are grown? And what if the star anise is old and losing flavour? How might you compensate? There are ways."

"I would very much like to learn," the young man says, looking more like a new puppy now than a beaten dog.

He says he will go to temple and pray for Hưng's full and speedy recovery.

Hưng cannot ask the young man to spare himself the effort. He will readily take all the help he can get.

———

Tư's parents are in the courtyard, his mother feeding her new chickens, the ground now covered in seed, his father squatting in front of the brazier pouring the tart juice he has extracted from tamarind pulp into the broth for a *canh chua cá*. He cooks this fish soup on days when Tư's mother says she just can't bear the thought of cooking or eating meat, usually days she has spent up to her elbows making sausages. Bình prefers cooking his hot and sour fish soup out here on the open fire; he bought the stove in the kitchen five years ago, but after using it once, declared he didn't like electric heat. He says it changes the taste of things.

Tư squats down beside his father and passes him a series of small white bowls. Bình tips diced pineapple, bamboo shoots, sliced red chilies, sugar, fish sauce, tomato wedges and fat cubes of white fish in turn into his rolling broth. They are engulfed in its aroma: the sourness bites the back of Tư's tongue.

"I've been thinking about how to get Hưng that money," Bình says, as he skims the surface of the broth with a slotted spoon, his wrist making a gentle figure eight.

"Me too," says Tư, tapping his temple. "The wheel is spinning but going nowhere."

"You told me about the prices that Bùi Xuân Phái's work fetches now. What if we were to sell my Phái drawing to these men Maggie is dealing with in California?"

Tư is astonished his father would even consider such a thing, having guarded and protected the drawing for so many years. "I could ask Maggie what she thinks it might be worth," he says tentatively.

"I leave the handling of it to you."

———

The following morning, Tư removes Bùi Xuân Phái's naked lady from the chest in his parents' bedroom and rolls her up carefully, wrapping her in newspaper, making sure every inch of her is covered. He holds her high above his head, not wanting her to be jostled about on these busy streets she has never walked down before, thinking how strange this bustling city would look to Bùi Xuân Phái if he were alive to see it today.

When Tư unrolls the picture for Maggie, she gasps and covers her mouth. When she finally drops her hands, she has the face of someone who has just eaten something extremely delicious.

She puts on plastic gloves, snapping them at her wrists like a forensics expert on *CSI*. She smooths down the curled edges of the paper, picks up her magnifying glass and studies every inch of it for what feels like an hour.

She uses words like *provenance* and *pedigree*. She talks about the purity of the drawing's lineage, having had only one owner all these years, and the fact that it was passed from Phái himself to Tư's grandfather Đạo, directly from one artist to another. She praises its condition as pristine and unadulterated. Pure. She commends them all, Đạo, Bình and Tư, for their care and respect in handling it.

"Your father's really prepared to sell it?" she asks.

"If it can get us the money for Old Man Hưng's shop, yes, he's prepared to sell it."

Maggie's eyes sparkle as she peels off the gloves and rubs

her hands together. "I think it would fetch well over ten thousand dollars," she says.

"Can we ask for twelve?"

"We can try," she says, picking up the phone.

This way of tackling things so directly, without apology or ritual, seems a bit reckless to Tư, but it certainly does move things along. He can just imagine what happens when deals go sour, though—no blessing to protect you, no Buddha or ancestor to make things right. This is one obvious downside to capitalism.

Maggie apologizes to Mr. Thanh for calling so late but says she has a proposal to make that she is quite sure he'll find of interest. She is in possession of a natural and fitting addition to the Võ collection—an immaculately preserved piece that could, in fact, serve as its celestial heart.

Maggie puts her hand over the receiver and gestures to Tư. "I want you to describe the piece to him," she whispers. "From your heart."

From his heart. Where feelings live. Subjective feelings. Gulp.

"One minute, Henry. I'm just going to pass you to someone. He's the best one to describe it." She passes the phone to Tư, taps her chest and whispers again: "From your heart."

"Hello," says Tư, clearing his throat. "Mr. Thanh? Yes, well, this is a drawing that has been in my family for fifty years. You have heard of *Nhân Văn*? No? Well let me tell you," he begins, launching into a brief history.

"Tư," Maggie whispers, tapping her chest again. "Heart."

"Um, Mr. Thanh? What I can tell you is that it is a very personal drawing. Very private. Like Bùi Xuân Phái must have loved this lady. She has her naked back to him and her hands to her face. Maybe they have just been intimate with each other. Perhaps she is crying."

Tư looks over at Maggie. She holds the tips of her index fingers to her lips and nods her head, her eyes a bit teary.

Mr. Thanh asks what they want for it.

"Twelve thousand dollars *and* the Lý Văn Hais," says Tư.

He doesn't dare look over at Maggie again. He hangs up the phone. Maggie reaches out to him and wraps her arms around his shoulders. She pulls him close, so close that he can feel the rise of her breasts and her sharp hip bones. Having never been hugged in his life, Tư's instinct is to turn into a plank of wood. Mr. Thanh has said he will confer with his associates and get back to them later in the day.

The wait leaves her feeling ravenous. Maggie orders room service, her favourite—a burger and fries. Eating a hamburger in the heart of Hanoi might seem like a contradiction, but it's the type of contradiction Maggie lives every day. She *is* that contradiction.

The phone rings just as she's swallowing her first bite. Maggie picks up the phone, wiping her lips on a napkin.

It's Professor Devereux—Simon—from the art school. He'd asked her to keep him updated. Said generously, "If there's anything else I can do." And she'd completely neglected to do so—she'd taken the name of the dealer in Hong Kong from him and run.

"I'm really sorry," she says. "I just got caught up in the chase. I hope there will be some resolution later today."

"If you're truly sorry you'll let me take you out for a drink," says Simon.

Maggie laughs, taken aback. He's flirting. Asking her out. She places a cool palm against a hot cheek.

"Do you know Bobby Chinn's?" he asks.

"The restaurant at the end of the lake."

"Why don't you meet me at the bar there at nine tonight. We'll celebrate your resolution."

Maggie laughs again, feeling foolish. And then she surprises herself by saying yes. "But how will I know it's you?"

"I'll know it's you, I'm sure of it."

Maggie rolls her eyes. Are French men really like this?

"I have an unfair advantage," he admits. "I found your picture on the Walker Center's website."

She does her own research as soon as she hangs up the phone, looking him up on the Internet. Simon Devereux has a PhD in art history from the Sorbonne. He wrote his thesis on French influences in Bùi Xuân Phái's work. His photo, though, is somewhat surprising. He's not Việt Kiều, but half Vietnamese: given his last name, his father must have been French. She pushes the tray of food on her desk away.

———

Every time he wakes she is there at his beside, old Lan but still beautiful, busy with some embroidery she sets aside as soon as his eyelids flutter open.

"I've forgotten all the poetry," he says.

"I'm sure you've just put it away for safekeeping," she says, patting Hưng's hand. "What about that first one from *Fine Works of Spring*. You knew it by heart."

"Even that, I'm afraid."

She leans over his bed. "The cherry blossom has lost its scent," she says in a voice as silken as when she was a girl. "The trees of the North have forgotten the season."

"You remember it?"

"I listened well," she says. "The bird that rests here is a carrier pigeon arrested in mid-flight."

"Oh, Lan," says Hưng, suddenly feeling very strange, wobbling inside like his organs have become unmoored.

"The bird has forgotten the message he's been sent to deliver. Ashamed, he begins to repeat the words of the morning's broadcast . . ."

"Oh, Lan. How I've missed you."

"Ah, Hưng, I've been here the whole time."

Maggie rushes over to Tư's house this evening, having just heard back from the purchasers in California. She feels euphoric: victorious and relieved, genuinely proud of Tư for being so convincing, nervous and giddy at the thought of meeting Simon Devereux later, embarrassed that the latter feelings should even be part of the mix. It's a drink, just a drink with a man she's never met. Today is the culmination of a year-long search for her father's work. His timing is uncanny.

She apologizes to Bình for dropping by unannounced, but he silences her with a smile, his silver-capped eye teeth sparkling in the light. "We are always happy to see you," he says, leading her across the courtyard by the hand.

Bình's hair is gleaming wet under the fluorescent light of the kitchen. Maggie notices a black smudge on Bình's neck, the same black on Anh's palms, and she's moved to think that a man with a glass eye is still concerned enough about his appearance to dye his hair.

Tư steps into the kitchen then with just a towel wrapped around his waist, his chest as hard and shiny as a polished apple. "Out of water," he says, before realizing Maggie is there. He folds his arms across his chest self-consciously.

"It's good news," says Maggie. "It worked. You made it work, Tư. I couldn't wait to tell you. They're going to give us $10,000 for the Bùi Xuân Phái—actually $9,998, they bargained for a luckier number—and my father's drawings."

"Whoa-hoa!" Bình shouts, leaping up and fetching the bottle of whisky that sits prominently displayed on a shelf. "It's never been opened," he announces proudly. It was a gift from his colleagues when he left the factory years ago.

Anh fetches four glasses, which Bình fills to the top. Maggie shudders at the mere smell of the whisky.

"Let us toast to the health of the old man," says Bình, raising his glass.

Maggie raises her glass and offers a toast of her own. "To the return of things that have been lost."

An Old Man's Destiny

Hưng admires the white length of his leg in its plaster, but curses it at the same time. He'll be stuck in this bed for several more weeks.

"You are longing to get back to cooking, aren't you," he hears Bình say as he and Tư approach.

"Even in my dreams I am making phở."

Bình sits down on the edge of Hưng's bed. "Wouldn't it be wonderful if you could have your own phở shop again," he says. "Just like the old days."

Why is Bình saying this? What is the point?

"What if you had that shop today?" Tư asks, joining his father.

"Today it would be very different," says Hưng, indulging them. "For one thing, we would have running water."

"And a refrigerator, maybe even a freezer," says Bình. "You'd get a lot more life out of your food."

"Those stainless steel counters are good," Tư adds, "really easy to clean."

"If you put the kitchen in the back and had a door to the alley, you could take deliveries," says Bình. "Anh could just send the meat up every morning."

Bình and Tư continue to build this fantasy shop, discussing square footage and the relative merits of various locations. Tư reckons you could fit twenty tables with four chairs each on the ground floor of your average tube house in the Old Quarter.

And then they introduce reality—the cost of it all—and Hưng stops them there. "Enough now. Don't agitate an old man's heart."

But they are grinning like children at Tet in the days when the government still allowed firecrackers. What is the matter with them?

Bình puts his hands between his knees and bends forward; he has a speech to make, it would seem. But what he says could do more than agitate an old man's heart; it could break it completely. "We have the money for your shop."

But where does such an extraordinary amount of money come from?

"It doesn't matter where it comes from," Bình says. "It matters that it comes as a gift. It matters that you accept it as a gift, because it is destiny, and one must not hide from destiny. What is rightfully yours, what was taken from you long ago, is being returned."

Hưng feels the weight of loss in this moment. Of those men who taught him more about the world than a simple peasant ever could have hoped to know.

"Perhaps it is too late," he says.

Hưng sinks back into his pillow and closes his eyes for just a minute. He thinks of Lan. Perhaps things do return, but never in the form that they left you. Lan is an old woman now, an old woman to his old man. The years of poverty have humbled her. She is a better person for it, Hưng supposes, but in some ways, he wishes she could have lived in a world where it was possible to be young and vain. Like Vietnam today. Like these spoiled children with their cellphones and gadgets and new clothes, and their desires for bigger, faster motorbikes and their dreams that they will go to Saigon and become famous. Will they be better for it? Sometimes hardship forces humility and virtue where it might not naturally arise.

Hưng is thankful he knows good children, children who possess the manners and values of old, like Tư.

Hưng pats the thin skin in the middle of his chest, feeling for the vial of MSG he now carries on a string around his neck. It is not nearly so expensive these days, but having done without it for so long has become a matter of pride. Everything is available now; it would be easy to become lazy.

Imagine if he did have his own shop again. Even though he would not be bound by deference to inheritance, he would still wish to replicate Uncle Chiến's shop. Forget these stainless steel counters and poured concrete floors Tư and Bình are talking about. Forget hiding the kitchen away in the back like some western restaurant. He'll be out there cooking in front of the open window, chatting to everyone who passes, inviting them in. He'll find a place with an old tiled floor that they can clean and polish. He'll nail rattan screens to the walls, a soft back against which to lean, a cushion to absorb sound, and he'd like some of those whirling ceiling fans the French used to install in their establishments.

He'll eschew the common trend of plastic tables and stools in favour of the old heavy teak furniture that tells people you are welcome here as long as you like. A man his age is likely to proceed more cautiously, if at all, knowing how Vietnam can do a somersault or backflip overnight and suddenly half the population is dead, in labour camps or prison or hiding in a bomb shelter or fleeing altogether because the country is tied to the yoke of some colonial master or native despot. Hưng hopes the seeds of Vietnam's destruction don't lie in this fever of capitalism that has infected the country, a fever that is beginning to infect him as well, but even if that is the case, he has lived long and hard enough to know Vietnam will recover. It always does.

He opens his eyes. These two men—his family—wait expectantly. "Give an old man some time to consider all this," he says.

He dreams of Lan wading among lotuses, only to awake to find her sitting by his bedside, picking at the seam of his trouser leg. "I'll sew it up again when your leg's all better," she says.

"Is it too late?" he asks.

"Too late?"

It's a good question. He is old, but not too old to contemplate running a business. He's been running a business all these years, hasn't he? Surely it would be easier to be settled in one place. His question has more to do with a fear of failure than anything else. He would wish to be able to recreate an environment like that of Phở Chiến & Hưng, but how can he hope to do so without his memory? So much from that time has slipped away.

"Tell me everything you remember, Lan. Please," he says, feeling the rise of panic. "Tell me names."

"Well," she says calmly. "It's hard to know where to begin. There were so many of them. What about Chiến Đạt and Huy Phước. Their poems always sounded very similar to me. And that Chinese man with the crooked nose who wrote stories about village life. And Xuân Quốc Quý, the mute who brought his brother along to say his words aloud."

Her recollection is extraordinary; she'd been acquainted with these men only through Hưng's descriptions of them, yet physical details and specific phrases that Hưng has absolutely no memory of spill without any apparent effort from her mouth.

"And, of course, Đạo's teacher, Phan Khôi," she continues. "He was always very serious, wasn't he? He might have been the founder of modern poetry, but by the time of *Nhân Văn* he was only concerned with essays and intellectual statements. I'm just a simple woman, but I much preferred Đạo's work. He had a passionate heart, that one."

It is as if decades have collapsed, and they are once again

sitting together on a woven grass mat under a weak moon and her skin is pearlescent, her hair long and loose around her shoulders, only she is the one telling the stories and it is he who is hearing them for the first time.

"I've missed you, Lan," he says again.

"I'm right here, Hưng."

The young man from the kitchen approaches the bed carrying a bowl of congee. He has brought two spoons.

"How would you like a job, Dǒng?" Hưng asks. "Working for me in a kitchen."

"I would like that very much, Grandfather."

There are two things he must ask of the young man, things he must ask of Tư and Bình as well. First, they must never again visit Hồ Chí Minh's mausoleum. It is very, very bad luck for business. And second, they must all go to the temple and ask the spirits for their blessings. The communists did such a good job of stamping out religion that young people today don't know whom to pray to. Buddha is no help with matters of money. Consult Buddha on matters of the heart. Ask the ancestors for help with business. This is responsible capitalism.

Lan holds out a spoonful of congee to Hưng. Hưng opens his mouth and closes his eyes.

Tư and his father have been eating inferior phở in the shop on Mã Mây Street for several mornings in a row, even going so far as to compliment the cantankerous old man who runs the place. Tư has given his father a lesson on the white lie and how it acts as a harmless social lubricant, and he seems to be taking quite naturally to this foreign practice. "Your broth has a very good aroma," Tư's father says, slurping it up with noisy enthusiasm.

"Do I know you," says the owner, "or do you have an evil twin at home?"

"Who taught you the recipe?" Bình asks the next day.

"Why do you care?" says the owner.

"Look, what are you doing here every day?" the owner asks toward the end of the week.

"It's a public place, isn't it?" says Tư.

"People like you make me want to quit my job."

"Actually," says Tư's father, seizing this opportunity, "we were wondering how much you pay to rent this place."

"Rent?" he bellows. "I own the damn building."

Tư's father proceeds carefully, scratching his chin. "Do you have any idea what the rents are like around here?" he asks. He lowers his voice and whispers: "I bet you could make fifty times the amount of money you make selling phở if you were to rent out the space."

"A guy said that to me once," says the owner, "but it turned out he wanted to open a nightclub. I don't want a nightclub in here, or some kind of opium den. My wife, kids and grandkids live upstairs."

"What about renting it to another phở cook?" Tư's father asks. "Keeping it as a restaurant."

The owner leans his chin on his broom handle. "Do you have anyone in mind?"

"Old Man Hưng," Tư's father says.

"I thought he was strictly a street seller."

"His fortunes have recently changed."

"Oh yeah?" says the owner, and Tư knows his father has this old bastard by the balls.

The Afterlife

For the first time ever, Tư's father asks him to drive the motorbike. Tư pushes it out into the alleyway and his father climbs on board behind him, saying, "My eyesight is not so good at night anymore." A great surge of passion for his family comes into Tư's throat, the recognition of his duty as eldest and only son.

They are off to see the old man at the hospital. Lan is there at his side as she tends to be more often than not, lifting Hưng's spirits with her presence. Tư has responded to Hưng's request for a notebook and pen, and day by day he is making notes, recording the words she feeds him line by line. They grow silent when Tư and his father approach the bed, sharing secrets.

This evening Tư recounts the story about the owner of the shop on Mã Mây Street, and Old Man Hưng chortles with satisfaction. The end of his time in hospital is in sight now that they have removed his cast.

"I'd like to see the shop as soon as I can manage," he says. "Me and my assistant cook."

Tư is taken aback. Did Hưng not teach him the recipe? Train him as apprentice? "Did you not like my phở?" he asks.

"You made a fine bowl," says Hưng, "but it takes a particular type of person."

"I'm not the right type of person?" Tư asks, truly offended now.

"Your life needs to depend on it," says Hưng. "Only a very poor person who needs a better life will marry himself to this kind of work. You have other choices, Tư.

"Want to see my leg?" he asks then, throwing back the covers and looking proudly at his yellow matchstick. He agitates to get up, reaching for Bình's arm. "Get my shoes for me, will you, Bình? They're under the bed. Latest fashion, eh, Tư?"

"Are you sure you're ready to walk?" Bình asks.

"I'm supposed to exercise it every day."

"That's different from walking on it."

"He's right, Hưng," says Lan, putting her hand on Hưng's chest. "Give it a day or two."

Hưng sighs, rolls his eyes, collapses backward. He's clearly not used to all this attention, all the fuss, being told what to do, but from the smile that returns to his face when he settles into his pillow, Tư thinks he is actually quite enjoying it.

———

Lan pats the papery, parched skin of Hưng's hand. "Bad dream," she says gently, touching his cheek. She strokes his mole with her leathery fingertips. "Do you ever think that without this mole your life would have turned out differently? You might not be here, for instance."

"But then I wouldn't be here with you," says Hưng. "Maybe that is why I was born with it."

Maggie leans against the frame of the doorway of the ward, holding a brown paper-wrapped package to her chest. She doesn't want to interrupt: Hưng is staring intently at the old woman sitting at his side. She is wearing faded black communist-era clothes and the same black slippers Hưng always wears, or used to. Her thin grey hair is pulled back in a bun, and they could be brother and sister if it weren't for the way she is looking at him.

It's a look of old love, of something knowing and decades deep. Something she wishes her parents could have shared.

The woman kisses Hưng's forehead, then slumps back in her chair. "Oh, Hưng," she says, immediately heaving herself forward to wipe away a tear clinging to the old man's lower lashes. "You old fool. I've known you for almost forty-five years; I don't think it's a sin if we're not married. Do you even know if it has enough room at the back? Not that we need much, but we'll probably only have room for one altar."

They are planning a future together, as much of a future as they have left.

Maggie asks the young man who is soon to be Hưng's apprentice to give the old man the package when his visitor leaves.

"But she never leaves, Miss Maggie. He is never on his own."

She will hold on to her father's framed picture for the time being, then. She has the others at her apartment, delivered in person two days ago by the dealer in Hong Kong, unwrapped by Simon shortly thereafter. There will be another occasion, a more appropriate one to give the old man this picture—at the grand opening of his new shop. The past will be revealed and given a place to hang in the present.

Phở Nhân Văn

The pots are new, and so is the stove over which Hưng is perspiring as he greets people on Mã Mây Street through the open window. Despite his limp, he can stand here for hours in these new shoes; they make him feel as if he could walk on the moon. In truth, his keen apprentice does much of the walking for him. Dǒng does the market run every morning, takes deliveries, carries the steaming bowls to tables, keeps the shop clean, swept and tidy.

Hưng admires his establishment every morning. He basks in the heavenly white of the newly plastered walls. Look at that fine fridge standing there. He likes its gleaming newness and won't ever remove the manufacturer's sticker. And hasn't Bình done an exquisite job of restoring the old wooden shutters and the latticework around the door? He's even created cupboards in the backroom for him and Lan according to Hưng's description of the closet he once admired in a room at the Hotel Metropole. Bình has also built a chest big enough to hold two altars: Đạo and Lan's grandmother are now getting acquainted. There have been no complaints from either of them so far.

Hưng is particularly proud of the sign. PHỞ NHÂN VĂN it says on the outside of the building, words painted by a local artist in exchange for one hundred bowls of phở. That artist sits now with colleagues and professors from the Hanoi University of Fine Arts at a table permanently reserved for them. A framed picture of two Indochinese tigers entangled in battle hangs on the wall above their heads—an inspired work by Lý Văn Hai, an alumnus of the school, Maggie's father—a sober reminder of the brutality waged between brothers in earlier times.

The second reserved table is for family. This morning, Bình, having discovered a particular talent for faces, is sketching Maggie's portrait. Tư is collecting the empty bowls, helping out as he does each morning, having recently quit his job in order to introduce Hưng to such capitalist concepts as improved margins and net profit per bowl. Phương, who holds the dubious distinction of being *Vietnam Idol*'s runner-up, is wearing headphones and tapping a pencil against a bowl. Maggie is reading a note from the charming young professor with the French name who sits at the next table. Lan, Hưng's aproned partner in the restaurant and all things, thinks she has been discreet as the go-between, dropping the note into Maggie's hands. She might think no one in this new family of hers has noticed, but Hưng watches Maggie's eyelids flutter as she looks over at the professor and bites down the smile of a woman newly in love.

Hưng has his moments of wondering whether this is the afterlife or the present life. But then he asks himself, Does it matter?

Author's Note

WHAT I REFER TO HERE as the Beauty of Humanity Movement—a liberal interpretation for fictional purposes—is more commonly known as the *Nhân Văn–Giai Phẩm* affair, after two publications *Nhân Văn* (Humanism) and *Giai Phẩm* (Fine Works).

This controversial chapter in Vietnamese history was first exposed to the West through the writings of Hoàng Văn Chí in *The Nhân Văn Affair* and *Hundreds of Flowers Blooming in the North*, published in 1959 by the Congress of Cultural Freedom in Saigon.

Đạo is an entirely fictional creation. The group of men involved in publishing the journals was, in fact, led by the great revolutionary poet Phan Khôi, who only appears as a minor character in this novel. I have attributed the essence of some of Phan Khôi's lines to Đạo, notably: "We believe absolutely in communism, the most wonderful ideal of mankind, the youngest, the freshest ideal in all history," and, "But if a single style is imposed on all writers and artists the day is not far off when all flowers will be turned into chrysanthemums," (page 150). The crimes of the Party listed on page 156 were articulated by Phan Khôi in one of his editorials.

Neil L. Jamieson's *Understanding Vietnam* (University of California Press, 1993) offers a thorough account of literature and communism in Vietnam, for anyone interested in reading more about the subject.

Very few Vietnamese novels have been translated into English. The exception is the work of the North Vietnamese writer Dương Thu Hương, whose novels were, in the 1990s, the first by a Vietnamese writer to be published in the U.S. These novels, which continue to be banned in Vietnam, offer rare insight into the conditions in Vietnam, and particularly Hanoi, in the 1980s.

Acknowledgements

With love and thanks to Heather Conway, Hà Quảng Phương, Trần Thị Lan, Drew Harris and Sherifah Mazwari for the shared experiences in Hanoi.

With gratitude to Maya Mavjee, Nita Pronovost, Jane Fleming, Martha Kanya-Forstner, Anne McDermid and Martha Magor for the editorial guidance and interest throughout the course of writing this book, and to the Canada Council for the Arts for support.

With thanks to Kris Risk for encouraging me to change directions and Chris Kelly for unfailing friendship and the occasional space in which to write. Thanks to the staff of Hanoi 3 Seasons, Kim's Café and Mimi's on Gerrard Street East for the phở and to Anh of Hidden Hanoi for sharing recipes and stories.

And to Sir Edward Fennessy (1912–2009) for always being my grandpa.

Camilla Gibb was born in London, England, and grew up in Toronto. She has a Ph.D. in social anthropology from Oxford University. *Sweetness in the Belly* was a national bestseller, a Scotiabank Giller Prize finalist, and winner of the Trillium Award. Her novels have been translated into fourteen languages and published to rave reviews around the world. Camilla Gibb lives in Toronto.

Camilla Gibb
on the Inspiration for
The Beauty of Humanity Movement

YOU NEVER KNOW WHERE a novel's going to come from. I don't, at least. I've come to have the feeling that the novel tells me it needs to be written, rather than the other way around.

A couple of years ago I was working on a book that grew out of an idea. I'd only ever entered a novel through character before, never through a concept, and now I know why. The greatest ideas can lack a pulse on the page; the brain is not necessarily the best organ for novels. The heart is a much better judge and creator.

Still, I persevered with that doomed book, unable yet to admit defeat. I was at the height of my frustration with it when I happened to go on holiday to Vietnam, a place I had wanted to visit for years. Vietnam was a revelation to me, completely unexpected. It was young and vibrant, its heart practically leaping out of its body, and it threw any preconceived notions I had about the place out the window.

The Western narrative of Vietnam is entirely dominated by the war, a war that remains very entrenched in the American psyche. The American War, as the Vietnamese call it, has had a lasting impact, but that war was a ten-year ideological battle fought on and above Vietnamese soil—not eighty years of French occupation, not a thousand years of oppression by the Chinese. Culturally and politically speaking, Vietnam's French and Chinese chapters of history have had far more influence on shaping the country and its struggles than the American War, but this isn't a story we know in the West. We know Vietnam only in so far as it concerns us.

It was a young tour guide in Hanoi named Phương who first offered me this perspective, one I would find reinforced over and over again as I travelled the length of the country. I was very struck by Phương—he had a good job with a reputable tour agency, possessed a very sophisticated command of English, and was highly skilled at negotiating that often awkward and bumpy terrain between cultures. Born into an era of economic renewal, Phương in many ways embodied the "new Vietnam."

He gave me permission to ask anything and, being a writer, and an anthropologist in a former life, I asked a lot—about Vietnam, about him, about his life. "Is this your dream?" I remember asking in the midst of one very long traffic jam, to be a tour guide, to interact with foreigners, to serve as a bridge between cultures? Did a young Vietnamese man today have the luxury of being able to dream?

It was a good job, he told me, but no, it was not his dream. What he had always wanted, he confessed, was to have his own phở restaurant—to serve Vietnamese beef noodle soup to a Vietnamese clientele, adopting the standards he had seen employed in the service of foreigners in the country, treating his own people with this same kind of respect.

In that fantasy, his whole family would be involved. His mother, a butcher, would supply the beef. His father would work alongside him, his fiancée, Lan, who was studying accounting, would do the books. The restaurant would support everyone into their old age. As Western as Phương seemed, he was very much a first-born son, loyal to his family and the expectations of his culture, governed by principles of Buddhism and Confucianism and by the fact that he was simply a very good guy.

This was the new Vietnam: at once versed in things Western, but committed to the work of developing Vietnam for the Vietnamese, not simply cultivating it for foreign consumption. And here was the seed of a new novel. A story I had not heard told before. Most significantly, here was the inspiration for one of the main characters—a character straddling these two worlds but increasingly conflicted by that divide.

"Who makes the best phở in Hanoi?" I asked Phương one day.

"There's an old man who doesn't have a restaurant or a license to do business," he said. "He has to keep moving locations because he is always getting fined by the police. People know where he is by word of mouth and they follow him.

They bring their own bowls from home and they just run away whenever the police turn up."

Who was this old man and how did he get to this place? I wondered. And so the novel began. An old man who is an itinerant phở seller. A young tour guide who is first among his devoted clientele. And a Vietnamese-American woman who turns up with questions about her father's disappearance during the war. The three of them bound by hidden histories that come to light over the course of the novel.

It has been three years since Phương and I first met, and I have been back once to Vietnam to see him and ask more questions. Phương now has his phở restaurant, in which I am an investor. He also has a son, Duc Bao, whom he and his wife, Lan, asked me to give an English middle name. Duc David Bao is now two years old. And I now have a daughter on the way, and Phương and Lan have likewise done me the honour. They have given her the name Thu—autumn—the most beautiful of the Vietnamese seasons, the season of blooming lotuses and the full moon into which she will be born, an auspicious name, they tell me, that will mark her "as perfect and beautiful and lucky as the moon."

This book is dedicated to Phương and Lan and Bao.

Winner of the Trillium Book Award
Shortlisted for the Scotiabank Giller Prize
A Globe and Mail Best Book
NATIONAL BESTSELLER

Set in Emperor Haile Selassie's Ethiopia
and the racially charged world of Thatcher's
London, *Sweetness in the Belly* is a richly
detailed portrayal of one woman's search
for love and belonging. Lilly, born to British
parents, eventually finds herself living as a
devout, young, white Muslim woman in the
ancient walled city of Harar in the years
leading up to the deposition of the emperor.
She is drawn to an idealistic young doctor,
Aziz, but their love has only just begun to fulfil its promise when
the convulsions of a new order wrench them apart, sending Lilly to
an England she has never seen and Aziz into the darkness of a
radical revolution.

Camilla Gibb brings to life characters facing extraordinary
hardship and loss with the unblinking honesty and emotional gen-
erosity that have made her one of Canada's most exciting young
literary talents.

"This is a rarity, a novel that transforms expectations. A hugely ambitious work executed with deceptive ease . . . utterly convincing, able to
transport us behind closed borders and back again." —*The Gazette*

Trade paperback: 978-0-385-66018-1
E-book: 978-0-307-37334-2

Anchor Canada

A *Globe and Mail* Best Book
NATIONAL BESTSELLER

A startling and ambitious novel, as funny as
it is poignant, *The Petty Details of So-and-
so's Life* tells the story of Blue and Emma
Taylor, who, despite an almost telepathic
connection, respond to the sudden disappearance of their explosive father in remark-
ably different ways. Emma sets off in pursuit
of a new family, and discovers a sense of
belonging in the most unexpected places.
Burly, tattoo-stamped Blue, haunted by the

brutal, disparaging voice of their father, embarks on a cross-country
search for the elusive parent. Emma and Blue share a most intimate
connection, one forged in the secret worlds and wordless communi-
cations of childhood. As they grow, they discover the limits of the
language they share.

Trade paperback: 978-0-385-65803-4

Anchor Canada